COLD JUSTICE

RICK POLAD

CALUMET EDITIONS
Minneapolis

**CALUMET
EDITIONS**

Minneapolis

THIRD EDITION April 2026
COLD JUSTICE Copyright © 2017 by Rick Polad.
All rights reserved.

10 9 8 7 6 5 4 3

Cover and interior design: Gary Lindberg

ISBN: 978-1-960250-43-8

Other Spencer Manning Mysteries

COLD JUSTICE

RICK POLAD

Preface

This is a work of fiction. Names, characters, places, and incidents are either the product of the author's imagination or are used fictitiously with the following exceptions.

Name the Dog Contest

Always embroiled in mystery, Spencer finds himself in the middle of a situation with a dog… and the dog needs a name. I decided to let my readers decide. The winner of the contest was Karen Bedore. Three runners-up were Helene Tipa Morrison, Nancy Knox, and Mooneen Gossett. All opted to take the prize of having their names used for characters in the book. Their names are used with their permission, and their names are all I borrowed. The characters belong to my imagination.

History in the Mystery

As in my previous books, Cold Justice weaves the rich tableau of Chicago crime figures into the story. Larry Maggio, my fictional head of Chicago crime, is also fictionally the grandson of the real-life crime boss Johnny Torrio, the man who taught Al Capone everything he knew. Wherever I mention historical crime figures and events, the information is historically accurate to the best of my knowledge.

Chapter 1

I had only been asleep for ten minutes when my phone rang at six a.m. Not a good start to the work week. But then my work week hadn't started on Monday. I had been out late on a surveillance job for a friend of my mom's until an hour ago, tracking down a deadbeat who refused to pay child support. Being able to pick and choose, it wasn't something I usually did. But Erma Blakely had played bridge with my mother, and her daughter, Tracy, had no one else to turn to. Child support deadbeats were lowlifes, in my opinion, and I was glad to help. I had told her I would find the guy if he was in Chicago, but if it led elsewhere I would turn that information over to the police and wish her luck. She said the police hadn't been helpful so far. I didn't doubt that. It wasn't something they spent a lot of time on.

But I had found the guy. With a little information from Tracy, I had assumed the guy had a girlfriend and started with the fact that some relationships start at work. He had recently quit his job and disappeared, but I paid a visit to Reynolds Pest Control and put my money on the young, pretty receptionist. I followed her home and, after four nights in the cold in front of her apartment building, found Mr. Deadbeat coming out at five a.m. with a smile on his face. I followed him to an address on the north side, which I would give to Tracy and the police.

My groggy hello brought a smart-ass comment from Lt. Powolski. I was too tired to explain, or even respond.

"Spencer? Spencer!"

"Yelling isn't going to help. I've been up all night freezing my ass off, and I'll be back asleep in ten seconds, so make it quick."

"You have that big inheritance, and you're out freezing your ass off? What's the matter with you?"

"Favor for a friend. You got something worth keeping me awake?"

"We arrested Joey Mineo."

That got my attention. "When?"

"Sometime while you were out freezing your ass off."

"No need for sarcasm."

"But fun nevertheless."

Joey "the Juicer" Mineo was the gambling and loan department for Larry Maggio, Chicago's current crime boss. Over the last few years we had developed a relationship based on something I couldn't put my finger on. I didn't agree with what he did for a living, but I had to admit he had a soft spot for kids and had been of some help in the Riverview case last summer.

"So what? What's this, the twenty-eighth time? And how many times has he been convicted? Oh yeah, none."

"You done?"

"Not quite. What did you get him for? Jaywalking?"

"Now?"

"Sure." I was trying to pay attention, but my eyes had closed right after I said hello, and my brain had already crawled back into my warm bed.

"Murder."

That woke me up.

"And why are you calling me?"

"Because he's asking for you. Get dressed."

"Pardon my wanting to get more than ten minutes of sleep, but why is he asking for me?"

"He says he's been framed."

I would have laughed if I hadn't been so tired. "Stosh, are you aware of how ridiculous that sounds? Of course he says he was framed. That's Criminal 101 along with 'I want a lawyer.'"

"Spencer, I think he was."

The little voice inside my head that kept me up nights thought so too.

***

I endured the eighteen-mile-an-hour wind and the twenty-two-below wind chill in between the house and the garage and was sitting in Lieutenant Powolski's office thirty minutes later with a cup of black coffee. His secretary, Kate, wasn't at her desk, so I left a box of Fannie May chocolates on her chair and pushed it in so the candy couldn't be seen by the masses. She'd know who it was from. I kept a supply in my freezer for such occasions. I couldn't begin to count the times Kate had pointed me in the right direction or cut through red tape. She had worked for my father and had told me if I ever needed anything to ask. She had been around for a long time and knew all the ropes.

"You look like hell," Stosh said as he straightened the stack of files on his desk.

"Feel like hell too—it's a matched set."

"You still on that child support job?"

"Yup. But about five this morning I got what I needed."

He nodded. "I'm kind of slow, so let me see if I got this right. You have an inheritance that has you set for life, you live the life of a pauper, and you're up all night freezing your ass off."

I took a sip and just looked at him.

"Huh? Am I right?"

I sighed and put the mug on his desk. "Let's talk about Joey."

He sat back and stretched. "Brought him in three hours ago for questioning. He'll be charged with first-degree murder."

I tried not to show how surprised I was, but that was pretty hard. "Try and convince me you're serious while I try and keep my eyes open."

Joey had been arrested more times than I could remember... for a wide array of imaginative charges, most having to do with gambling and loan sharking. Joey had a strict moral code that he lived by, and it was a pretty good roadmap if you ignored the crimes he sanctioned. He once told me he didn't force people to bet on a horse, and he didn't force people to sign an IOU. He was doing them a service. I had pointed out that by taking money from a poor father Joey might be taking food out of some kid's mouth. He told me if I ever knew of such a kid he'd show up with dinner—for the kid.

But he refused to touch other things, like prostitution and anything to do with kids. And his employees were not allowed to gamble or have anything to do with horses, for two reasons. One, that was *his* business. And two, if his employees bet and lost, somebody would have a hold on them, and Joey figured that also meant someone would have a hold on Joey. He had told me that his men knew from the beginning that there were transgressions that wouldn't be forgiven.

He had never been convicted, but as far as I could remember they hadn't tried tax evasion. They hadn't tried murder either. He had beaten them all because he was careful and because he had other people do his dirty work, and they had never sold him out—they had grown accustomed to breathing. Joey had moved up to the gambling chair when Larry Maggio took over the organization in 1973. Before that, Joey was the driver for Sam Giancana, a long-time Chicago mob boss who was murdered in his home.

"So what's the story?" I asked.

"Can't tell you all the story yet. We're waiting on his lawyer, and I don't want to take any chance on screwing this up. But we have an eyewitness who puts Joey on the scene putting two bullets into a now dead guy."

"Who's the dead guy?"

"Max Schloff."

I nodded. "Max Schloff, part of the mob, fine upstanding citizen except for drugs and prostitutes."

"But a dead citizen and an open case."

"Which you're working on just as hard as all the others."

He just stared at me.

"Who's the witness?"

He shook his head and pursed his lips.

"Reliable?"

"A witness."

"Who I'm guessing isn't… say… the mayor."

No answer.

"When did this happen?"

"Friday night—11:20."

"Okay, let's go back to the framed part. First, Joey doesn't carry a gun… maybe doesn't even own one. He tells other people what to do. Second, he has alibis for every second of his life. I don't think he even pees alone."

Stosh nodded and leaned forward to put his arms on the desk. "Which is one of the reasons I believe him. We catch most criminals because they're dumber than rocks. Joey is smarter than you and I. No way he'd let this happen."

"So what do you think?"

He shrugged. "I agree with him—he's been framed. And it's a good one. There's more that I can't tell you yet. A jury would be out for ten minutes except for they'd miss the free lunch."

"Yeah, hard to resist greasy chicken. Is he here?"

"Yes. Probably go to Cook County Jail after the prelim unless he gets bail. But he may not get it."

I stood and said, "Can't see how this is anything but a waste of my time. He'll be out of here in no time."

"Don't know, Spencer. He looked worried."

"This should be interesting."

Stosh raised his eyebrows.

"It would be a great cover to build a rep as the guy who never leaves the office. Take care of business without telling anyone else, and sleep easy every night."

Stosh nodded slowly.

"Max was a loose cannon," I said. "Maybe he crossed some lines, and Joey took care of business."

"Maybe. And maybe he was framed."

I stretched. "Maybe. If he was, by whom?"

"I'm guessing that's what he wants you to find out."

"And what about Chicago's finest?"

"We have a crime and a witness. We're following that. Something else turns up, we'll follow that too."

"But since you have an open and shut case maybe justice looks the other way."

"You're defending Joey?"

I took a deep breath and let it out slowly. "I'm too tired to know *what* I'm doing. There are many things Joey has done that he's never been convicted of. Maybe you get him for the wrong thing, and that's okay."

He didn't answer.

"Who's the arresting officer?"

"Detective Piletti."

I nodded. "Time for a chat."

He bent his head down, stretching his neck. "Have fun with that."

As I walked out he said, "Hey, Spencer."

I looked back.

"Close the door."

I did and stood, wondering what was on his mind.

"Sit."

I did, but he just gave me a serious look and said nothing.

"So?"

He took a deep breath. "I'm going to share something, and I don't want it repeated."

"Sure."

"The papers will say Schloff was killed in an alley."

"Okay… so?"

"He was killed on the second floor of a warehouse on Cambridge."

I looked at him with raised eyebrows. "You going to explain?"

"We got the tip for the warehouse and, since Joey's name was mentioned, were hoping to keep it quiet as long as we could. But

Jennings from the *Tribune* happened to be in the neighborhood doing what he does and stuck his nose in. I had a chat with him, and
he agreed to print the alley story and sit on it for a week unless we
clear it before."

"Really? What did you bribe him with?"

"Bribe is a nasty word, Spencer. I just reminded him of some
favors and promised he'd be the first to hear when we know
something."

"Any particular reason for the alley story?"

"Nothing specific. I just had a feeling, and we gave it a shot.
Misinformation is sometimes useful. You don't tell nobody. And
nobody means nobody."

I nodded. "Why are you telling me?"

"Because in the past you've proved to be helpful. It may be useful while you're shaking those trees. Who knows what's gonna fall
out."

"Okay. Thanks."

Stosh was a 'by the book' guy who didn't play hunches. I'd pay
attention to this one.

***

I sat waiting in the empty interview room for ten minutes before the
door opened, and a guard walked in ahead of Joey Mineo. Another
guard followed behind. Joey wore cuffs. It was the first time I had
seen him without a suit. He looked like a shaved poodle, and his face
had lost the normal confidence that was part of his demeanor, but I
couldn't pin down what it had been replaced by. One of the guards
left, and the other stood in a corner. Not being his lawyer, we didn't
get a private conversation. If it weren't for Stosh I wouldn't even be
having a conversation.

He nodded at me as he sat at the bare wooden table. "Manning."

"Joey." *He could have thanked me for coming*, I thought with a
little chip on my shoulder. Most of me wanted to be home in bed.
"I'm working on no sleep here, Joey. Why me?"

"Because I'm good at what I do, and you're good at what you do. I've been set up, and I got no idea by who. I need someone who's good at what *you* do. The cops ain't gonna put a lot of effort into this."

I let that lie. "If you've been set up, I would think *your* people would be more help than me."

He just stared straight through me. "You gonna help me or not?"

I knew I would. I couldn't pass this up, but I didn't want him to think I was at his beck and call. And, given his response to my last comment, I realized he didn't know whom he had been set up by.

"They got a witness, Joey. Why should I believe you?"

"I don't know who the hell the witness is, but I never killed nobody, specially that crumb Max Schloff."

"Or had anyone killed?"

He didn't answer.

"How many times you been convicted, Joey?"

"Not a damned one."

He sounded proud.

"And how many of those times were you guilty but got off because you have good lawyers?"

"The system said I was innocent, Manning. And I'm innocent now. If you're not going to help, quit wasting my time."

I stared back at him. "I'm not cheap." That was true. Most of the time I was free, but I wasn't cheap.

"Stop by the office. Tell Marty to give you five grand. That enough?"

That was more than enough. "For starters."

He nodded and tugged at his collar. Even without a suit he was dressed better than most men, but it wasn't all quite pulled together.

"And I need some information."

"What kinda information?"

"Like a list of your employees."

"For what?"

"Because you're not sure who set you up, and it's easier to start ruling out the friends we know than the crowd of guys who hate you."

He nodded. "Ask Marty."

"I'm asking you."

"Well, I'm not in a talkative mood at the moment. Something about the surroundings."

We stared at each other for a minute. "No guarantees, Joey."

He shrugged.

"Then there's the problem that if this is a frame it's a pretty good one. Someone went to a lot of trouble and put a lot of thought into this." I paused. "Someone doesn't like you," I said with a slight smile. "How many people have you pissed off over the years?"

He didn't answer.

"This is like finding a needle in a haystack, Joey. I'm good, but I may not be *that* good."

"You like challenges, Manning. And, just like me, you never lose."

"So far. Hate to ruin my record."

We were both quiet for a minute.

"I don't know, Joey."

"How about justice, Manning?"

I laughed. "Really? How do you make your money?"

He ignored me. "Really. I didn't do it, so there is some guy out there who did. There's a murderer out on the streets. The public ain't safe."

I laughed again. "Since when did you become interested in the welfare of the public?"

"Hey, I'll get you a room full of people in the neighborhood who'll tell you they ate at Christmas because of me."

I knew that was true. "This is someone dedicated to you, Joey. No one else is in danger here." I was right, but so was he. Justice had never caught up with him. So maybe it was okay if justice caught up with him for the wrong thing. But there was a guy on the street who might get away with murder if Joey was being framed.

"Okay. I'll take the five grand. You talk to your lawyer, and I'll be back this afternoon and we'll chat again."

He just nodded, trying to look his usual crime boss self, but he didn't quite pull it off. The look in his eyes wasn't all that sure.

Chapter 2

The office was only a few blocks out of the way home, so I stopped to check in with Carol. Piles of snow from the storm two days ago were starting to turn dirty. Didn't take long in the city. A gray, end-of-January day didn't do much to warm up the fifteen-degree temperature, and another storm was on its way, but the days were getting longer. A few more minutes of sun every day would soon turn into spring.

I had hired a plow service to clear the spaces in the rear of the building, and they had done their job. When I got the door open I saw Carol turning around to make sure it was me.

"Morning, Spencer."

"Good morning, Carol. Beautiful day."

"Yes. I figured you'd be home sleeping after last night."

"Something came up. But I'm heading there soon."

I hung up my coat on the rack in the hall, and as I turned into my office I heard a low growl that stopped me. Carol turned toward me, looking sheepish.

"Did you growl?" I asked.

She beckoned me toward her and pointed to the front of her desk.

I walked around and discovered the source of the growl. Lying curled up on the floor in front of the desk was a black and white

Alaskan husky with a red bandanna around his neck. I glanced at Carol and she scrunched up her face.

"I don't know what the policy on pets is," she said with a smile.

"I don't either. Don't think there is one." I bent down and held out my hand. He sniffed it and didn't seem to object. "Is there a story here?"

"Billy found him curled up in front of our door this morning. He was shivering."

I reached out and rubbed his head. "I would think so."

"We brought him in, got him warmed up, and gave him some food. I took Billy to school and brought him over here."

He didn't object to my rubbing his head. "No collar."

"Nope. Do we have to report him?"

"I'll check with the police and see if there are any missing dog reports."

"What if there aren't? Billy wants to keep him."

"Of course he does, but one step at a time, beautiful."

"He wanted to name him, but I wouldn't let him. He looked so sad."

I put my hand on her shoulder. "If it helps any, you did the right thing. Naming something makes it yours and would have made it even harder to say goodbye."

I picked up a dart from the tray on her desk and threw it at the board I had hung on the west wall. I almost missed the board. There were two hooks... one at regulation height and one at Billy height. I left my weak effort in the cork and headed for my office.

As I entered the hallway, she asked, "Are you going home?"

I laughed. "If I don't get some sleep I won't be able to think."

"Do you have something to think about?"

"I do." I filled her in. Her jaw dropped more with every sentence.

"That's big news, Spencer. But there was nothing in the *Trib*."

"No, not yet. They're making sure they have their bases covered. Check the evening edition. It'll be the whole front page... no matter *what* happens."

"This is so exciting! Maybe the biggest case in the history of Chicago, and we're in on it."

I laughed. "Calm down, Carol. This city has some history that puts Joey Mineo way down on the list of biggest cases." I saw her look of disappointment and said, "But it sure beats a stakeout in the middle of a cold night."

She smiled. "So what's the next step?"

"Pick up a check and have a chat with a couple of guys in an ice cream parlor... after a few hours of sleep, that is."

"You could sleep upstairs."

I had also rented the second-floor apartment above the office. I had brought in a bed and a change of clothes to use for quick naps. "I could also use a hot shower and some breakfast. I'll be back this afternoon. Will you be here all day?"

"I will now. I don't want to miss any of this. Billy is coming here after school. He'll be happy playing with the dog. You'll check and see if any have been reported?"

"Right now."

I called Stosh.

"After what I just gave you, you're asking about a dog?"

"Life goes on, Stosh. Besides, the dog's more important."

He said he'd find out and have someone get back to me.

"Get back to Carol. She's manning the phones."

He hung up.

Chapter 3

Joey ran an ice cream parlor with a soda fountain that was a front for whatever else kept him busy from day to day. The name on the sign over the door was "Ice Cream Parlor." Brilliant.

While working on the Riverview case, I'd had several conversations with Joey that brought me into the guarded room at the back of the parlor. I was hoping this visit would get me something besides a check.

A little bell rang as I opened the door, and the moose sitting at the back of the room guarding the door to Joey's office looked up from the paper spread out on a round table. He was a large, barrel-chested man with more than one chin and wore a brown suit that was at least a size too small. I had the feeling he was not comfortable in suits, but Joey, the best-dressed man in town, liked his help to look respectable. He wouldn't be able to move his bulk very quickly, but I was sure the gun under his jacket would be out in the blink of an eye if need be. An unlit cigar was held between his teeth. Joey didn't like smoke. It ruined his clothes. Despite several visits, I didn't know the moose's name. Finding out was on my list.

There was a woman sitting at the counter. She was about thirty, and her legs weren't long enough to reach the foot rail. A round face, short black hair, and no makeup left the impression of someone who didn't leave an impression... except for the fact that I was pretty sure she had been sitting at that same counter the last time I was here during the Riverview case. We had locked eyes in the long mirror on the back wall as she watched me walk to the back office. That was the only time anyone besides the moose and the guy behind the counter had been there. This time she didn't look up from the paper she was reading as she picked up a cup of coffee. I sat down next to the moose.

"Boss ain't here," he said. The cigar didn't move.

"I already know that."

He had no response, except for squinted eyes—I had confused him. I got the feeling he thought that if I knew Joey wasn't there, then I shouldn't be either.

"You gotta name?" I asked.

Still no response.

I tried again. "Marty in?" Marty, who shared the back office, was Joey's bookkeeper. That wasn't quite true. There weren't any books—they were all in Marty's head.

"Why do you want to see him?"

I shrugged. "Maybe talk about where Joey is."

"He don't know."

"We've already been down this road. I do. Maybe Marty would *like* to know. Whaddya think?"

"You packin'?"

"Nope."

"And you won't mind if I check."

"Suit yourself." I took off my coat and he checked.

The moose knocked on the door to the back office, and ten seconds later a horizontal window slid open. Moose explained and Marty opened the door, then sat on the couch. The plush red chair behind the oak desk seemed ominously empty.

"Manning," he said with a slight nod.

"Marty." I nodded back.

He said nothing. No suit for Marty. Not visible to the public, he got by with a still classy, burgundy cardigan sweater and very expensive shoes.

Looking to start a conversation, I asked, "So what am I doing here?" I turned the chair in front of the desk to the couch and sat. Since Marty didn't bite, I continued. "You know where Joey is?"

"You here to see Joey?"

The ice was broken. "Well, if I was looking for Joey I wouldn't be here, 'cuz here he isn't. But since I do know where he is I figured I'd share."

Marty did know the cops had Joey. Joey lived with some of his boys who would have called Marty as soon as the cops left. But he didn't know why or where.

The blank stare I got was why Marty was so valuable to Joey. Every transaction for every one of Joey's accounts was in Marty's head. If anyone wanted to see Joey's books, the response would be, *there aren't any*. After all, it was just an ice cream parlor… and for that there were probably books that showed the company was run at a loss.

After enough silence, he said, "So share."

"You know the cops have him."

That didn't phase him.

He crossed his legs. "What for this time?"

"Murder."

Marty laughed. Not just a chuckle, but a loud, long laugh that probably woke up the moose on the other side of the door. "Well that's a new one, Manning. Who's he supposed to have killed?"

"Max Schloff."

More laughter. "Max Schloff? That two-bit piece of garbage?"

I nodded. "That's the one."

"That's absurd. Where is this supposed to have happened?"

"In an alley."

"How?"

"Shot."

He laughed again. "The boss doesn't carry a gun, and he certainly wouldn't be in an alley. Lawyers will have him out by noon."

"Not this time."

"What the hell does that mean?"

"That means they haven't charged him yet. Just holding him for questioning."

"Which means they don't have the evidence. You want a cigarette?"

"Nope."

He lit one and turned on an exhaust fan.

"I thought Joey didn't like smoke."

He just blew out a cloud and stared at me. I knew Joey wasn't there. He didn't have to point out the obvious.

"Actually it means just the opposite," I said. "They've got him cold. Eyewitness."

Another laugh but not quite as loud. "So why isn't he charged?"

"They're being careful."

His eyes narrowed. "So why are you here?"

"Joey hired me. Told me to tell you to write a check for five grand."

"Did he actually say 'write a check'?"

I saw the problem. "No. He said for you to give me five Gs. I added the check part."

He stared at me for less than ten seconds, then set his cigarette in a crystal ash tray, walked to the other side of the desk, and bent down. He came up with a stack of hundred dollar bills and handed them to me.

"That was easier than I thought it would be," I said.

"Whaddya mean?"

I shrugged. "I could be making up a story."

"And you could be trying to swim on the bottom of the river, but I figure you're not that dumb."

"Good to know." I folded the bills in two and added them to the six bucks in my pocket. I didn't count it.

"So what else you need, Manning?"

"For starters, a list of the people who work for Joey… names, addresses."

He blew out a cloud of smoke. "You're kidding, right?"

"Nope. Why? Is that a problem?"

"You don't exactly see our names on billboards. Stay alive longer that way. And out of jail. Understand?"

I told him I did, but that his boss didn't have that luxury at the moment and was looking to me to fix that.

"And you think one of us has something to do with this?"

"I don't think anything yet. But I need to start somewhere, and talking to the people he spends time with seems like a good idea. Maybe somebody saw or heard something that might help."

"Don't think the boss would want me to give out names."

I shrugged. "Do you think the boss would like to look at life in prison?"

"It was somebody mad at the boss. You're looking in the wrong spot."

"You just gave me five grand, Marty. I get to decide how to earn it. *If* he was set up—"

"What the hell you mean, if? He wouldn't do something that dumb. Who cares about that bastard Schloff? And I've never seen the boss with a gun."

Marty was sitting up straight on the edge of the couch. I waited for him to calm down as he blew out some more smoke. I wished Joey was here. I wasn't all that fond of smoke myself.

"What do you know about Schloff?" I asked.

"He was a worthless piece of garbage."

"Did he work with the outfit?"

He glared at me. "First of all, there isn't an outfit. Second, Schloff was a loser… nobody wanted him around."

"Okay, Marty… give me a name. Give me the man Joey pissed off who would want to set him up."

He laughed. "*The* man? I could give you a hundred."

"My point exactly. So here seems to me a better place to start. I'm not accusing anyone… just gathering information. Looking for a place to start." I didn't know if he had something to hide or was just frustrated because he didn't know where to start looking any more than I did.

"How about this, Marty? You give me names, and I talk to them here."

He blew out a cloud of smoke and said, "Okay, Manning. You and me talk to them here."

I smiled. "No, just me. Who's going to talk with a pipeline to Joey sitting in the room?"

After a bit more verbal jousting he finally gave in.

"So who are we talking about, Marty? There's you and the moose guarding the door and the soda jerk. Who else?"

"Nobody else… and the guy behind the counter is just a soda jerk. He comes to work and goes home."

"But in between he sees everyone who comes in here. What's his name?"

"Jimmy Smith."

"Smith? Really?"

He shrugged.

"That's what's on his paperwork?"

"What paperwork?"

A knock on the door drew his attention. He walked over and slid open the window. I couldn't hear the conversation. When he sat back down I asked what was up.

"Seems the boss is in jail."

"So I've heard."

He just stared at me.

"How long has Jimmy worked here?"

"Going on six years."

"Who hired him?"

"What do you mean, who hired him?"

I spread my arms, palms up. "Pretty easy question. Who hired him?"

"The boss hired him. Who else?"

"And the boss would be…?"

"I don't have time for games, Manning."

I noted that he didn't answer the question and moved on.

"And what about the muscle outside the door?"

"Mike DaVita. Ten years."

"And how about you?"

"How about me what?"

"Last name?"

He took a deep breath and sighed, giving in. "Sparin."

I looked at him with raised eyebrows. "Shortened from what?"

After glaring at me for a sufficient amount of time to make his point, he said, "Sparini."

"And you've been here...?"

"Forever."

I knew that was the best I was going to get.

He got up as someone knocked twice on the door.

"Yeah?"

"Lunch is here."

"Be right out."

I had one more question. I didn't think it would work, but I tried anyway. "And how about his bodyguard?" No one I knew of had ever seen Joey with a bodyguard. The line was either the guy was the best there ever was, or he didn't have one. Joey was known to be on the frugal side. The threat of a bodyguard didn't cost a cent.

"That's not something I can talk about, Manning... no matter how much you just got paid."

"So you're saying there *is* a bodyguard?"

"I'm saying you wanna talk bodyguard you gotta talk to the boss."

I knew that was the end of that road. "And how about a driver?"

"Kid named Danny Primo. Been here about a year."

"Okay. I'm going to have another chat with Joey this afternoon. I'll ask him about the bodyguard."

"You do that."

"Anything you want me to tell him?"

He ignored that. "When's he getting out?"

"No clue. When I left there they hadn't charged him yet. They have to do so or let him go. I assume his lawyers are working on it."

He just nodded.

"I'll let myself out." I looked back as I closed the door. He was staring at the wall. And if it wasn't him who had set up Joey, he was probably hoping he got to the guy before me.

I closed the door, turned to the corner, and said, "See ya, Mike."

He looked surprised.

The soda jerk watched me walk out into the gray day. The girl at the counter was gone.

Turning up my collar and pulling on my gloves, I glanced up at the apartments over the grocery across the street. A curtain fluttered in a second floor window. And, being winter, the window was closed. Someone was watching the neighborhood. For some, that was all there was to do, especially on a day like today.

I turned into the wind and headed back to my Mustang, thinking about all the cement and bricks that had taken the place of the prairie. Progress. Trees had been replaced by black streetlamps, straight and unmoving in the wind. It had started to snow again, and the wind drove stinging flakes into my face. On my way to the parlor I had heard on the radio that the temperature was fifteen, and the wind chill was ten below... like fifteen wasn't bad enough. Life in the Windy City.

***

All it took was a few snowflakes to make a mess of traffic. Luckily, I had the parking spaces behind the office. Street parking was bad enough in good weather. Parking bans on the major roads when it snowed made spots on the side streets pretty valuable prizes. People would reserve their spots by placing furniture in the street. One person just around the corner kept a couch on the parkway in front of his house that he would move into the street. Of course, there was nothing legal about that tactic, and heated arguments added tension to the winter discontent.

I solved my problem by paying We Care Lawn and Plow to keep not only my parking spots clear, but also the alley behind my building, much to the pleasure of the rest of the tenants on my block.

I heard the typewriter when I walked in the back door. I got a hello from Carol and another growl from the dog.

"You need to teach that dog who buys the dog food around here." I bent down and offered my hand. I thought I saw him squint as he ignored it. "Anybody looking for me?"

"As a matter of fact, yes. A Larry from Motorola stopped by. He has something for you."

"What?" I went to high school with Larry. He was a big shot in communications and was the one who had set me up with my pager a few years back.

Carol shrugged. "No clue. He wouldn't tell me. Just wanted to know when you'd be back."

"What did you tell him?"

"That I had no clue. He smiled and said my days of being clueless were about over."

"And that means?"

"There are many things I have no clue about, Spencer. Add that to the list. I'm amazed you pay me for being so clueless. He said for you to call when you got back. Said you have the number."

"I do. Anything on the dog?"

"Nope."

I handed her the cash and told her not to worry about getting it to the bank in this weather. Walking the three blocks would be like the Donner party trying to make it across the mountains. Well, maybe not quite that bad.

She said there was no way she was going to be responsible for five thousand dollars—she'd brave the weather.

Chapter 4

I was about to call the precinct station to check on the dog when I heard the front door open and Carol say hi to Rosie, my love interest detective on the Chicago police force. We had spent two weeks over Christmas up at my cottage on Moonlight Bay in Door County. Aunt Rose had outdone herself with the dinner feast, and leftovers had lasted a week.

I walked out of my office and found her squatted down, petting the dog.

"What a sweetie, Spencer!"

I smiled. "Thanks, I try."

"Idiot. What's his name?"

Carol took over. "We don't know. Billy found him last night in the recess by our front door."

Rosie unzipped her coat, and Carol offered her some coffee.

"We've reported him. I was just going to call the station to see if anyone had reported him missing," I said.

"I suppose that's the right thing to do," said Rosie with more than a note of sadness. "Looks like he's pretty happy here."

"He is," Carol said. "Except he growls at Spencer."

"Smart dog." Rosie continued her petting. "Seems a shame to try and find someone who left a dog out in the cold."

"Agreed. But you don't know what happened. Any number of things could have gone wrong. Probably a very worried owner out there somewhere."

"No collar."

"No wonder you're a detective. Yes, strange, but still, we have to check."

Rosie stood. "You available for lunch?"

"Sure. You working?"

"All done. I'm going to the range."

"Okay. I'd join you, but after lunch I'm going to the station to have another chat with Joey if he's still there." Rosie and I had been in the academy together and were at the top of our class in firearms. We had continued our competition and were pretty even as far as who won.

"He was when I left," she said. "I'll go with you… we can check on the dog."

"You pet the dog… I've gotta make a call first."

I called Larry and got no more information than what Carol had told me. He had something for me and was being very secretive. He said he'd be back at two.

***

My first stop at the station was O'Malley's desk, where I asked about the dog.

"Business must be pretty slow, eh Manning?"

"It's a favor. You got anything?"

He uncovered a sheet of paper. "Yup. Lady called this morning. Name of Nancy Knox. Dog got away from her last night."

"How do you let your dog get away in below zero weather?"

"Well, don't be too hard. It's a working dog."

"Working?"

"So she says. Probably some poor blind lady."

"The dog had no collar."

"I don't explain them. I just do the paperwork."

"Okay, thanks." There would be one unhappy little boy, not that he'd be able to keep him anyway. Carol's building didn't allow pets.

Rosie asked the desk sergeant about Joey. He had been sent to County. That meant he had been charged. I told her I wanted to talk to Stosh, and she said she'd come up to his office in ten minutes.

***

Rosie and I chatted on the way back to the office. The wind had picked up, and blowing snow brought traffic to a crawl. It gave us a chance to talk, and I told Rosie about my little voice.

"I'm betting on your little voice, Spencer. It's always been right in the past."

"But it's Joey the Juicer. The things he's done that we don't even know about would fill a book."

"Yup, interesting ethical problem," she said as she honked at a cab that cut in front of her and fishtailed once before recovering.

"What are your thoughts, Rosie?"

"I like to see bad guys off the streets, Spencer, but I just arrest them and hand them off to the courts. What happens then is out of my hands."

That was the same thing Dad had always said. "I was more thinking about the philosophical problem. They got Capone for tax evasion."

"Ah, yes, but he *did* evade taxes. So he went to jail for something he was guilty of. What if it was a frame? Would it be okay because of all the other things he did that he got away with?"

Traffic wasn't moving. A ten-minute drive was going to take an hour. "A part of me would like to think so."

"And that opens a door to a very slippery slope. Pretty much throws our whole legal system under the bus."

"So what's the answer?"

Rosie laughed. "I don't worry about the answer. I just do my job. I arrest—"

"I know. You arrest them and hand them off. Aren't you interested in what happens to them?"

"Don't have time. I read the papers, but business is good—I'm busy enough just taking care of my piece of the puzzle."

"So, what if Joey is being framed?"

"I'm not worried about Joey. He has better lawyers than I could ever dream of affording. And I hear he has a pretty good private detective working on it."

I watched the wipers battling the snow. They were losing. "I'm wondering about that."

"I bet you are. But I know you like things to be right. And if Joey didn't do it, then who did? And is it okay for whoever that is to get away with murder?"

"Yeah, thought about that."

"And since you like the challenge of the puzzle, you'll do it just in case it isn't Joey."

"But if it *is* Joey, his five grand will buy him a jail cell."

"You're his best bet right now, Spencer. Have a plan?"

"Same as usual, Rosie. Talk to everyone involved… shake the trees and see what falls out."

"Who do you talk to? His enemies would make a long line."

Traffic started to move, and we made it through the light.

"Most murders are committed by family or friends, right?"

"Right. Upset spouse or other relative. Personal issues."

"He's not married. His family is in that ice cream parlor. A frame is something personal, and personal means someone you know."

"Could be."

"Could not."

"Could not. Wanna catch a movie tonight?"

"Sure. I've got steaks in the fridge. Come over about six. If I'm not home yet warm up the grill."

"Okay. You're not going home?"

"I'd like to on a day like today. I'm going to the office to see what Larry wants and then head over to County."

We stopped at the Happy Dog, a few blocks from the office, for dogs and fries.

***

I didn't hear any growling when I came in the back door. I shook off my coat and asked Carol if she had heard from the dog lady. She had. The lady had shown up an hour ago and taken the dog.

"Oh, Spencer. I feel so sorry for that dog. That was the meanest lady I've ever met."

I laughed. "A lady who lost her dog is the meanest lady you've ever met?"

She glared at me. "Was I speaking French?"

I sat down on the edge of her desk. "Okay, I'm sorry. Tell me about it."

"She was rude and arrogant and not at all thankful that we had found her dog… and kept it from freezing, by the way. She scolded the poor dog, and when she walked up to him, he backed away from her."

The front door opened, and a shivering Larry came in with a box under his arm.

"Hi, Spencer. Nice weather—"

"Hang on, Larry. We're in the middle of a crisis. Go ahead, Carol."

"Well, that's about it. I wanted to take him and run out the back."

"I'm sure you read her the wrong way. People don't treat their dogs like that, especially a working dog."

"Spencer! I didn't read anything wrong. She put a collar on him and snapped a leash and actually dragged him part way to the front door… and what do you mean, a working dog?"

"The police told me he's a working dog."

"Meaning what?"

"Meaning she has some kind of disability the dog helps with."

"Since when is being a despicable piece of garbage a disability?" She was still glaring at me.

"Well, it's not. What was wrong with her?"

"I just told you."

"Okay. Dogs are used for people who are blind, or have trouble walking, or can't pick things up—"

"Or need a beer from the fridge," Larry said.

Now *I* glared. "Like I don't have enough trouble here?"

He shrugged.

"There must have been something, Carol. Think back."

"I'd rather not… she makes me sick."

"Try."

She calmed down a bit, stopped glaring, and shook her head. "There was nothing, Spencer. There was nothing wrong with that woman." Then her face lit up. "You're an investigator. Would you investigate her?"

"For what?"

"For being a jerk. And for mistreating animals. Get the anti-cruelty society to look into it."

I glanced at Larry. He was watching with amusement.

"What would they look into?"

"She dragged him across the floor! And she left him out in the cold to freeze."

I took a deep breath. "Okay. If I look into it would you calm down and get back to work?"

She squinted. "You're just saying that to shut me up, but okay… if you promise to do something."

"I promise. Station says her name is Nancy Knox. I didn't get an address. Please call and get that."

"I already have it," she said, looking proud of herself.

"You do?"

"Don't look so surprised. I'll have you know I work for a private investigator. Her address is 3620 Paulina."

"She gave you her address?"

"I told her I needed it for our records."

"And she gave it to you?"

"Yes, after I told her if she didn't she couldn't have the dog."

"Wow," said Larry, "Remind me not to get on *your* bad side."

"Well, that was smart, but she probably made up the address. We can get the right one from the police."

"She didn't make it up."

"And how do you know that?"

"I told her I needed to see her driver's license."

Larry was nodding with a satisfied smile.

"Okay, give me a note, and I'll see what I can find out." I turned to Larry. "Now, what's this big surprise?" I stood.

"Well, I plan on changing your life."

"Don't know how to take that. I had a secretary a while back who had the same plan." I wondered what was in the box he held in his left hand and nodded to the office.

"So," I said as I leaned back in the chair, "change my life."

He put the box on the desk and told me to open it.

The box was a little bigger than a shoebox, and inside was something that looked like an army walkie-talkie.

"I'm dying to know how a walkie-talkie is going to change my life."

He shook his head. "It wouldn't. But this will. It's a portable cellular telephone. Installs in your car and charges while you drive. You can take it out of the car, and it stays charged for a few hours."

I wasn't convinced this was life changing. "Let's talk about the portable part. Do you have a model that comes with wheels?"

"Funny man. This is the next big thing in communications. It's going to change the world."

"Uh huh."

"That's the same thing you said about the pager. You came to rely on that as I remember."

I pulled it out of my pocket and held it up. "Now *this* is portable. Fits in my pocket."

"Well, one of these days that phone will fit in your pocket too."

"What kind of drugs do you take?"

"Make fun. Give it a try." He handed me a card. "Here's the guy who will install it in the Mustang for a small fee."

"Ah, a catch."

"A gift. You don't want it… I'll give it to Carol."

I nodded slowly. "Okay, thanks. I'll let you know how it works out."

"I already know how it works out. Welcome to the modern world."

I wasn't so sure I was going to like the modern world.

Chapter 5

Joey had the best lawyers money can buy, but they couldn't help him this time. The DA evidently liked the evidence and had put her career on the line with a first-degree murder charge. Joey had been booked and moved to the county jail. A top organized crime conviction would make her career, and it sure looked like she would get it. But there was that little voice following me around, whispering in my ear. And, since I had taken Joey's five grand, I figured I should listen. It was singing the same tune as four hours ago—Joey wasn't this dumb.

I wasn't happy about having to drive to County to see him—the parking was terrible, and so was the weather. A normal twenty-minute drive had taken an hour. I parked in front of the bleak building and dreaded getting out of the warm car. The seemingly hopeless grip of a Chicago winter held its normal pall over me. I stared at the gray walls and thought that there was little difference between outside and in. It was dismal no matter which side of the wall you were on. But I also knew there was one huge difference. I could walk in and walk back out again. For Joey, there really was no relief from the interminable winter inside the gray walls.

I stared out the window at the snow falling heavily and thought about my plight. One of the perks of my life was that I really didn't need a job. I had mixed emotions about the money Mom and Dad had left me, but one of the benefits was that I didn't need to work and could stay home on days like this. I grabbed my snow brush, apologized to my baby-blue Mustang, resigned myself to the blowing snow, and opened the door.

***

I had asked Stosh to call ahead and add my name to the list of people who could get in to see Joey.

When I went through check-in, the guard asked me why I had brought a snow brush into the jail. It wasn't the first time I had been asked. It seemed perfectly clear to me, but no one had ever told me it was a good idea. I explained that if the brush is inside the car you get a seat full of snow when you open the door to get the brush. Makes more sense to be able to brush off the door before you open it. I got the usual stare and put the brush and my coat in a locker.

It took ten minutes of paperwork and another half hour of waiting before I was led into the interview room where Joey sat on a straight-back wooden chair with a look of despair. It didn't take long for jail to take a man down a few pegs. The cocky, self-assured purveyor of crime didn't look so cocky. His fashionable, never-a-crease-in-the-wrong-spot, perfectly color-coordinated three-piece suit was replaced by drab orange, one-piece prison garb. I knew it wasn't the jail door or the tiny space with nothing other than a toilet and a bunk that had brought Joey down... it was the orange suit. Joey was a product of the clothes he wore as much as he was of the position he held in the Chicago crime outfit.

We looked at each other for a good minute before he asked, "You get your money?"

I nodded.

He shrugged. "Then why am I still here?"

"I'm good, Joey, but you were just arrested this morning."

"You need to get me out of here, Manning, and I don't mean tomorrow."

Normally I would ask about lawyers, but I knew he had the best money could buy, and they were already working on bond. Joey was only a cog in the Chicago crime machine, but it was a machine that took care of its cogs. Having one of its cogs in jail where frustration can lead to deals being made was never a good thing from their point of view.

"I give you a few days, Manning. But when do I get out on bond? The suits tell me they're working on it, but they're not the ones in the clown suit. I've been arrested before, and I was out before the next meal."

"This is different, Joey. Murder makes this a new ballgame."

"Yeah, I get it, but I didn't do it. You gotta find the piece of garbage who set me up."

"If that person exists, I plan to."

He straightened in the chair. "Are you telling me you don't believe me?"

"I don't believe or disbelieve. I just look around for the truth."

"What about bond?"

"Not my job. But I'm guessing that's going to be tricky with an eyewitness."

"You find out who that is, Manning. He'll tell a different story once my boys get ahold of him."

I folded my hands on the counter and leaned in. "Come on, Joey. The police have been after you for years, and now they have an eyewitness who puts you at the scene with a gun in your hand. That person is going to have better protection than the president."

"But you can find out. You got friends."

"I wouldn't even ask. That's not what friends are for."

He gave me a surly look.

I did plan on asking. And I did plan on seeing how far Stosh would bend, but I wasn't going to tell Joey that. I was pretty sure Stosh wasn't going to bend much, if at all.

"So what's the plan, Manning?"

"I talk to people and retrace your life and everyone who knows you."

He cracked his knuckles. "Who do you talk to?"

"You and your boys for starters. Speaking of which, Marty wasn't too willing to have a conversation and seemed to think the rest wouldn't either."

"So?"

"So, while I'm not getting cooperation, you're getting free room and board."

"I'll pass the word."

"You do that. Tell me about Friday night, about 11:20."

Stosh had told me that an eyewitness said he saw Joey Mineo shoot Schloff at 11:20 Friday night on the second floor of a deserted warehouse on the north side. I had asked questions and got no answers. That was all I knew. But the papers were saying it happened in an alley, so that's what I shared with Joey.

"I was in my place all night. And I wouldn't even think of walking into an alley. Are you nuts?"

"Maybe. But that's not the issue. Do you have an alibi for Friday night?" I knew Joey could get someone to swear to anything, any time. I told him so and also told him that I needed to know the truth if I was going to get anywhere.

He shrugged and reluctantly said, "Not for 11:20."

"Tell me about the night."

He shrugged again. "What's to tell? Same as any other night. Me and Marty decide it's too cold to have dinner at Gibsons, so we go back to my mansion and have them deliver. I don't know why the hell I live in this icebox."

"Gibsons delivers?" Gibsons steakhouse was one of the best in the city, maybe in the country. While looking into Joey, I had learned he had his own table there. I wasn't impressed—so had my dad.

"Everyone does everything for the right amount of money."

I had looked into Joey a few years back just out of curiosity. His 'mansion' was a remodeled three-flat on the north side looking out over Lincoln Park. Word was, he lived on the top floor, and his boys had rooms on the second. The first was used for living, kitchen, dining room with a fancy chandelier, and a plush game room with a mahogany poker table.

"So you're home… then what?"

"What? You're keeping a diary? Home is home. That's all you gotta know." He stared.

I returned his stare. "I can return the cash."

"Never thought of you as a pain in the ass, Manning."

"You never thought from behind bars before."

We stared for another moment before he continued.

"You wanna know how much time I spent in the head?"

"If it's pertinent."

"The steaks came about six. We eat."

"Who is we?"

"The boys."

I stared some more. It was becoming our means of communication. He understood and sighed.

"Mike, Danny, Marty, and me."

"This would go faster if I didn't have to tell you to keep going after every sentence."

"What?"

"Tell me about the evening. I want to know everything that happened and what time."

He stretched and shifted in the chair. "We watch some TV. Wanna know what?"

My stare got the point across.

"Danny takes Marty home and gets back around nine. We play poker till ten thirty."

"Marty doesn't play poker?"

"We don't let him. He knows what everybody is holding before they even pick up their cards."

The guard interrupted and told me I had ten minutes left. I nodded. "So poker ends. Then what?"

"Then we go to bed."

"What time?"

"What time what?"

"Did you go to bed."

He shrugged. "I watched a little Johnny Carson. Saw him introduce Tony Randall and don't remember anything after that. So I'm
asleep before eleven."

"What about Mike and Danny?"

"I ain't their mother."

"They go home?" I knew they had rooms on the second floor but
didn't want Joey to know that I knew.

"Home is the second floor. Somebody wants me, they gotta go
through them."

"Any witnesses to your being in bed after eleven?"

"Now, how the hell would I have witnesses?"

"No idea. But if Jimmy had brought you warm milk at eleven
thirty that would be helpful."

"Hey, you want Jimmy to bring me milk every five minutes,
that's what happened."

"I want what happened to happen. Would it be possible for you
to get out of the house without the others noticing?"

He looked disappointed. "Thought you were working for *me*,
Manning."

"I am. But I'm working to find the truth. If you did it, I'll find
out. If you didn't, I'll find the guy who did."

"You sound confident."

"No sense in planning to fail. Could you get out?"

He shrugged. "If they were asleep and I was quiet going down
the stairs."

"One last thing."

He stared.

"Who are your boys? Marty is the accountant, Mike guards the door
to the castle, Jimmy is the soda jerk, Danny is your driver. Who else?"

"Nobody else. You got it."

"I'm missing one."

He looked puzzled.

"Who's your bodyguard?" I hoped I could catch him off-guard.

"No chance, Manning." He didn't miss a beat. "Not information you need to know."

"And maybe getting out of here isn't something you need to do. Your bodyguard may have seen something you missed."

More stares. I'd have to come back to the bodyguard. I got a warning from the guard. Our time was almost up.

"So this is your normal routine? Eat, play cards, go to bed around eleven?"

He nodded.

"Okay."

The guard walked over.

As I stood up, I said, "One last thing. After dinner, you have any idea what Marty did?"

"Why you asking that?"

"Just asking."

He shrugged. "Not a clue."

"Okay, see you around, Joey."

"Yeah, great. I'll just wait here for you."

The snow had stopped falling and was now just blowing. I brushed off the driver's door, started the car, turned on the heater, and cleaned the rest of the windows. By the time I was done, the inside of the car had started to warm.

As I was brushing the windows, I thought about something I had meant to ask Joey. He and two other men lived in his house. It seemed odd that none of them had wives or girlfriends. I put it on the list of things I needed to know more about.

Chapter 6

I needed a hot cup of coffee and my couch. But I also needed to talk to Stosh. If the station wasn't on the way home I would have put the talk off until Wednesday.

I climbed the stairs two at a time and made my way halfway down the hall to the office with the nameplate "Lt. Powolski" next to the door. Kate was at her desk in the outer office.

"Hello, Spencer. What brings you back here on a day like this?"

"Would you believe I missed you?"

She laughed. "No. He's indisposed but should be back shortly. Go on in and have a seat."

I sat on the more comfortable looking of the two wooden chairs, closed my eyes, and fell asleep. My eyes opened wide when I was startled by a thud and my chair jolting.

"Oh, sorry. I tried to be quiet. Did I wake you?"

"How is kicking my chair being quiet?"

Lieutenant "Stosh" Powolski was a part of the family. He had been a sergeant on the south side when my dad was chief of police. I had grown up calling him Uncle Stosh. He and Aunt Rose were the only family I had left after my folks were killed a few years back. He was a surly, obstinate pain in the ass, and everybody loved him. For years, we had played gin rummy almost every Saturday and some weekdays. He was a walking encyclopedia on Chicago crime history and the biggest Cubs fan in town.

"Make it short, kid. I'm going home."

"Just saw Joey. He's not happy."

"I'll try not to lose any sleep over that," he said as he slid folders into the cabinet behind his desk. "Where are you going with this?"

"Not real sure. I'll start talking with the crew in the ice cream parlor and try and find a thread. He's got no alibi for the time of the shooting. Says he was asleep by eleven. And since there's no Mrs. Joey, there's no one to verify that, like that would matter anyway."

He looked at me like he could care less. "You know that there are very few people in this city who mind seeing Joey behind bars."

I nodded. "Even most of the criminals don't mind. Joey doesn't have many cheerleaders."

His desk cleared, Stosh stood and walked to the coatrack in the corner.

"How long do you think he'll be in County? What's the chance of bail?"

"Hearing is tomorrow morning. It'll depend on the judge, but the DA is not in favor."

"His attorney will argue that he's in danger in jail and isn't a flight risk."

"All the guys walking with a limp will smile about that."

"Okay, different question. What's the chance we'll get a judge who's not being paid off by Larry Maggio?"

"Slim. But I wouldn't mind bail. Joey thinks he can beat anything. He's not going anywhere."

I thought as Stosh put on his coat. "I agree—he's not going anywhere. But maybe he's safer in jail."

"How so?"

"If he is being framed, someone's out to get him."

"Agreed. But, making that assumption, they didn't shoot him… they set him up. They don't want him dead—they want him in jail where he can sit and stare at bars for the rest of his life."

"Why would someone go to that trouble?"

"The list of people he's pissed off is longer than we can imagine. Who knows why?"

"But Joey's into money. The people on his bad side knew what they were getting into—they came to him. He didn't beg them to borrow money from him. Sure, they were upset, but that's something you forget and get on with life. There's gotta be something bigger."

"Well, you have fun figuring that out. Me, I wouldn't be sad if you didn't."

A part of me wouldn't be either.

"You wanna get some dinner?" he asked.

"No thanks. Rosie is coming over. I have steaks ready for the grill. And she's prettier than you."

"Can't argue with that."

"Gin Saturday?"

"Sure, kid."

***

Rosie had the grill heating, and I realized I was hungry. I was also glad she was there. We had danced around the meaning of our relationship for years, but lately it had settled into enjoying being together without analyzing it. I hung my coat on a hook in the hall and got a hug from the chef. Two New York strips were on a platter on the kitchen island. I had carried in the box with my new portable phone and set it on the kitchen table.

"Steaks are ready to go on. Get cleaned up and you can take care of the asparagus."

"Sounds great. Be right back."

She was walking in from the porch when I got back to the kitchen.

"Spencer, do you ever use the telescope?"

Dad had bought me an eight-inch dobsonian scope for my tenth birthday, and we had spent hours looking at the sky. I had once considered being an astronomer, but advanced degrees in physics weren't in my future. But when Dad told me about all the discoveries amateurs had made I decided to just have fun. He had taught me a lot. The celestial objects were old friends, but old friends that held memories I didn't want to face yet. I didn't know if I ever would.

"I used to. We used to drive up to Michigan or Wisconsin where it was really dark."

"Is there anything to look at tonight?"

"There's always something to look at."

"Would you show me? I've never looked through a telescope."

"Maybe another night, Rosie. It's pretty cold." It was actually a good night for viewing. There was no moon, and there was a clear view of Orion from the backyard. The nebula in Orion's belt was spectacular. But I just wasn't ready to move the telescope from the corner.

We ate in the living room watching the news, just as Mom and Dad and I had done almost every night. The six o'clock news led with a major story about Joey. He did his best to keep to himself and wouldn't like all the publicity. But then he didn't have a lot to say about it at the moment. The reporter interviewed one of Joey's attorneys, who stated with a straight face that Joey had been framed. The ABC station ran old footage of one of Joey's previous arrests and gave his history as the loan guy for Larry Maggio, Chicago's current crime boss. The reporter emphasized that this was different from the last eighteen times Joey had been arrested—this was murder. He had no more facts than what I already knew, but managed to stretch it out to five minutes. An unknown eyewitness had seen Joey shoot a man, later identified as Max Schloff, in one of Chicago's dark alleys on the north side. After some information about Max Schloff, whom the reporter described as a lifetime jack-of-all-trades criminal with more arrests than Joey, he signed off with the statement that a hearing would be in the morning.

"So how did the chat with Joey go?" Rosie asked.

"Swears he was framed but has no idea about who. If it wasn't Joey I'd feel sorry for him."

She laughed. "After talking with him, you still think he was?"

"I do. This is just silly. Joey isn't this dumb, or that brave. If he wanted to kill Schloff he'd have someone else do it. What do *you* think?"

"I agree. As much as I'd like to see him take a fall, this smells bad. But despite the smell, if the witness holds up it could stink like a barn full of steaming manure and end up with a guilty verdict."

"Thanks for the imagery." Trying to ignore her smile, I savored the last bite of steak, finished off the asparagus and mashed potatoes, and asked Rosie if she knew who the witness was.

"I don't, but I wouldn't say if I did. I like my job. There's a tight lid on this. I don't even know if it's a man or a woman."

"Do you think Stosh knows?"

"I'd bet he does, but I'd never ask. Are you playing your usual gin game Saturday?"

"Yeah. I'll see what I can get out of him."

"That will be nothing, Spencer. He likes his job too. What's in the box?"

"What?"

"The box behind me on the table."

I told her about the portable phone and opened the box.

"Hard to call that portable," Rosie said. "Does it come with a wagon to haul it around in?"

I laughed. "I mentioned that to Larry. But he was too excited to pay attention to my raining on his parade. He says it's the wave of the future."

"Yeah, as long as you have a wagon."

I shrugged. "It may come in handy."

As we were cleaning up the dishes, Rosie asked if I'd been shaking any trees.

"Not yet. But Joey's family are those guys who hang around the ice cream parlor. I'm going to have a meeting in the morning with my operatives and put some eyes on the ice cream crew."

I washed and Rosie dried.

"And I'm going to look into a certain Knox lady who has some mysterious handicap and a working dog to prove it."

Rosie smiled. "Spencer Manning to the rescue. Can I be Dulcinea?"

"You already are. I am devoted to you, my lady."

She looked up with watery eyes and lips that asked to be kissed. I obliged. I put on a Jobim record that added soft Brazilian ambience, and we settled on the couch where I forgot about Joey.

Chapter 7

As the weatherman had promised, Wednesday was bright with sunshine that would warm the temperature to twenty. A heat wave.

I got to the office at a little after nine. Carol was working on files. I got settled in my room in the back and gave her a slip of paper with six names… four men and two women I had used on previous cases for surveillance, and asked her to set up a meeting for two this afternoon.

I watched the traffic on Diversey for a minute through the big plate glass windows—commuters on a conveyor belt only to do it all again tomorrow—and listened to the discordant sounds of automobile engines and honking horns… the music of the city. I returned to my office, settled in my chair, and called Ben Tucker, my retired ex-DA friend who had quit a year ago at the ripe old age of thirty-two. He now spent the warm months playing golf and the winter buying new clubs. He had retired with a good reputation and a list of contacts, and whenever I needed something he knew the right person to talk to. At the moment, I needed some information and a connection in whatever department at city hall took care of dog permits.

He answered on the third ring. He was glad to hear from me.

"I was going to call you and suggest dinner and lively conversation," he said.

"And maybe turn that conversation to a certain Joey Mineo?" A good portion of Joey's eighteen arrests with no convictions had been Ben's. He would love to see Joey in jail, but I knew Ben would have liked to have been the one who put him there.

"Maybe. You never know where a few beers will lead. But you called me."

"Yeah. I need backgrounds on four guys who work for Joey. Can you still help?"

When Ben worked for the state, he had access to every record the state had and was willing to share.

"I can, but it'll cost you."

"If it's still dinner at McGoon's, we're good."

"How's tonight at six?" he asked.

"Great, but make it seven."

"Bring the names with you. I'll start the ball rolling tomorrow."

"Thanks, Ben. One more thing." I told him the story about the dog. "I want to get a look at permit records. I'm hoping you have a name that can get me through red tape."

"You've been hired on one of the biggest cases of the decade, and you're worried about a dog?"

"I have a boy and a dog he loves and a lady who mistreats the dog and appears to be working the system. If I had to choose between the dog and Joey, I'd take the dog."

Ben laughed. "I know you would. I would too."

"No, you wouldn't."

"Okay, no, I wouldn't." He laughed again. "Give me a minute."

I listened to background jazz as I waited. John Coltrane.

"Ready?"

"Shoot."

"Mooneen Gossett." He gave me a number. "Drop my name. She'll save you a trip downtown."

"Great. Thanks. See you at seven."

"Yup."

Carol leaned into the doorway when I had hung up. "Three of your four people are coming at two. I got a disconnect message for Ralph."

"Okay, thanks, Carol. I'll get you another number."

Under Ralph's name in my address book was a number for the pool hall where he spent most of his time. I left a message for him to call Carol.

Without Ralph I'd have to take one of the four ice cream boys, probably Danny Primo—he had never seen me. I had other people I had used, but after these four the quality went down, and I wanted the best for this job.

I called the number for Mooneen and was told she was in a meeting and wouldn't be available until after lunch. I said I'd call back. The city ran on meetings. I had a feeling it would run far better without them.

Along with the phone, Larry had given me the name of a mechanic who would install it in the car for a fee, and that's what I did with the rest of my morning. For fifty bucks I had a phone in my car that would charge while I was driving and that I could carry around with me—once I got a wagon. I headed back to the office and called Carol from the car to ask what she wanted for lunch. When I told her I was calling from the car, she said I shouldn't be talking and driving at the same time. She questioned the safety of the concept. I told her it wasn't going to matter much… this was a fad that wouldn't catch on.

***

I called Mooneen at one minute after one. She answered. I explained who I was, who gave me her name, and what I was looking for. She said she'd put me on hold and be back in a few minutes. It was twelve.

"Mister Manning?"

"Still here."

"Sorry that took so long. Our records are not easily accessible. I found the application for Nancy Knox, but there's something odd about it."

Odd was good. I didn't want this to be a case of an upstanding citizen who did everything right.

"What's that?"

"Well, under the reason for wanting the license for a guide dog it just says 'health reasons.'"

"Why is that odd?"

"Because it's usually not that vague. It will say blind, or wheel-chair... something like that."

"Do you have a guess why it's vague?"

"I do."

I took a deep breath. Technically she had answered my question, but she knew I wanted her guess.

"And what would that guess be, Mrs. Gossett?"

"It's Miss, and I can't say. But since you're a friend of Ben's, if you'd be willing to meet for lunch..."

Ah, the hand was out. "Sure, how about tomorrow?"

"That would be fine. Do you know Spiro's deli? A block up from city hall?"

"No. But I'll find it. Noon?"

"A little after. Let's meet in the back booth. I'll see you tomorrow."

"Okay, thanks."

I wondered what the mystery was and why she was hesitant to talk on the phone. I'd have to ask Ben more about Mooneen.

***

I jotted some notes about Joey and wrote down the names of the operatives. Next to their names I wrote who I wanted to pair them with and some notes and a description of their subject. I decided to assign Jimmy, the soda jerk, to Morrie, and Marty, the accountant, to Paul. That left Danny and Moose and an easy decision who to give to Rebecca. Danny had never seen me so Rebecca got Moose. Helene, one of the most interesting ladies I knew, and Chester com-pleted the team. Both of them were in their eighties. I used them for easy surveillance jobs that didn't require moving around. This job was perfect. I needed someone to watch the parlor during the day and the house at night. Chester had been a night watchman and had never gotten used to sleeping at night.

There was a Chinese restaurant across the street from the parlor where Helene could spend the day—Chin's, and there was a small parking lot on the side where we could park. I had already cleared it with the owner. He was skeptical at first, but fifty dollars a day and a paying customer for lunch convinced him. I also told him we'd use the restaurant for lunch meetings at least once a week. That would work out perfectly. We could meet without a break in surveillance. I had already asked Carol to call Larry and arrange for phones for everyone but Helene.

They had all arrived by ten after two. Chester wore a plain brown tie with his white shirt and plain brown suit. The shade of brown in the tie changed, but I had never seen him in anything different. I wouldn't be caught dead in a tie and had included that in my will. If I found out I had been laid out with a tie on, God help someone.

While Carol served coffee I filled them in and assigned them a person. I told them everything I knew, which wasn't much, ending with my belief that Joey had been framed.

Paul sat up straight in his chair and stretched. "So you're betting it's one of these four?"

"No bets yet. Hoping."

"Yup. Betrayal starts at home. But what's with all these guys living in the same house and no wives?"

"Well, only two them. Free rent?"

"You have photos?" asked Rebecca.

"Not yet, but I'll get them today. I'm going to park outside the ice cream shop and get some shots of them as they leave. Stop by here tomorrow after noon and get them from Carol. The parlor closes at five. You can pick up your guy then. I've only been at the parlor a handful of times, but all three are there from ten to five. They never leave. I'll also get backgrounds."

"How about lunch?" Paul asked.

"I was there yesterday. Lunch was delivered. But we'll set up a schedule. One of you will always be at the parlor in case someone leaves. Helene will be across the street in the Chinese restaurant and will call in a backup if that happens. Chester will watch the mansion from five to midnight. So surveillance of Mike and Danny ends at five. But be available if you're needed."

Morrie raised his hand. I usually used only one operative on a case. But when I had used two or three Morrie was always very polite.

"Morrie, I've told you you don't have to raise your hand."

He shrugged. "I can't help it. It was the nuns."

I smiled. "And?"

"So these four schmoes are his whole crew?"

I knew where he was going. It was the question of the decade.

"As far as I know."

He nodded and after ten seconds asked, "You don't know nuthin' about a bodyguard?"

"Just the rumors."

"Seems strange… a high-end crime guy with no bodyguard."

"It does. But people have watched Joey, including me. No one anywhere near him."

"I've heard the rumors," said Morrie. "Just plain strange."

"I have a theory," I said. "Joey is one cheap bastard. If people think he has the best bodyguard on the planet, he's covered, and it costs him nothing. Back to the plan. This is no different from the usual tail job—photos, times, who they meet, where they go, what they do. Timesheets and expenses to Carol at the end of the week. Let's meet back here at two on Friday. Any questions?"

"Usual pay?" asked Paul.

"Ah, glad you asked. No. Double pay. Joey parted with some serious cash."

No one complained.

"Oh, one more thing. Carol will be your contact, as usual. But I now have a phone in my car, so she can get ahold of me quickly if something happens. Let me know about even the smallest thing."

Morrie smiled. "Phone in your car. What'll be next? Phones in your pocket?"

Everyone laughed.

"Hardly," I said. "The one in my car barely fits in the car. It's the size of a shoebox. I'm getting phones for all of you... except Helene. They'll be portable, and you can charge them at home or plug them into your cigarette lighter."

We all chatted for a few minutes before they got their coats. I sat on the edge of Carol's desk as they left.

"Interesting group," Carol said.

"They are that. Put a meeting here at two on Friday on the calendar. And would you please set up an appointment for me? I'd like to see Larry Maggio Friday morning. If he's available around ten that would be perfect. And lunch Thursday."

"Okay, I'll call. Who are you having lunch with?"

I told her about Mooneen.

"Thanks for looking into that, Spencer. Billy is heartbroken about the dog. He worries about him."

"I do too," I said. "Something wrong there. I don't like the impression you got of that woman."

"Nope, she was a mean one."

I gave her a brief rundown of the plan for the operatives. She knew the drill.

I stayed at the office thinking about the case, making notes, and listening to WGN on the radio. A few minutes before three, one of the reporters broke in with the news that a judge had ruled no bail for Joey. That surprised me. I figured Joey's money and the lawyers it bought would get him out. I figured the amount would be high, but I had figured he would be out. Ten minutes later the phone rang.

"Spencer, it's a Mr. O'Brien. Says he's Mr. Mineo's attorney."

"Thanks, Carol."

"Spencer Manning," I answered.

"Hello, Mr. Manning. Terry O'Brien, Mr. Mineo's attorney."

Well, he was *one* of Mr. Mineo's attorneys. And not the lead one, whose name I didn't remember.

"What can I do for you, Mr. O'Brien?"

"Mr. Mineo is wondering what progress you're making."

I sighed silently. Not much patience on Joey's part, but I guess if I was staring at bars in a baggy orange suit I'd have little patience too.

"Given that I only got the case yesterday, there's not much to report."

"I understand that. But Mr. Mineo may not. We need to tell him something. He'd like to see you."

I thought of several things to tell him but kept them to myself. "Tell him I've hired operatives who are looking into some people of interest."

"What people of interest?"

"That's all I've got, counselor. When I have more, I'll let you know."

"I understand." He gave me his direct line.

"While you're on the line," I said, "I just heard the judge disallowed bail. I'm surprised."

"We are also. We're working on it."

"I bet. But jail may be the best place for him if you believe someone is out to get him."

"And jail may be the worst place for him if you believe someone is out to get him."

"Good point. I wonder which is correct," I said.

"Let's hope for the first since that's what we're stuck with for the moment."

"Let's hope. Please keep me informed, counselor."

"I will."

I got my coat and said goodbye to Carol.

"What was that about?" she asked.

"Joey is wondering why I haven't solved the case yet."

"How impatient. Does he expect miracles?"

I laughed. "He hopes for one. I would guess that living in a cell raises the impatience bar."

"I guess. Mr. Maggio isn't available at ten. He can do eleven."

I nodded.

"Okay. I'll call and comfirm."

"Thanks, Carol."

"Are you coming back today?"

"Nope. Going to get photos of the Joey gang and then dinner with Ben."

"Good luck. Hi to Ben."

"See you tomorrow, Carol. Tell Billy I'm on the case."

She smiled. "I will. That'll make him happy."

***

I parked across from the ice cream parlor at four. I had driven by slowly and saw Jimmy behind the counter and Moose in his usual chair in the corner. I assumed Marty was in the office and Danny would show up sometime before five to chauffeur them home. There were two women sitting at a table with a kid and a man and woman sitting at the counter. I couldn't see any of their faces. At 4:50 a black Lincoln pulled into the spot in front of the parlor next to a fire hydrant. Joey evidently had his own personal spot. Nice of the city to put a hydrant there. The Lincoln was driven by a young kid whom I assumed was Danny. I took his picture.

Shortly after he squeezed into the space, the customers started to leave. More pictures. The last one out was my lady at the counter whom I had first seen when I was working the Riverview case. She was wearing a coat but had no gloves or hat. Her hair was black and straight, bobbed right at jaw level. As she was waiting for traffic I got some good photos. As she stood at the curb, she looked directly at me for a few seconds, but her expression didn't change from a deadpan stare. When the light turned red and traffic stopped, she crossed and went into the three-story building across the street that had apartments above storefronts. A grocery was directly across the street. To the left was a laundromat and to the right the Chinese restaurant, Chin's. I watched the building, and a minute later a light came on in a second-floor window above the grocery store. It was the same window with the curtain that had fluttered without a breeze.

***

dropped the film off at a photo shop and was on my second Guinness at the bar in McGoon's when Ben showed up.

"Sorry I'm late." He caught the bartender's eye and pointed at my glass. "You'd think having lived here my whole life I'd be used to the cold, but every winter is just as bad."

"Nothing keeping you here."

"Nothing but what's keeping me here."

"And what's that?"

"No clue."

We both laughed. When his beer arrived the hostess showed us to a table.

"Well, this turned into an interesting day. Makes me wish I hadn't retired."

"I bet." I knew Joey was a prize that Ben would love to have. "Breck seems to be sure of herself."

"She's good, Spencer. And she doesn't go out on limbs."

The waiter arrived and we both ordered steaks.

After a long drink, I said, "Joey's good too. Often arrested, never convicted."

"Thanks for reminding me. Did you talk to him?"

"Yup. If it helps you any, he's miserable. Can't understand why he's not out on bail. I thought it would be high, but I thought he'd get bail. You have any thoughts on that?"

"Nope. Just a judge who isn't in somebody's pocket. Probably get overturned."

"I don't think it matters. Joey's not going anywhere."

"Agreed. But I'll sleep better tonight knowing he's behind bars for even a few days."

I grabbed a roll. "You think he did it?"

Ben laughed. "That's the ironic part of this. There were many cases that he should've done time for. Open and shut. So I'd sure like to see some justice. But this isn't Joey. He didn't do this."

"Everyone I've talked to agrees."

"Which is where you come in. Given his history, how do you feel about getting him off?"

"Jury's out. Lotsa mixed feelings. Justice would be nice, but I don't know if it counts as justice if you get convicted for doing something you didn't do to make up for all the things you did."

"That'll keep you up at night," he said as he raised his glass.

"It didn't keep me up last night. Don't think I'll let it tonight either."

We chatted about the case over steak and potatoes. I told him what I knew about Joey's crew and explained my surveillance plan. Ben had used all of my people and agreed they were the best in the business. I told him I hadn't heard from Ralph and asked if he could recommend a fourth. I needed to be doing things other than tailing Danny.

"Only one," he said as he pulled the last piece of meat through the juice.

"Who?"

"Me."

I laughed but stopped when I realized he was serious. "Really? You were just complaining about the cold."

"Not happy about that, but I'd like to be a part of this."

"You do realize that everyone at this table agrees that Joey didn't kill Schloff."

He nodded as he chewed.

"So you want to be a part of maybe getting Joey off?"

He thought for a few seconds. "Maybe not."

"Yeah, maybe not." I gave him a sideways look. "Any maybe you couldn't get him in court, so you set him up in a frame."

"Don't say that too loud."

"You're not denying it?"

He just looked at me with a little smile.

I took a deep breath and rolled my eyes. "Okay, I can use the help. I'll have photos in the morning. Carol will have them by noon. Danny lives with Joey along with Moose. The kid drops them off at ten and picks them up at five." I gave Ben the license number of the Lincoln and Joey's address.

"Okay. I'll stop at the office at noon. Reports to Carol?"

"Sure, but if you need me, I have a new toy." I told him about my portable phone. He agreed that it wouldn't catch on.

As I paid the bill I told him I had talked to Mooneen and asked him how old she was. He said I'd find out.

I ended the night early after a phone call with Rosie. I mentioned the alley in passing. She didn't correct me. I didn't know if she didn't know or wasn't talking. I figured I could tell Rosie, but Stosh had said nobody means nobody. I guessed that included Rosie.

I turned on the news as I got ready for bed. The weatherman was describing the arctic air that was going to move in by morning. Something about a dip in the jet stream. Below zero by sunrise with winds picking up during the day and a wind chill of twenty below. It would be a good day to say inside. Great timing.

Chapter 8

The garage was heated so the Mustang started easily Thursday morning. I just had to walk twenty feet to the garage, but that was brutal. The thermometer on the back wall of the porch showed five below, and the wind was blowing hard out of the north. The sky was blue with bright sun that did nothing for the temperature. People in the southern hemisphere were complaining about the heat.

The parking garage was a half block from Spiro's. Luckily the wind was at my back, but the cold blew right through me. There were three people in the restaurant, one woman sitting by herself in the back booth. It was Mooneen Gossett. She didn't look anything like the picture I had from her voice. I didn't have a definite picture, but I had envisioned a young woman. Mooneen was old enough to be my grandmother.

After some small talk about the cold that gave complete strangers something to talk about, we ordered sub sandwiches at the counter. The counter man asked if she wanted her usual.

"So you come here often," I said.

"Yes, it's a popular spot. Usually packed at lunch, but today only the brave wander out."

My winter braveness had ended in December. I was ready for spring. I told myself I was doing this for Billy.

"How long have you worked for the city?"

She laughed. "Too long."

Our number was called and I got the sandwiches.

"Thank you, Mr. Manning."

"My pleasure. How long is 'too long'?"

"Oh, I lose track, but it's been about thirty years." She smiled at the amazement on my face.

"I bet you could write a book."

"I probably could."

We ate and talked about the current Harold Washington regime. As the first Black mayor of Chicago, he had won with the support of Blacks and White liberals who saw him as a reform candidate. Voters weren't happy with the chaotic leadership of Jane Byrne, the first woman mayor, who had been elected because voters remembered two disastrous snowstorms in 1979 that had dumped thirty-five inches of snow on the city in two weeks. Michael Bilandic, who had taken over when Richard J. Daley had died in office in 1976, was blamed for the aftermath of the storm— roads weren't cleared for days, trash pickup had stopped, el trains bypassed stops, and other city services came to a halt. All that, of course, was not Bilandic's fault, but he was the guy sitting in the seat.

The papers were full of the bad blood between Mayor Washington and the city council, and I asked how that was affecting the everyday business of the city.

Mooneen shrugged and, with a resigned look, said, "Doesn't affect me too much. Hard to make dogs political, but the big things are a mess. Politics is politics. It will never again be the same as when Mayor Daley was here."

"You mean never as corrupt?"

She shook her head. "Oh, it will always be corrupt. But the city worked when Daley was mayor. It was corrupt as hell, but he got things done and took care of the people."

"Maybe there's another Daley in our future."

"Maybe. But he'll never be like his father."

I took a bite and turned to the dog.

"So back to my question, Mooneen. You said you had a guess for why the form says 'health reasons' without listing the reason."

"Yes, I do."

She finished the last bite of her sub and said, "Bribery, or she knows somebody."

I wondered why that guess rated a free lunch. "And you couldn't have said that over the phone?"

She wiped her mouth, folded the napkin, and set it next to her plate. "I could not. There are ears all over that place and rumors that phones are bugged." Seeing the look of wonder on my face, she continued. "I know, who cares about dog permits, but the atmosphere of distrust and backstabbing is everywhere. I'm close to retiring. I'd like to do that on my own terms rather than get a pink slip."

"Okay, so what do you think health reasons means?"

She looked straight at me with a determined look. "I think it means there's nothing wrong with that woman and that she knows someone who pulled some strings."

"Can you tell who approved the application?"

"Normally, but not in this case. The signature is illegible."

"Do you know when the application was processed and who would have normally handled it?"

"I do. It was two years ago, and that would have been me. But it wasn't me."

"So who else might it have been?"

"Any of eleven people in the department."

I realized I was spending more time on a dog permit than on Joey, and I had to get to County.

"Eleven people for dogs?"

She laughed. "We handle other things too."

"Was there a date on the application?"

"Yes, another week will be two years. And I have a question for you."

I figured she'd earned a question. "Shoot."

"Why are you so interested in this?"

I explained what had happened, and she looked disgusted.

"That's just plain wrong, Mr. Manning. I've learned to look the other way at how people abuse the system. But to abuse an animal… just plain wrong. Someone who drags a dog belongs in jail."

I agreed. "Tell me, why would someone who doesn't really need the dog want one?"

"What do you mean?"

"Well, if you want a pet you just go get a pet. Is there any special benefit she gets out of having a guide dog?"

Mooneen looked disgusted. "Sure. Special parking, early admittance to events, things like that. But hardly worth going to the trouble."

"Unless you have a special pipeline that cuts through the red tape."

Mooneen just shook her head. "It's just disgusting. These dogs are in demand. They don't have enough to go around. She's taking that dog from someone who really needs it."

"I agree. But let's try and give her the benefit of the doubt for the moment. Maybe there's some reason we're missing."

"Maybe. Thanks for lunch." She pushed back her chair and stopped, looking thoughtful. "I might be able to do one more thing. It'll take a couple of days, but I'll look into records and see if she's in the system prior to this current application."

"I'd appreciate anything you can do, Mooneen. Thanks." I gave her my card and we stood. As I put on my coat, I said, "One more thing. I wonder if I could get a copy of the application." I helped her on with her coat.

She laughed and opened her purse. "You'll have to forgive my old memory, Mr. Manning." She handed me a folded piece of paper, saying, "I thought you might want it, so I made a copy. I just forgot to give it to you."

I returned the laugh. "Not a problem, Mooneen. Thanks much." I held the door, and we headed in opposite directions. While my car was warming up I looked at the application. The dog's name was Spot. He didn't have any spots.

***

The same guard was at the counter when I walked into the jail. I filled out the form, showed my ID, and got ready to wait. Luckily I was the only one there. We both commented on the cold, and as he handed me my pass he said, "At least you don't need your snow brush today."

I was impressed. Someone working in a jail should be observant, but that probably wasn't always the case. He told me it should only be ten minutes. It was five.

***

I watched Joey walk into the room, dejected and slump-shouldered. If a man is made by the clothes he wears, Joey had fallen to the bottom of the ladder. He looked mentally beat-up and defeated. His eyes were dead, and dark lines accented the bottoms. If it were someone else I might ask how they were doing, but I could tell how he was doing just by looking at him. And most of me thought that was okay. He deserved this and far more.

As he sat down on the other side of the glass, he laid into me. Or at least he tried to. There wasn't much authority left in Joey's belligerence. I almost laughed. But I was working for him so I kept a little respect.

"Manning, I'm still here. What the hell are you doing?"

"What I usually do. I have operatives looking into some aspects of this, and—"

"What aspects?"

"Nothing I want to share at the moment." He would have gone nuts if I would have told him the aspects were his men. "But there's one person who isn't working on it at the moment and that's me."

He just stared at me with those dead eyes.

"I got a call from a Mister O'Brien. He said you wanted to see me."

"Damned right. I want to know what's going on… and not just you got aspects. Why the hell aren't you working on it? I hired you, not some losers."

"I'm not working on it because I'm sitting here talking to you."

"Well you—"

"Me nothing, Joey. I do things my own way. And that doesn't include visiting you, unless I need something. There's nothing I can discover looking at you through this glass. So, unless you think of something important, like who your bodyguard is, I'll make sure O'Brien is kept up to date with anything important. If that's not okay, I'll return the five Gs." A big part of me was hoping he would take me up on that, but he didn't.

"Okay, okay. Calm down. This is driving me nuts. You gotta get me outta here, Manning."

"First, I'm doing everything I can. Second, this is only the second day. This is all about wearing out shoe leather. One step at a time and see where things go. I've got the best people working on it." I hadn't left a case unsolved yet, but there was always a first time. I wasn't going to tell Joey that, but I did have another thought.

"How many times have you been arrested, Joey?"

"Including this one? Eighteen."

I nodded. "And how many times convicted?"

He looked up with what little pride he had left. "Zero."

"Right. Let's assume that some of those eighteen you were guilty of, but your lawyers were smart enough to get you off."

"I was never guilty!" There was a little fire left in those dead eyes.

"Just for this purpose let's cut the crap. You were guilty of some of those and others that never led to an arrest."

"I ain't admitting nothing."

"Not asking you to. Just asking you to consider a point."

"What point is that?"

"Let's also assume that you were framed for the murder of Max Schloff."

"We don't have to assume. I was! I wouldn't waste a breath on that Schloff crumb. What's your point?"

"What if whoever did the framing is just as smart as you? Or even smarter? What if they're smart enough to get away with this?"

He squirmed in the chair, and I was smiling on the inside. I didn't mind at all adding to his discomfort.

"That's why I hired you, Manning. You gotta be smarter than them. How many cases have you solved?"

"All of them."

He nodded. "So what's the problem? Solve this one."

"So you're not firing me?"

"No, I'm not firing you. Get the hell outta here and find who did this."

He stood up, and the guard walked over to his chair. Joey turned without saying another word.

***

As I unlocked the car door my fancy phone started ringing. I picked up on the fourth ring.

"Manning."

"Spencer, it's Carol."

"Hi, kiddo. You win the prize for being my first call."

"And what would that be?"

"You get to work for the best PI in Chicago."

"Great! Who is it?"

"Nice." I started the car. "What's up?"

"Are you coming back to the office?"

"Wasn't planning on it. Do I need to?"

"Not since you have that phone. Ben called. He has some information. He'd like you to call him tonight."

"Okay. Thanks. Nothing on the backgrounds yet?"

"No. I'll let you know as soon as I get something."

"I know you will. Just anxious."

I tried backing out of the spot and realized I couldn't look over my shoulder holding the phone with the cord stretched across the gear shift. Another reason this would never catch on. So I put the Mustang back in park and let the car warm up.

"How was your lunch?" she asked.

"Nothing much. But she's going to dig a little deeper."

"I hope she finds something. I really don't like that person."

"I hope so too. I can't imagine someone you wouldn't like this much. She must be pretty nasty."

"That's putting it lightly. I'd say a bitch."

"And that's the first time I've heard that word come out of your mouth."

"And you may never hear it again."

I laughed. While we talked, I was staring at the temperature gauge. It wasn't moving.

"One more thing, Spencer. I confirmed your appointment tomorrow at eleven with Mr. Maggio."

"Great, Thanks Carol. I'll stop in the office first."

"Okay. See you then."

"Hi to Billy."

The gauge had started to move. I turned the fan up to high and backed out of the spot. It was just a little past four. I had plenty of time to get some food before picking up Rosie at eight. We were going to see the new *Star Wars* movie.

***

I put a pan of tomato soup on the stove and called Ben.

"Hey, Spencer. I've only got a few minutes. The backgrounds should be done sometime tomorrow morning. They'll fax them to your office."

"Thanks. That's it?"

"No. I picked up Danny Primo this afternoon about two when he left the flat. He made some stops and picked the boys up at five."

"So?"

"So, one of the stops was a liquor store on Clark Street. He parks a few doors down and goes in. Two minutes later, in walks Jack Eigen. And ten minutes later they walk out together, talk for a minute, shake hands, and leave in opposite directions."

"Jack Eigen. I haven't heard that name in a while. He's got a long record as I remember. What do you know about him lately?" I made a ham sandwich while we talked.

"Yeah, all two-bit dumb crap. But he did time for every one. When I left we hadn't heard from him in six months. But I bet his parole officer would like to know who he's hanging around with."

I agreed. "But maybe it was just a chance meeting."

Ben laughed. "And maybe the Cubs will win the series this year."

"You never know."

"I know."

"Yeah, you and everyone else. Talk to you tomorrow. Stay warm."

"I plan on it. Nice night to stay home."

"Yup. Wish I could."

"You're going out in this? Hot date with Rosie?"

"Yup, and a fluttering curtain."

"I'd ask what the hell that means, but I gotta go. Hope it's worth venturing out in fifteen below."

"Me too. See ya, Ben."

"Adios."

The soup had been simmering. I poured it into a mug, sat at the kitchen table, and ate while trying not to think about the temperature. My trek could wait until tomorrow, but it had to be at night, and tomorrow wasn't supposed to be much warmer. It was a great night to go to a movie. The place was almost empty.

***

I dropped Rosie off and headed south. There were very few cars on the road. It took twenty minutes to get to Joey's ice cream shop and park in his private spot by the hydrant. I sat for a few minutes looking across the street at the window with the curtain that had fluttered without any wind.

I zipped my jacket, pulled on gloves, and headed across the street. The building had three floors. The curtain was on the second. Only two names were listed for the second floor. There was a Michael Masters and an L. Hands. I was looking for the name of the lady with the short dark hair who spent her days in the ice cream parlor. I wondered why, and the best place to start was with her name. A first name would have been nice, but getting that wouldn't be hard.

I sat in the car for five minutes looking up at the window, hoping to catch a glimpse of my mystery woman. She didn't show. Before I drove away, I looked back at the window and said, "Hello L. Hands."

A half hour later the Mustang was back in its warm garage, and I was sipping coffee and watching the news. I checked the phone book for L. Hands. There was no listing. A call to the station in the morning should take care of it with a little help from Kate. The weatherman said the cold spell should break soon. He was forecasting fifteen above by Friday. It's not often fifteen above sounds like a heat wave. He said if it made us feel better, it was forty-eight below in Yakutsk, Siberia, the world's coldest city. It didn't make me feel better.

Chapter 9

Friday dawned bright and sunny. It had warmed to seventeen above. People waiting for buses and walking to their offices from the train were more stalwart than I, who wasn't happy about walking from the heated house to the heated garage.

I called Kate while waiting for traffic to clear. She said it would be nice to work on something easy and would get back to me after lunch with the name. I figured if I left by nine that would give me enough time to take care of a few things at the office and get to my Maggio appointment at eleven.

Carol was at the coffee machine when I arrived and handed me a hot cup.

"Thanks, my woman Friday. How was the commute this morning?"

She laughed. "The commute is like rolling out of bed. I almost could. Living right across the street is wonderful. It's the two block walk getting Billy to school that's the tough part. But at least the wind has calmed down. Nice to only have to deal with the temperature."

I took a sip. Carol's coffee was good, but it wasn't like Mom's—nothing ever is.

She poured herself a cup and said, "The backgrounds are on your desk. Everyone picked up the photos yesterday, and you have an eleven o'clock appointment with Mr. Maggio."

I knew she didn't approve of my dalliance with organized crime, but she hid it well.

"Good. Thanks. I'll be here until about ten." I stopped halfway to my office, reached into my pocket, and pulled out Mooneen's permit copy. "It's not a case, but would you make a file for the dog lady and put this in it?"

"I already did. What is it?"

"A copy of the handicap permit."

She took it. "This is going to help?"

"You never know." I watched her looking it over.

"Hard to read the signature."

"Impossible to read the signature. Tends to keep people anonymous."

I made it to my office, settled into my cushioned chair, and opened the file.

***

Michael DaVita… Moose. Sixty-two years old. Born in Chicago on the south side. His listed address was Joey's on Lincoln Park West. Married when he was twenty-two. Divorced two years later. One daughter, no address. The report listed an expired driver's license. That had happened twelve years ago, in 1972. He had a current gun permit. Next to employment were the words "self-employed." He had been arrested three times. Two were gambling related. One was a DUI. The only one that had stuck was the DUI. He had been given probation and during that time had let his license lapse. Not much there, but I didn't expect much.

The sheet on Marty Sparin had even less. Thirty-eight years old. Born in Detroit. His current address was listed as 3711 Kenmore. That put him within walking distance of Wrigley Field. A previous address was also in Chicago. He owned a 1982 Buick and had just renewed his driver's license. No arrests. He had a degree in business from the University of Chicago. No marriage listed. He had a gun permit that had an original date of 1969, sixteen years ago.

The driver, Danny Primo, was twenty-four years old. His address was also listed as Joey's. He had two arrests in the last two years for petty theft, and there was a recent outstanding speeding ticket. He had a year left on parole. His parole officer wouldn't be happy about Jack Eigen. Born in Chicago. His last place of employment was a car service station on the north side. I wondered how he got the job with Joey and thought he must be related to someone. Joey didn't pick up kids off the street.

Jimmy Smith, the soda jerk, had an address only a few blocks from Marty on Southport. He was fifty years old, had a valid driver's license, and had never been arrested.

Carol had made copies of each sheet. I left the copies with her and walked to the front window to watch the bundled pedestrians. There weren't many. As I turned and started toward my office to get my coat, the phone rang. I sat on the edge of Carol's desk and listened to her "umhmm" and "thanks."

She hung up and looked up at me. "That was Kate. Your mystery lady's first name is Loretta."

"Okay. Thanks."

"Does that help?"

"Not yet. But more information is better. Please give Ben a call and see what he can find out about Loretta Hands and please make reservations for two at McGoon's at seven."

"You don't want to use the same guy we just got the reports from?"

"No. I have a feeling about her. Ben has sources that will go deeper than these reports."

"Okay." She smiled. "Good luck with Mr. Big."

I got my coat and headed downtown.

***

Larry Maggio's office was on the fifth floor in an all-glass building in the high-rent district on Michigan Avenue. We had first crossed paths a few years back when a case led me to a picture gallery he owned. I had been invited by two large men in a limo who strongly recommended it would be in my best interest to have a chat with Mr. Maggio. The meeting had been cordial, and he had said to call if I ever needed anything. I try and not need things from the heads of organized crime, but this time I was working for Joey, which meant that I was working for Maggio.

Traffic was light, and I found a spot on the first level of the parking garage. I was fifteen minutes early and stopped in the lobby to warm up. The elevator door opened opposite Maggio's glass wall.

The same smiling secretary was at the desk and said Mr. Maggio was expecting me, and I could go right in. She told me I could hang up my coat and announced me on the intercom. I knocked and let myself in. I couldn't remember if the same hired help was sitting outside the door, but he was doing the same thing as the last time... reading the paper with one eye and watching me with the other.

Maggio stood and walked around his desk. He held out his hand, and I took it.

"Hello again, Manning. Have a seat."

Nothing appeared to have changed since my last visit. The view out the windows to the south was still spectacular, the bar behind the desk was well-stocked, and Maggio was dressed immaculately.

He folded his hands on top of the glass-topped desk. "I'd offer you a drink, but last time you refused."

"Well it's still hard to turn down Glenfiddich 15, but before lunch is a bit early for me. I'll take some water."

"To tell you the truth, me too. Next time make the appointment for afternoon." He smiled.

I said I'd do my best, but I had no intention of making a habit of visiting Larry Maggio.

He filled two crystal glasses from the pitcher on his desk and said, "I assume this is about Joey. Have you seen him?"

"Yes. Orange isn't a good color on him."

"No, that must be killing him. I was shocked he didn't get bail."

"Perhaps not so shocking given who he is."

"Perhaps. O'Brien tells me Joey knows nothing about it and says he's been framed. Do you have any ideas on that?"

I took a drink. "I would have to agree. Joey's not that dumb. First, if he did do it, he'd have an alibi set up. And second, he wouldn't do it. He'd have someone else take care of it. Can you tell me anything?"

He took a deep breath. "I would agree he's been set up, but the list of possibilities is long."

I nodded. "Tell me about Max Schloff."

We were interrupted by the sound of sirens coming up Michigan Avenue.

"Not much to tell. A nickel-and-dimer we used at times. He was harmless. He wanted to play with the big boys, but he wasn't very bright. I think there was something wrong with him. The boys made fun of him but would help him out sometimes if he needed a few bucks. Nobody would have any reason to kill him."

"One person did. And maybe the reason was to put Joey behind bars."

"I hear there's a witness. You know who?"

"Nope. That's being kept very quiet."

"Bound to come out sometime."

"Yup. At trial if not sooner. The cops are being very tight about it."

We stared at each other for a minute before I said, "I have a few ideas, if you wouldn't mind answering some questions."

"I might and I might not. Go ahead and ask."

I leaned forward and fingered the glass. "How secure is Joey's job?"

He raised his eyebrows. "What does that mean?"

I shrugged and thought about how to put my questions. I usually liked my clients, but this one represented everything I thought to be wrong with the world. "Two things. Are you happy with him?"

He sat back in his chair. "I'm not sure what that means, Manning."

I thought some more, staring at the sunlight sparkling in the crystal glass.

"Is he doing his job? Causing any trouble for anybody?"

Maggio stared at me, deciding how to respond. "Given that his *job* isn't something you agree with, all I can say is, from my side of this desk, no one here has any problems with Joey."

I nodded slowly. "Okay. How about this? Anyone looking to take over his job? Anyone think Joey's been doing it long enough, and it's time for a new face in his chair?"

He thought some more. It was like we were dancers both wanting to lead but couldn't figure out what the rhythm was.

"Again, from this side of the desk, I see no problems. Nobody who works for me is that dumb."

I disagreed. There's always someone who wants to move up the ladder, no matter what the job. But I kept that thought to myself. "It would make sense. If this is a frame, someone wants Joey out of the way. There are two ways of doing that. Putting him in jail is one. The other is more permanent."

He nodded. "I do see your point, but I see no evidence of that. If someone wants him out of the way, it isn't someone in my... company."

"What can you tell me about the... employees at the ice cream parlor?"

"What do you want to know, and why?"

"Let's start with the why. Most crimes are committed by a relative or friend of the victim."

He shook his head. "I've already told you there's no one who works for me you should be concerned with."

"I have to be concerned with everyone. And if it's not one of them, the list of people who want to get even with Joey is endless."

"I don't agree, but I see your point. What do you want to know?"

"How long have they been... with you?"

He laughed. "We don't exactly keep employee files."

"Give me a rough guess." Wondering how much he knew about his employees, I wanted to check what he said against what Marty had told me.

Leaning forward, he said, "Okay. DaVita is the longest, about ten years. Marty a little less, Smith about five years, and the kid just a little over a year. But you're barking up the wrong tree."

The times matched. He was more hands-on than he let on. "I have to bark up every tree. And as I already said, outside those trees the forest is huge."

The intercom buzzed, and he pushed a button.

"Yes, Ashley?"

"Your next appointment is here, Mr. Maggio."

"Thanks. Tell him it'll just be a minute."

I guessed I was done.

He looked up at me. "Any more questions?"

"Just one. What do you know about his bodyguard?"

He laughed again. "Not a thing. I don't micromanage. Officially, why would Joey need a bodyguard to run an ice cream parlor?"

"How about unofficially?"

"Same answer. And why would you care?"

"I'm just trying to help here. I start with a list that includes everyone and cross them off. A person in the 'ice cream business' might have a bodyguard, and that bodyguard might know something."

He smiled. "Do you box, Manning?"

"Used to. Why?"

"You're pretty good at sparring."

"I do my best."

"Always nice chatting with you, Manning. If you need anything else, call."

And we'd continue dancing around my questions.

I had never gotten much information out of Maggio, and I wasn't fond of associating with him. Meeting with the head of organized crime in Chicago conflicted with my upbringing by a dad who was chief of police. But information is information, and a few years back a sentence from Larry Maggio had helped me solve a case. He had said he didn't micromanage, but I was betting if he knew when Joey's crew were hired he also knew about a bodyguard.

I checked in with Carol from the car and told her I'd pick up sandwiches for lunch. She told me Ben couldn't make the meeting at two but would make dinner.

***

Morrie was the first to arrive. He was always fifteen minutes early. I had tried to convince him that if he could always arrive fifteen minutes early he could arrive on time. It wasn't a concept he could understand. While we were chatting about the Cubs' chances, Carol stepped in and told me Ralph was coming but would be a little late. Paul gave me his opinion on the changes the Cubs needed to make to get back to the World Series in 1985. He had been at the series in forty-five, the last time the Cubs had won the pennant. They hadn't won the series since 1908. Hope springs eternal.

Everyone but Ralph had arrived by five after two. I handed out the profile sheets and asked for reports. No one had anything out of the ordinary. I told them about Ben's seeing Danny and Jack Eigen together.

"There's a name you never stop hearing," Paul said. "Eigen can't stand it if a week goes by without his name on the police blotter."

"Yeah, not exactly how you want to make a name for yourself," replied Morrie. "But I can't imagine the kid has anything to do with this. He's strictly penny ante."

"Maybe he's branching out," said Rebecca.

Morrie just shrugged.

I heard the front door open and Ralph introduce himself to Carol. He sat on the chair in the corner, and, after briefly catching up with the three he knew, I introduced him to Helene and Chester. I filled him in and gave him Danny. That would free up Ben if something special came up.

A little after two thirty I heard the door open again. A minute later Larry entered my office carrying a large box. Everyone but Helene got a portable phone. I had offered to buy them, but Larry offered them free if everyone agreed to record where they were using them and if they had any reception problems. He explained that the network of transmission towers was in its infancy, and they needed to find out where it worked and where it didn't.

They all acted like kids at Christmas with a new toy. I told them we'd meet Monday at Chin's for lunch at noon. I saw them all out and sat in front of Carol's desk. She gave me a hurt look.

"So, how come I don't get a car phone?"

"Maybe because you don't have a car."

"Men. All they have is excuses," she answered with a slight smile.

"And sometimes they sign checks."

Her smile grew bigger. "You have a point. What's your plan for the rest of the afternoon?"

"I'm going to the parlor and set up a meeting for Monday to have a chat with the boys. I've got some time to fill before I meet Ben at seven."

"So you think one of Joey's people is behind this?"

"I don't think anything yet, Carol. I'm just watching and shaking some trees. You shake the right tree sometimes something falls out."

"You mind if I close up at four? I'd like to take Billy for some new clothes."

"No problem. You don't even have to ask. Just let me know."

"Maybe not, but I always will."

I just nodded. Carol was the best part about this job.

***

The boys were the only ones at the parlor. It was a good thing Joey didn't depend on ice cream to make a living. Moose just got up and knocked on Marty's door and waved me in. I wondered how good I should feel about being one of the boys. Marty still wasn't thrilled about my talking to the group alone.

"What are you doing about this besides bothering us, Manning?"

"There are a few other angles, but none are promising." Actually, there were no other angles after Maggio had added nothing to the pot. "You and Joey have given me nothing else to go on."

He stood up from behind Joey's desk and lit a cigarette. I wondered how much he liked the desk. History was full of guys getting used to other guys' desks, sometimes with the help of a bullet or two. Maggio had told me a while back that he was a businessman—guns were a thing of the past. Maybe Marty had traded a gun for a frame.

He reluctantly agreed to a meeting Monday and said he'd make sure Danny stopped by.

I nodded to Moose on the way out. He nodded back. Jimmy was washing glasses and didn't bother to look up.

The sky had clouded over, and a wind out of the north was adding to the cold. As I crossed the street I glanced up at Loretta's window. It was just another window. Nobody looking out and no curtains moving.

There wasn't enough time to go home so I headed for McGoon's. I could get a parking spot and watch the customers over a leisurely Guinness or two.

***

It was only a ten-minute drive, but I had forgotten it was Friday and that the working crowd would be quitting early and celebrating the end of the work week. The tiny parking lot behind the pub was full, and I had to park a block away on a side street. And I was lucky to get that. The walk in the cold air was invigorating, but I was glad it was only a block. The sky had clouded over, and they were predicting more snow overnight.

I smiled at the maître d', Nathan, as I unzipped my jacket.

"Nice to see you, Spencer. You're early."

"I am. Gonna settle at the end of the bar and watch the crowd."

"Fine. Are you meeting the lady?"

I laughed. "I wish. No, just Ben. Please point him in my direction when he gets here."

"Sure thing."

The bar was crowded and noisy, but there were three stools at the end farthest from the dining area. Jack placed a Guinness in front of me as I was hanging my jacket over the back of the stool.

"My thanks to you and your brewmaster, Jack."

"I'll pass that along, Spencer. How's the crime game?"

"Never a lack for business."

"Yup, two jobs with good job security… murder and alcohol."

I raised my glass.

The TV over the back of the bar was running the nightly news. I was watching with half my attention. The other half was thinking about how to approach the parlor gang on Monday. I knew they weren't going to be happy about the chat, but it was worth a try. Then the half that was paying attention to the news made the Monday meeting even more problematic. The channel seven news anchor was talking about all of Joey's prior arrests and lack of convictions and ran a taped statement by his lead lawyer about how they were still trying to get him released on bond.

I knew that would make Joey a happy man. I was pretty sure he wasn't concerned about being convicted. When it came to arrogance Joey had more than his share. But being locked up in a cell was killing him. I couldn't bring myself to feel sorry for him. But his being in a cell made my job easier—Joey wouldn't be sticking his nose into the investigation. And I was pretty sure he wouldn't be happy about my talking to his men. If he got out and was there on Monday, my talks probably wouldn't even happen.

Before the story was over, the couple three stools over left, leaving a wide space between me and two guys talking about the Blackhawks. I caught Jack's eye and raised an empty glass. He gave a tiny nod, finished wiping the bar, and pulled another.

I was nursing that smooth bit of Ireland—Dad had called it the nectar of the gods—and watching the weather report, when someone sat down next to me. But it wasn't just any someone… it was someone with short black hair whose feet didn't touch the bar rail. Except this time she was looking considerably more memorable. Maybe it was the makeup, or the multi-colored scarf, or the gentle smell of baby powder. I didn't know if bulls really were attracted to the color red, but if they were they would have approved of her lipstick. I wondered several things, including why she showed up here and why she sat next to me when there were five empty stools. Perhaps it was my magnetic personality and good looks. Perhaps not.

I kept my eyes on the news and heard her order white wine. When Jack brought it he gave me a quick look that included a nasty little gleam in his eye.

She picked up the glass and said, "I hope you don't mind my taking this seat."

"Nothing to mind. But there are several open. I'm wondering why you picked that one."

She smiled an enticing smile and said, "I don't like drinking alone. It's always nice to have someone to talk with."

I took a drink and didn't respond.

She kept trying. "I haven't seen you here before. Do you come here much?"

Before I could respond, the news anchor came out of a commercial with more about Joey with his photo in the bottom right corner of the screen.

I swirled my beer, nodded to the TV, and decided to stir the pot. "Interesting story. Do you think he did it?"

She laughed and leaned toward me. "Oh, I wouldn't know about such things. I don't have much faith in the justice system. People have been getting away with murder since the beginning of time. Why should this time be any different?"

"He'll get a trial, and they have an eyewitness. Seems like a good case."

"And I imagine he's got the best lawyers money can buy. And maybe a few judges too."

"You're pretty cynical."

I finished my beer and Jack raised his eyebrows. I told him I'd wait for dinner.

"Just realistic. By the way, my name's Jamie."

"Nice to meet you, Jamie," I said flatly. I tried not to look at her, but I couldn't help staring at her eyes. They matched the color of her hair—as black as ebony.

The newsman did the talking for the next few minutes. Sometime in those minutes Jamie managed to change her position so that her leg was touching mine. I didn't admonish her leg. It reminded me of Sarah Dingle in sixth grade. When she had sat next to me on the bus she dropped a book on the floor. I gallantly picked it up. Somehow, by the time I handed it to her, she had moved closer to me, and her leg was touching mine. I didn't mind, but at the time I didn't really know why I didn't mind. I didn't mind now either, but now I knew why. People often touched in a crowded bar. But there were still four seats left on the other side of her.

She finished her wine and asked, "Do you have a name?"

"Yup."

Before she could respond, Ben walked up.

"Hey, Spencer. Am I intruding?"

"No, we were just chatting about names." I introduced him to "Jamie."

"Always interested in those of the female gender," Ben responded with his usual charm. "I hate to intrude, but Nathan has our table ready."

Jamie laid a five on the counter, swung around on her stool and said, "Looks like I'm the one who's intruding. You two have a nice dinner." She turned to me, swung her purse over her shoulder, and said, "Maybe we'll see each other again, Spencer."

I silently swore at Ben. "Maybe we will."

"Well, bye."

I watched her walk away in the mirror. She didn't look back.

As we walked to the dining room, Ben asked, "Where was the Spencer charm? You treated her like you wanted her to leave."

"You get the table. I'll find you."

I waited for a group to clear the foyer, walked back to the bar, and waited for Jack to turn around.

"Hey, Spencer, nice lady."

"If you mean she gave you a nice tip, then I agree. Have you seen her in here before?" Even a customer who had only been in once would be remembered by Jack.

He shook his head. "First time during *my* shift."

"That's what I thought. Thanks, Jack."

"Sure thing, Spencer." He turned to a waitress.

I found Ben at a table at the back of the restaurant section. Two glasses of Guinness were already on the table.

"So what the hell was that about? 'Maybe we will?' What happened to 'I look forward to it'?"

"Well, two things, and both are females."

He took a long drink and said, "Both? I get Rosie, but it doesn't hurt to be nice. Who's the other female?"

"Loretta Hands." I sipped my beer.

Ben let out a startled "Loretta Hands" as Jane arrived at our table.

"Hi, gents. Nice to see you both."

"Hello, dear Jane," said Ben. "You look as lovely as a spring morning."

She curtsied and asked if we wanted menus. We both declined and ordered steaks, medium rare.

"Back to Loretta," said Ben. "You lost me. What did that have to do with Loretta Hands?"

I took a long drink, took a deep breath, and said, "I'm not quite sure. I can answer that better after you get some background on her."

Nathan seated two couples at the tables next to us. The place was filling up.

"Well, I already have some background on her. And I think *some* is all we're going to get."

"Seems the night for being cryptic. What do you have?"

He took a deep breath followed by a long drink.

"Loretta Hands. Born in Chicago in 1956. Address on Diversey. Rents. The rental agreement was signed three years ago. No prior address. She has a driver's license but does not own a car. She has a gun permit that dates to 1977."

"Okay. What else?"

He stared some more. "That's it."

I was about to take a drink but stopped and set my glass down. "What do you mean, that's it?"

He shrugged. "That's it, as in there's nothing else. This is the most average American there is… except for one thing."

I looked around the room. There wasn't an empty table, and the noise level was high. People enjoying the end of the week. All of a sudden I wasn't.

"Yes… one thing," I said. "Why does an average American girl get a gun permit the first chance she gets?"

Jane arrived with our steaks as Ben continued. "Why, indeed. But I bet we could come up with several reasons."

The steaks were sizzling on the metal plate, and the baked potato and sautéed green beans rounded out a perfect meal. Luckily, the rise in my curiosity level hadn't affected my appetite. Jane was back two minutes later with more beer.

"Anything else I can get you gentlemen?"

"Only some lucidity, my dear Jane," said Ben.

Her smile disappeared. "Some what?"

"Not to worry. You have provided for our every need."

She squinted at him. "You'd think I'd be used to you two by this time."

Ben raised his glass. "Hopefully the romance will never become as predictable as your fine service."

"I'm sure that will be the case, especially if I can figure out what you're talking about."

Ben laughed and raised his glass again as she picked up the tray.

"You've got to stop playing with her, Ben."

"Not playing in the least, Spencer. I'd follow her to the ends of the earth."

"Right. And that might be romantic if she hadn't already forgotten about you."

He shrugged as we cut into the steaks. They were done perfectly, as usual.

As he chewed, Ben asked, "How does this mystery woman fit into the Joey picture? I'd like to meet her."

"The mystery gets more mysterious. You already have."

His eyebrows raised as he chewed.

"That was her at the bar."

"You introduced her as Jamie."

"I did. That was the name she gave me."

As we finished the meal and another beer, I explained how she fit into the picture.

"Do you think she's anything more than a person who lives across the street?"

"Too early to think, Ben."

"Hard not to think so. If she isn't, there's sure something else she's hiding. And she's very good at it. She sure isn't your average girl across the street."

"Agreed."

"Do you have someone on her?"

"I'm out of people, so no."

"How about me?"

I finished my Guinness. "If you're willing. But as far as I can tell she has no job and no set schedule. She spends a lot of time in the parlor."

"I'll see what I can do."

Jane brought the check, and I paid.

***

I turned up my collar as I walked back to the car. The sky was clear and the air was cold. I pulled into the garage and stopped in the backyard to look at the sky. Jupiter and Mars were within one degree of each other in the western sky. No moon and cold, crisp air made for perfect viewing. I thought of taking out the telescope, but the cold trumped the viewing. And I still wasn't ready to dig up memories.

Chapter 10

Lieutenant Stanley Powolski had been on the force two years longer than my dad when Dad became chief. He had been a sergeant for as long as anyone knew and had turned down every chance at promotion. He had no desire to be anything but a sergeant. He had finally accepted a promotion to lieutenant but only for the raise. Francine, his wife of thirty-seven years, had developed cancer, and the extra money came in handy.

I had called him Uncle Stosh ever since I started talking. When I started high school I dropped the uncle, but he would always be family. And with Mom and Dad gone, he and Aunt Rose were the only family I had left. He had taught me how to play gin when I was three. We played for Lifesavers. He also got me started on beer. That was a few years after the gin. The only beer in his fridge was Schlitz, "the beer that made Milwaukee famous."

I had given up trying to explain to him that the beer in his fridge wasn't the same as the beer he had grown up with. In the late forties Schlitz was the best-selling beer in the country, much to the dismay of Anheuser-Busch, which started new campaigns in the fifties. The lead went back and forth until Busch took over for good in 1957. Schlitz's owners fought back by cutting costs. They made small changes that they thought wouldn't be noticed by their customers. They replaced malted barley with corn syrup and used cheaper hops, ignoring the warnings of their brewers about what would happen if they fooled with the quality of the beer. For a while their market share grew faster than any other beer. They also shortened the aging time and had to add a silica gel to prevent a haze from forming as the beer chilled, because there wasn't enough time for the protein to settle out.

In 1976 the FDA started to talk about listing ingredients on bottles and cans. They certainly couldn't list silica gel, so they added a new anti-haze agent. That caused an unexpected problem—it reacted in the bottle with the foam stabilizer forming a layer that looked like mucus. The owners tried to tell consumers that it wasn't harmful, but Schlitz was done.

I later expanded my beer selection, but at Stosh's house it was Schlitz. The owners had at least one loyal drinker.

I got to his bungalow a little before noon and found him in his recliner, reading.

"Hey, kid. I hope you're hungry. I've got plenty of meat."

"I could eat a horse, but I'd prefer pastrami on rye. What are you reading?" I knew the subject, just not the book. Two shelves of Stosh's bookcase were filled with Chicago crime history. There wasn't much he didn't know.

"New book by Brinkman. He takes another look into old unsolved crimes. Supposed to have new information, but I'm not holding my breath."

"Why do you read all that crime history?"

"Takes my mind off the *new* crime history." He shook his head. "Eight shootings since six last night—five dead. We're ahead of last year."

It wasn't a new problem. Dad had dealt with it for years.

"One good thing about the mafia—they just shot their own... or at least that was the plan. These bastards throw bullets around like confetti. One of the dead is a little girl who was sitting in the back of a car going to a birthday party."

"I know it's frustrating, Stosh. Is there an answer?"

He shrugged. "We just keep arresting them if we can find them. The people in the neighborhoods won't talk because they're scared and don't trust us to protect them. Did you see the blurb in the *Trib* this morning?"

"You mean by the superintendent?"

"Yup." He picked up the paper and leafed through it to a page with a picture of a pair of handcuffs and read the quote. "Our policemen don't come from Mars. They come from the community and then tend to represent the views of the neighborhoods from which they sprang." He shook his head. "We shouldn't have to explain that we're the good guys."

"Things aren't going to change. Is sprang a word?"

He just glared at me. I was used to it. "And God forbid we look the wrong way at one of these gang bastards. An ACLU lawyer will be knocking on my door."

"Why not just lock someone up for life if they commit a crime with a gun?"

"Easier said than done, Spencer. The solution is to get the kids off the streets with jobs and stronger families and keep them out of the gangs. They need more options."

We relocated to the kitchen and laid out the sandwich fixings. Pastrami, roast beef, and ham from the deli down the street and a choice of bread and rolls. I had a taste for pastrami, but by the end of the afternoon I'd have one of each. He took two bottles of Schlitz out of the fridge. We took our sandwiches and beer into the front room and ate on trays. We'd play cards and watch whatever sport was on and find some place for dinner. But tonight I was abandoning him for Rosie—she was off at five. She had a new partner and had been spending more time than I thought necessary breaking him in. She had broken a couple of standing dates to help Gabriel get situated. Gabriel?

As he was pulling in his tray, Stosh asked, "So, you think your boy will be out soon?"

"Don't know. But I wouldn't mind not having to drive to County to listen to his whining. But I was hoping to talk to the boys at the parlor Monday. Joey being there would not be good. I had enough trouble with Marty."

"You think you'd get anything out of them anyway?"

I finished my first bite and washed it down, trying not to think about the mucus. "Only by mistake. As you know, you never know what someone will say if you ask enough questions."

"Sometimes they don't even know they said something important."

"And sometimes neither do we."

He talked while he ate. "You doing anything else besides talking with the boys?"

"They're all being watched. So far we've got Danny Primo, the driver, running into Jack Eigen at a liquor store."

"Anything to that, you think?"

I shrugged and picked up the second half of my sandwich. "Probably not, but I'm not fond of coincidences."

"But they do happen."

"Sure. The world works at random. They do happen. But each one needs to be ruled out."

"Okay, probably not a coincidence, but probably nothing to do with Joey."

"Probably not. The big problem with following these guys is they don't spend all their time in church and volunteering at the Salvation Army. Everything they do looks suspicious because everything they do *is* suspicious."

He turned on the TV. We were in between seasons. Football was done, and baseball was a few months away. And golf didn't come on until three. The only thing on was bowling, but sport was sport. I cleaned up, got us each another bottle, and he set up the card table. By three he owed me six-fifty. Even at a penny a point it mounted up.

"So dinner with Rosie?" Stosh asked.

"Yeah, for a change."

He gave me a strange look.

I folded my cards. "What do you know about this Gabriel she's been spending too much time with?"

"What I know is, I've been able to live to this ripe old age by minding my own business." He dealt.

I picked up the cards, arranged them, and drew. "Gin."

"Crap."

"And what the hell kind of name is Gabriel?"

"Calm down, Spencer. The kid is new in town, and Rosie is being kind and helping me out. We're still short-handed what with Steele pulling that trigger. She'd do the same if it was a woman."

"Probably. But I bet her name wouldn't be Gabriel."

I shuffled and dealt. I knew I had no holds on Rosie, especially after the way I had treated her in the past, but we had something more than casual. I wasn't sure exactly what that was.

"You're not seeing anyone else, are you?" he asked.

I shook my head. "No, but it seems someone is seeing me."

"Care to explain that?" He discarded the queen of hearts. I picked it up and told him about Loretta, or Jamie, or whatever her name was today, at the bar.

"I'm thinking you're being stalked."

"Yes, odd."

"I'm also thinking you like it."

"Who wouldn't?"

He shrugged. "Maybe Rosie."

"Yeah, well, Rosie's busy these days."

"Now, Spencer, you're over-reacting."

I shook my head and picked up his next discard. "I just don't understand women."

"Join the club. Francine was the only woman I ever understood, but only about 10 percent of the time."

"What about the other 90 percent?"

"I read a lot."

As I picked up another discard, he said, "Why don't I just give you my hand?"

Before I could respond, the phone rang. Stosh threw down his cards in disgust and got up. His phone ringing was hardly ever a good thing.

"Powolski."

His expression didn't change as he quietly said one word—
"Shit." He hung up and headed for the closet. As he pulled out a
coat, he said, "If you're coming get your coat."

Wondering what was going on, I scrambled as he grabbed his
shoulder holster.

I knew better than to ask and waited as he drove west. As we
ran through a yellow light at Cicero, he said, "Somebody shot our
witness."

I let that sink in before asking if he was dead.

"Not sure. Reynolds couldn't find a pulse, but he couldn't find
his wallet if it was in his pants."

I had ten questions but didn't ask. He had enough to think about
at the moment without dealing with me. His witness had been kept
in a safe location that even detectives like Rosie didn't know. It
was the biggest secret since Hoffa's disappearance. Obviously Stosh
knew—we were on the way there. And evidently so did someone
else. And obviously the safe location wasn't all that safe. But I had
shown them *that* a couple years ago.

As he turned right onto Kildare, I saw the street lit up like
Christmas with an ambulance and plenty of police cars. The street
was lined with parked cars on both sides squeezed in between piles
of snow. Stosh stopped in the middle of the street behind four squad
cars, and we walked three buildings north.

***

We walked up two flights to the top floor. The small apartment
was full of cops. I exchanged nods with the ones I knew. Rosie
was talking to Reynolds near the couch. Her back was to me. Another detective, who I assumed to be Gabriel, was listening. Stosh
squeezed his way into the bedroom, and I followed. Next to the window, one brown shoe was sticking out of one end of a white sheet
that covered the rest of a body. Broken glass covered the floor. The
ME was packing his bag and looked up as Stosh stood next to him.

"Lieutenant."

"Doc."

Stosh knelt and picked up a corner of the sheet and pulled it back. The face of an old man looked surprised. I would too.

"Any question about this?" Stosh asked as he stood.

"Nope. Two shots into the heart. Somebody was a good shot. He was dead before he could think about it."

"I'm guessing you have plenty to keep you busy, but please make it a priority."

"Right."

Two medics lifted the body onto a stretcher. The lieutenant ignored me as he followed Doc out of the room. I took a few steps to the window and looked across the street. The block was mixed apartment buildings and simple, single-family homes. The building directly across the street was four stories. With the angle the bullet had entered the body and the height of the victim, they'd be able to narrow down which window the shot had come from. As I looked, two detectives came out of the apartment building across the street and walked toward me.

"Spencer."

Careful not to step on glass, I turned around. "Hi, Rosie. I guess the secret got out."

"I guess it did. The lieutenant won't be fun to be with."

"Nope. Glad I'm having dinner with you instead of him."

She took a deep breath. "About that."

I was sure my disappointment showed.

"Clements asked if we could stay and help process the scene. It'd be good experience for him."

"Of course it would." My tone wasn't exactly supportive. I assumed Clements' first name was Gabriel.

"Why are you answering like that?"

"Not your case, and you're off in an hour. Sorry if I sound disappointed."

"You sound more than disappointed."

"I *am* more than disappointed. But you do whatever you need to do."

She gave me a frustrated look and walked out. I spent another minute at the window, then sat on the couch in the main room and listened to Stosh talking to Reynolds and the detectives whom I'd seen coming out of the apartment building across the street. I had missed some of the conversation, but I wasn't concerned about it… he'd fill me in at the dinner we were now going to have.

There were four apartments facing the street. Someone was home in two of them, the ones on the second and fourth floors. Their identification confirmed they lived there, and they said they had not been out of their apartments in the last hour and had not seen anyone strange. They had all heard what sounded like a shot but figured it was a car backfiring until the police showed up. No one was home in the other two apartments. The manager had opened the doors. Nothing appeared out of order, but the crime lab would go over them after they finished with the murder scene.

I got up and joined the group.

"May I ask a few questions?"

Stosh introduced me to the one detective I didn't know and raised his hand, telling me to go ahead.

"How many detectives did you have here at any given time?"

Reynolds answered. "Me and West traded shifts. And there was a uniform and a detective in the apartment across the hall at all times. We had a camera put in the lobby and the back stairs. No one came in the building without our knowing about it."

"There are two bedrooms. The interior one has no windows. I assume that was your witness room. What was he doing in the room by the street?"

Reynolds shook his head. "That was our room. Glunner was told never to go in there."

"So, why was he in there?"

"I don't know. Maybe he was trying to make another phone call."

Stosh interrupted, his anger showing. "Another? What the hell are you talking about? He made a phone call?"

Reynolds looked embarrassed. "I found him on the phone once. I was in the head, and when I came out I found him on the phone.

He hung up when he saw me and told me he was just trying to call a friend who would be concerned about him."

"Jesus, Reynolds," Stosh said. "Get the phone records. He must have placed the call. Find out where to."

"So, how did he get in there this time?" I asked.

"I drink too much coffee," Reynolds said with a sigh.

"While you're drinking your next cup," Stosh said, "find out where Joey's boys were an hour ago and which one of his flunkies saw them there."

"Right, Lieutenant."

As we walked to the squad car, I said, "If we had my car with the fancy phone I could find out about the boys."

"How so?"

"I have tails on them."

"And your tails have phones?"

"Yup."

"Back upstairs. You can call from the apartment."

I had my hand on the door handle, and we talked over the top of the car. "Well, I can't."

"You can't?"

"I don't know the numbers."

"Well, that's a big help," he said as he got into the car.

I told him the numbers were in my car. I also told him he was buying dinner.

As we pulled away, he said, "We'll stop at my place. You can call."

I did. Chester said Joey, Mike, and Danny had been in the house all day. Lunch had been delivered a little after noon. Marty also had not left his house.

***

Stosh turned left on Cicero, headed north, and got on the Edens Expressway at Foster. Neither of us said a word. I knew he'd talk when he was ready.

"Do I get a say in what's for dinner?" I asked.

"Nope."

"Do I get to know where?"

"I've got a taste for ribs."

I nodded. That was okay with me. Since we were heading north, I knew where we were going. Skokie. "I'll never argue about Carson's."

The hostess seated us by the fireplace and said Ryan would be right with us. Saturday nights were always busy, but we were early. We ordered beer and a full rack each, and I watched him staring into the fire.

"Nobody knew about this, Spencer."

I took a drink. "I assume you mean nobody you knew about. I also assume your statement is out of desperation rather than facts."

"What the hell are you talking about?"

"Well, obviously there were people in your command who knew. And, unless one of them did this, obviously someone else knew too. At least they can't pin this one on Joey."

"Not directly." He took a drink and swirled his beer.

"Tell me about him," I said.

"Martin Glunner. Seventy-three years old. Lived off of social security in a rundown apartment building."

The fire felt good on my back. I was counting the days until spring. "How did all this happen?"

"He showed up at the station two days after the killing and said he saw who killed Schloff. He had no trouble picking Joey's picture out of the book."

"What was he doing there?"

"Said he used to hang there when he was on the street. He lived in an apartment now but would go back to see friends. Said he heard footsteps and was going to call out when he saw Schloff come around a corner, followed by Joey about twenty feet away. Glunner hid behind a concrete column and watched. He said Schloff swore to Joey that he'd pay next week. Joey didn't say a word—just pulled a gun out of his pocket and shot him."

"And you buy all that?"

He shrugged. "No reason not to."

"Does he have a record?"

"Nope. Not even a traffic ticket."

"Any ties to the mob?"

"Not that we know of. But Schloff was an errand boy for Giancana. After Giancana got it, nobody wanted anything to do with him. He didn't fit in."

"Yeah, most of humanity doesn't fit in. I had a chat with Maggio. I asked him about Schloff. He didn't mention the Giancana connection."

Stosh smiled. "And you're surprised by that?"

"No. Just interesting. And if Glunner was on the street, how did he end up in an apartment?"

"Says he was helping support a sick sister. When she died he had enough to rent a place."

As I was thinking about all that, the ribs arrived. Part of the experience was taking in the look and aroma before the first bite. Garlic mashed potatoes and asparagus filled out my plate. My stomach could only take about a minute of waiting before I cut into the best ribs in town.

After the first bite, I said, "And you realize that if Joey was set up, all that is crap, right?"

Stosh was further into his dinner than I. We had discussions about looking at good food several times in the past. He just nodded.

"You checked out his story?"

"Of course. He even described the graffiti on the pillar next to where Schloff was shot. He described how the body was lying on the floor."

"And if Joey was set up that picture looks a lot different."

I thought some more as I ate. "Did you check on the sister?"

He said a muffled "what?" through a mouthful of food.

"His sister. Did he have one?"

Ryan stopped to ask if we wanted more beer. We did.

"That was on one of my detective's list."

"And?"

"Still working on it," he said, somewhat aggravated. "Spencer, this was an airtight witness. Everything we checked was perfect."

"How often is something perfect?"

"Not often, but sometimes we get a gift."

"One of Dad's rules was beware of gifts."

He nodded again.

"Would you let me know about the sister question?"

"Sure. I'll put Glunner's murder aside and put everybody on that for you."

I thanked him without returning his sarcasm. "So, two dead. If we assume Schloff was killed to frame Joey, then Glunner was part of the frame and a victim of the first rule of murder—don't tell anyone, and if someone else is involved get rid of them before they can talk about it."

"Yeah, not very pretty, and maybe the answer to your apartment question."

I nodded as I ate. "It would have been easy. I'll fix you up in an apartment. All you gotta do is say you saw someone get shot. Of course whoever did it would have left out the part about dying."

"Yeah, a minor detail."

I was still slowly savoring the ribs as Stosh finished his last bite.

"So, tell me about this Gabriel," I said.

"He's a new detective. What else do you want to know?"

Before I could answer, Ryan started clearing the table and asked if we wanted dessert. We both declined.

"Rosie seems to be spending a lot of extra time with him."

He gave me his tough cop look. "Ah, I should have known. I forget, how many years have you kept Rosie wondering?"

"Beside the point."

"Not at all. Rosie is helping out her partner because Rosie is dedicated to her job. She's dedicated to you, too, but you evidently haven't figured that out yet."

Ryan dropped off the check. I finished my beer and pushed away from the table.

"Don't worry about Rosie, Spencer. Let it go."

I wanted to point out that this was advice from a guy still sleeping in his recliner because he couldn't face the bed he and Francine had slept in, but I did realize that even if it was the same point, the situations were a lot different. I just nodded.

We talked about the murder of Glunner on the ride home.

"There's something we haven't mentioned," I said.

"And that is?"

"You have a leak."

He just gave a disgusted grunt.

"Would you pass on the bullet information when you get it?" I asked.

He ignored me. "Back to your stalker." He took the entrance to the expressway and headed south. "Who knew you'd be at McGoon's?"

"Me and Ben. Why?"

"Three possibilities. She has been stalking you. Someone told her about your dinner. Or she just happened to be there, and you don't like coincidences. So, who else?"

"Nobody, I…"

"Who else?"

"Carol. She made the reservation. But there's no connection there."

"That you know of. Come on Spencer. They go to the same hair dresser, they met at the laundromat, their kids go to the same school. They—"

"Okay, okay. I'll ask."

He pulled into his drive and let me out. There was a light dusting of snow on my Mustang.

"Cards Wednesday?" he asked.

"Okay. But I'll talk to you before that."

"I am blessed."

"You're a pain in the ass."

"*I'm* a pain in the ass?"

I slammed the door, and he pulled up to the garage.

As I waited for the car to warm a bit I made a mental list of things I was waiting for. The bullet trajectory would just be interesting. They had already narrowed down the apartments. There was nothing I could do that the police wouldn't do, but it would be good to know where the bullet had come from. The phone number would be more interesting. And I needed to talk to Carol. I looked at the phone under the dash and decided not to put a frozen block of plastic up to my ear.

I had planned to spend Sunday hibernating with the paper and a book. I was in the middle of *The Long Goodbye*. I had read it several times, but a reread of Raymond Chandler was better than many other books I had read just once. A part of me was intrigued by Jamie, or Loretta or whatever she was going by today. Maybe I'd brave the cold, have lunch at McGoon's, and see if she showed up. I knew I might be walking into the lion's den, but Abraham Lincoln had put his political enemies in his cabinet so he could keep an eye on them. I didn't know if Jamie was a friend or foe. If she was a foe, I'd learn more by spending some time with her. And she would be a pretty pleasant foe. If she was a friend... well, I wouldn't turn down another friend. And Rosie was busy.

***

There was a message on my machine from Rosie. She'd call back tomorrow. While I was at the phone, I called Carol. She had just put Billy to bed. He had asked about the dog. I'd have to make time to look into that some more. I told her about Jamie and asked if anyone else could have known about the dinner reservations.

"No, I don't... wait, there was a woman who came in as I was dialing McGoon's and sat in front of my desk."

"Shorter than you, bobbed black hair and a round face?" I asked.

"Yes. How did you know?"

I ignored her question. "Did she leave a name?"

"Nooo." Her silence was full of questions.

"Damn. That would have been interesting."

"What do you mean?"

"She collects names. Would have been interesting to see who she was then." I thought for a few seconds. "I used to collect stamps. Collecting names would be cheaper."

"What are you talking about?"

I told her about my mysterious stalker. "Could she have known where you made the reservations?"

"I suppose, if she was nosy. I wrote 'McGoon's' and 'seven' on my notepad."

I silently swore. "What did she want?"

"Said she needed to see you. She was recommended. She asked if you'd be back in the office. I said you were done for the day, but you would call her. She wouldn't leave a name or number."

I didn't respond while I thought.

"Is something wrong, Spencer?"

"No. Just answers I don't have yet. If you see her again, call me."

"Okay, but you have me worried. Did I do something wrong?"

"It's okay, Carol. Get some sleep, and I'll see you Monday morning."

I got ready for bed and then called Rosie. There was no answer. I fell asleep wondering about my stalker and decided to have Sunday lunch at McGoon's.

Chapter 11

McGoon's wasn't as crowded as it was during football season. I had spent most Sundays at the bar with friends watching the Bears. It had been a good season. They had won their division but had lost the NFC championship game to the 49ers. The prediction for the next year by the football pundits was to win the Super Bowl. But predictions were easy to make.

I ordered bangers and mash with Irish brown bread and ate at the bar. There were only two other people at the bar so Jack had time to help me solve the world's problems. We had figured out how to bring about world peace when he asked if I had seen the new TV show, *Jeopardy*.

"No. Heard about it. Like a trivia game, but you have to ask questions, right?"

"Right. They get some smart people."

I took a drink. "Sounds odd. Bet it won't catch on. *The Sixty-Four Thousand Dollar Question* only lasted three years."

He glanced away and then nodded toward the door and winked.

"What's that about?" I asked.

"You'll see." He gave me a sly smile and walked away.

I figured out what it was about before she sat down next to me and dangled her feet above the foot rail.

"Well, we meet again," she said with a smile.

"Yes, small world. Jamie, right?"

"Right. I'm impressed. And you're Spencer."

"I am today."

She laughed. "Some days you're not?"

"No, just some days people have other things to call me."

The waiter arrived with my lunch.

"What brings you back here so soon?" I asked.

"Probably the same thing that brings you back."

I figured that was exactly right, but I didn't know why. "And what would that be?"

"The food is terrific. Bangers and mash is one of my favorites."

I wasn't going to share. She put in an order and asked if she could join me. Jack set a glass of white wine in front of her and winked at me again.

I hadn't given enough thought to what I would do if she showed up. My only plan was to let her talk and see what was on her mind. As I ate, she spoke first.

"You from Chicago?"

"I am. How about you?"

She laughed. A nice laugh. Inviting. "I'm not really from any-where. We moved around a lot."

"Army?"

"No. My father just didn't like staying in one place."

The bar was filling up. Jack brought me another beer.

"So you have family here, then," she said.

"Well, not anymore."

I cut a slice of sausage and forked it into some potatoes. I was surprised when she let that lie.

"What do you do to make your fortune, Spencer?"

That was one of the things I should have thought about. I decided that since she obviously already knew, the truth was best.

"I'm a private detective."

Her eyes widened in feigned surprise. If I didn't know that she already knew that, my male ego would have been duly stroked.

"That's exciting! That's pretty amazing about the murder of that witness."

That was something I *had* thought about. There must be a connection between her and Joey. She frequented his parlor. But that could be for any number of reasons. A group of guys who lived together and a pretty girl across the street. Maybe she was waiting for the soda jerk job to open up. Or maybe she just liked ice cream.

When I ate without answering, she continued. "With the only witness dead, do you think they'll let him go?"

"No. Not right away. But I bet the DA isn't happy."

"No. Probably not. But it's a shame to see a guilty man go free, especially that way. Sounds like the mob is alive and well in Chicago. I thought things had changed."

"Things haven't changed since Cain and Abel."

Her food arrived, and she cut into the sausage. "That's a pretty grim outlook."

"I read the papers." I ate my last bite of sausage and eyed hers. She was right about one thing—the food was excellent.

"Who do you think killed him?" she asked.

"Killed who?"

"The witness."

"No clue."

As she cut some sausage, she asked, "Do you think they'll catch him?"

"If they get lucky."

"What do you mean?"

"This wasn't an angry shooting. It was planned and thought out. Very unlikely that there are any loose ends."

"I wonder how many crimes the police don't solve."

"A lot."

"Maybe I shouldn't feel so safe."

I just smiled. We had talked our way through lunch, and I hadn't learned anything useful. Jack asked if we wanted refills, and we both declined. If the circumstances had been different this would have been the point in the conversation where I asked her back to my place or she asked me to hers. I knew neither was going to happen, but I wondered if she was waiting for me to ask. I thanked her for the company, and she said she hoped we would meet again. I knew we would, but I had no idea how or why.

The checks came and we left money on the bar. Jack nodded to me with a smile.

***

I had settled on the couch with the Sunday *Trib* and fallen asleep somewhere through the sports section. The phone woke me around three. It was Rosie asking if I wanted to meet at McGoon's for dinner. She was buying and said she had a taste for bangers and mash. I told her about lunch… well not all about lunch. I suggested she come over for pizza, and she accepted. We watched some mindless TV and talked about Joey. She wondered how long it would take his lawyers to get him out on bail. Now that the witness was dead, my guess was by noon on Monday. Hers was Monday afternoon. I planned to visit the parlor in the morning for a chat with the help. I didn't ask Rosie about Gabriel, and she didn't ask about Jamie. But then she didn't know about Jamie.

She left early, and I went to bed with *The Long Goodbye*.

Chapter 12

The sun was out Monday morning, but the thermometer was still sitting at eleven degrees. I waited for rush hour traffic to clear, then headed for the ice cream parlor. I wondered whether Loretta would be there. She had worked herself into an interesting corner. I figured she thought I wouldn't have remembered her from the parlor. But if she showed up there again it would be somewhat suspect. She hadn't denied knowing Joey, but she hadn't offered that she did. And at the very least she knew *of* him and would normally have mentioned that.

The ten o'clock news led with a story about Joey's lawyers going back to court this morning. I parked in the restaurant lot and walked across the street. The same familiar cast were at their places inside the parlor. Moose was at his table with an unlit cigar between his lips, and Jimmy was toweling glasses behind the counter. Both looked up as I let in a rush of cold air. Neither spoke. I figured that was about what I should expect from the chats.

As I took off my coat, Moose said, "Hey, Gumshoe." He got up, rapped twice on the door, and announced me when Marty slid the panel open. He didn't ask about a gun. I let myself in and sat in the armchair with the green cushion.

Marty was behind Joey's desk with a cigarette going in the ashtray and didn't bother with greetings. "You think the boss'll get bail what with somebody taking care of the snitch?"

I gave him my best disapproving look and decided not to bother arguing his choice of words. "You never know. Depends on the judge. But if I were to put money on it, I'd say yes." His blank expression didn't change. I couldn't tell if he would be happy about that or not. It would be good to know.

I watched him for another minute. The only change was when he picked up the cigarette and blew smoke up toward the ceiling fan.

"So, what's the deal, Manning? I have things to do."

It didn't look like he was doing much. The desk was clear.

"I came for a chat with the boys. Might as well start with you."

He shrugged and blew some more smoke. "Unless you want to talk about baseball or the shameful rate of crime in this city, we have nothing to say."

"I'll give it a try."

He shrugged again. "Your time."

"Who's been running things with Joey gone?"

"Who do you think? Same person who runs things when the boss is here."

I wondered if Joey would agree with that. "So, if you run things maybe you'd like to sit behind the desk *all* the time instead of just when Joey is a guest of the county."

"I'm not stupid, Manning."

"Not saying you are." I knew Joey would be lost without Marty to run the business, but I also knew Marty respected the mob structure. "But if Joey were gone, I'm thinking you wouldn't mind."

"Every working stiff likes to get somewhere in life. If the boss were gone and Mr. Maggio thought me a good replacement, I wouldn't turn it down."

That was a safe answer, and it didn't give me any insight into whether he would be willing to have a hand in helping his boss to be gone. Maggio had told me that the old days of the mob were over and that he ran a business. Marty fit that picture... Joey didn't. I was sure Maggio would prefer Marty and was well aware of Marty's value to the 'company,' which made me wonder about Maggio. But I was also sure Maggio realized the value of Joey.

Every once in a while they had to break a few legs... just business of course.

I looked at the fully stocked bar Joey kept behind his desk. Marty made no offer. But it was too early for me anyway.

"Marty, let's say you had to pin this on one of the boys. Who's your best guess?"

He shook his head, inhaled, and blew out a cloud of smoke. "Try a different song, Manning. I'll admit my motive, but what reason would the other three have? They know nothing about the business. They're just hired help."

I planned on asking each one of them that question. Someone might answer.

"Are we done here?" Marty asked.

"You and I are. How about you send in Mike?"

"Mike's not going to be happy about that."

"I'll try and worry about that."

As he stood, I asked, "What's with Mike and Danny living with Joey?"

"What's with you asking?"

"Just wondering."

"Keep wondering." He left the room and several minutes later was back with Moose. He sat behind Joey's desk, and Moose sat on the couch.

I looked from one to the other. "I need to talk to Mike alone, Marty."

"That's not going to happen."

"What are you afraid he'll say?"

"I'm not afraid of anything because he has nothing to say."

He wasn't talking to me—he was telling Mike. "Then what's the problem?"

He stared at me for a minute and then got up and walked out with a glance toward Mike.

As soon as the door closed, Moose said, "I got nothing to say, Gumshoe."

"Yeah, I heard. Joey's in a bind. You don't want to help?"

"I would if I could, but I don't know nothing." The cigar was still clamped between his teeth, like a mother dog picking up a pup with her mouth. It wiggled as he talked. And even when he wasn't talking it moved. It was like someone playing with a pencil.

"Joey has made a lot of enemies. Do you know any in particular who would go to this trouble?"

"Nobody's that stupid."

"Plenty are that stupid, Mike. You see everyone who comes and goes. No threats?"

"Lots of threats."

"Anyone in particular stand out?"

He just shook his head. "You're barking up the wrong tree."

"I agree with you, Mike. I don't think this is any of Joey's customers. But that leaves one of his employees."

He took the cigar out of his mouth and suddenly sat up straight. "If you're saying I had something to do with this, you're nuts."

"I'm not saying that at all. But you yourself ruled out the customers. So that leaves you four."

A look of confusion showed on his face. He was struggling with that concept.

"That's a lotta crap."

"Look at it logically." I knew that was asking a lot. "Who would benefit from Joey being put in jail?"

He leaned back on the couch and replaced the cigar. "None of us are that stupid either." His eyes squinted a bit. "Except maybe…"

I gave it thirty seconds before I asked, "Except maybe who?"

He didn't answer, but his eyes squinted to slits.

I had to keep him talking, so I made an educated guess. Danny was the obvious choice. Everyone else spent the day together.

"Danny?"

He opened his eyes and nodded slowly. "I always wonder what the hell that kid does all day long."

I knew at least some of what he did and was anxious to hear more at lunch.

"So if you had to pick one of the group it would be Danny?"

"I ain't saying nothing. You done wasting my time?"

I ignored that. "Do you think Joey would meet someone in an alley alone and kill them?"

He laughed. "The boss wouldn't go anywhere near an alley. He wouldn't want to get his suit dirty."

"When was the last time you saw him with a gun?"

"I've never seen him with a gun." We just looked at each other for a few seconds before he asked if I was done.

"Who's the bodyguard?"

"He ain't got no bodyguard."

"That's pretty hard to believe, Mike. A guy who makes enemies as part of his business would be pretty dumb to walk around alone."

"The boss ain't dumb."

"Again, then logic would say he has a bodyguard."

"I don't know nothing about logic. I know there ain't no bodyguard."

"You see all the customers. Do you know anything about a short woman with short black hair, about thirty?"

"The boss doesn't have any lady customers."

"I've seen her at the counter eating ice cream."

"If they don't go into the office I don't pay attention. Now you done?"

"Sure. Send in Jimmy, please."

Halfway to the door he stopped and turned around. "I gotta say one thing, Gumshoe. You gotta lotta nerve coming in here and trying to pin this on us."

"Just doing my job, Mike. If he was set up, and I think he was, it was someone he knows. And the only people he knows are you four."

He stood and started toward the door.

"One more question, Mike." He turned back with a glare. "Could you get out of the house at night without the others noticing?"

"What kind of question is that?"

"Just wondering—could you?"

He shrugged. "Sure, I suppose."

"And so could Joey?"

"I guess. Why do you wanna know that?"

Seemed obvious to me. I let him wonder.

After a hard stare, he walked out. Jimmy came in a minute later. He was clenching his hands and fidgeting. I watched him do it for a few minutes until he finally asked what I wanted.

As I explained my theory about the setup, his fidgeting became more extreme. I was surprised he didn't fall off the couch.

"How long have you worked for Joey?" I asked.

"About five years, but I don't know anything. I just watch the counter... you know, ice cream and sodas."

"But you're always here. You must know something."

"I just work here, mister. I've never even been in this room."

"You didn't know what goes on here when you took the job?"

"Honest to God. I just do the ice cream. I never even see these guys except here."

I believed him the first time, but I spent ten minutes trying to get him to change his mind. He didn't. Moose wasn't about to make ice cream cones, so they needed somebody to wear the white apron. I asked him how he got the job.

"I was out of work. My sister was dating a guy who knew somebody looking for a counter man. I got hired."

"And you didn't wonder about the guy sitting at the table with a gun or the parade of customers who walked into the back room without buying ice cream?"

"I just wanted a job, mister. I mind my own business."

I still believed him, but there *was* a question he might know something about.

"There's been a lady coming in. Sits at the counter. Short black hair, round face, cute. You know who I mean?"

"Yes. Name's Jamie. Nice kid. She's a regular." He had settled back to his normal fidgeting.

"Can you tell me anything else about her?"

"Likes strawberry ice cream."

"She ever go in the back room?"

"Nope. Sometimes gets a table but usually sits at the counter."

"She ever talk to Mike?"

"Never. Just ice cream."

"She ever ask about me?"

The fidgeting ramped back up. He'd be a terrible poker player.

"No. I... Why would she ask about you?"

Since she had stopped at the office, she had somehow found out my name and that I was an investigator. Someone had told her. I watched him fidget for another minute.

"This is how it is, Jimmy. My job is to find out who framed Joey. You're telling me you can't help me with that. Right?"

He nodded vigorously. "Right." He looked relieved.

"But here's the problem I've got. If someone lies about one thing I have to wonder if they're lying about another." He didn't look so relieved anymore. "Do you follow me?"

"No... no, I don't. I'm not lying about nothing."

"Well, from where I'm sitting you have to be." I watched him fidget some more. "Would you like me to explain?"

He nodded, hesitantly.

"Jamie stopped by my office. So she had to get my name from some-body. And you said she never talked to Mike or went into the office?"

Another hesitant nod. He was still perplexed. He knew he was trapped. He just didn't know how or why.

"So, if the only person she talked to was you, you must have been the one who gave her my name."

He was trying to think, staring at his shoes.

"And if you're lying about that maybe you're lying about Joey too. I'll have to tell him you're holding back something. How do you think he'd like that?"

"Please, mister. I'm not lying. I just..." He thought for a few seconds. "Just that she made me promise."

"Okay, I appreciate a promise. But some things are more serious than a promise. How did she get my name?"

"She gave me a big tip and said there was a guy who had come in here a few times and gone into the back room. She described you and said she was interested. Thought you were good looking."

He looked up at me, and I nodded for him to continue.

"Wanted to know your name. I didn't see any harm. Names aren't secret."

I agreed but found that ironic seeing as how we were talking about someone with more than one. "How much was my name worth?"

"A ten spot."

I was disappointed. I was worth more than that.

"And how did *you* know my name, Jimmy?"

"Marty told us you'd be in to ask questions."

"Okay, that makes sense."

He was wringing his hands. "You aren't going to tell the boss, are you?"

I handed him a card. "No, but if you see anything or think of anything give me a call."

"Okay, mister." He got out fast, and Marty closed the door and sat behind the desk.

"You solve the case, Manning?"

"Yeah, the butler did it." He didn't appreciate my humor. "Can you get Danny here?"

"The driver?"

"You got another Danny?"

"No and no. He comes back at five to drive everybody home."

"What does he do in the meantime?"

"Errands and who knows what else."

"Don't you wonder about an employee who disappears all day?"

"He's never given us anything to wonder about. He just drives the car."

"You've never wondered who he's seeing in his spare time?"

"He gives me something to wonder about it will be taken care of."

"You know Jack Eigen?"

"I know of him."

"So does Danny."

Marty didn't react. I wondered if that was enough to make him wonder.

"I'd like to talk to him. When can you arrange that?"

"Be here at five. If he's still working for us you can talk to him."

"I can talk to him either way."

"If he's talking, you can."

I left without following up on that. It was 11:40. Just in time for lunch.

Chapter 13

I walked to my car and called the office. There were two calls, one from Ben and one from Mooneen at city hall. Ben had information and was going to be late to lunch. I told Carol I'd be back in a couple of hours.

I entered the restaurant through the side door off the parking lot. Mr. Chin said hello and said everyone was in the party room in the back. Everyone was there but Ralph, who was tailing Danny, and Ben who would be late. Helene would watch the parlor until Chester finished eating, and then they would switch. I had filled Mr. Chin in on our need for privacy. After the food was served we didn't want to be interrupted. If we needed something we'd ask. After giving him two fifties, he had no problem with that. A waiter took drink orders and explained the buffet. They would bring refills if needed. That wouldn't be needed—there was enough food there for lunch and dinner. I had eaten there when I first approached Mr. Chin. The food was excellent. We talked while we ate.

I filled them in on the interviews. Everyone agreed that Marty would take Joey's position if for whatever reason Joey wasn't in the picture. They also agreed that he probably wouldn't be the guy to make that happen, but the "probably" left the door open. Whoever was doing this didn't care if they ended up dead. And none of us could think of why anyone would think that way.

We all had full plates from the buffet. I was working on my egg drop soup.

"Chester, why don't you go first so you can relieve Helene."

He pulled out his notebook.

"My surveillance was from five to midnight. There was only one incident. Last night, just a few minutes after I got there, the front door opened, and Mike walked out. He stood on the porch for a minute and lit his cigar. He walked to the corner and then turned west a coupla blocks to a house at 342 Belden. He looked up at the house for twenty seconds or so and then put his cigar out in the snow and left it there. He walked up to the door and knocked. The door was opened by a woman who looked late twenties, thin, about five foot eight, long brown hair. He reached into his overcoat, pulled out an envelope, white business sized, and handed it to her. She took it and let him in. He was there for an hour and ten minutes when he walked out and back to Joey's. He lit another cigar on the walk back and put it out on a porch post. That one he kept in his mouth. He entered the house at 10:32. There's a garage behind the Belden house off the alley with a dark green Oldsmobile Delta 88, four-door sedan in it."

"Do you have any idea what was in the envelope, Chester?" I asked.

"I do not," he answered in the same matter-of-fact tone of his report. "Do you want to cover the woman?"

"Not at the moment. Mike is the one we're interested in. But I'll run the address and see who owns it."

Paul sat down with a second plateful. "A man walks to a house in the dark, hands an envelope to a woman, and goes in. Hard not to figure there's money in the envelope. And not hard to figure what for."

"Agreed," I said. "But not a fact. Morrie, what... hang on. Chester, did anyone else show up at that house while you were there?"

"No, just Mike."

"Okay. From now on, when the boys are buttoned up in the mansion, switch to the house on Belden. I'd like to know if anyone else is visiting. And if Mike comes back, you'll see him. Go ahead, Morrie."

Morrie reported that Jimmy Smith was out four times over the weekend, two to local stores and two social events. He had met people for dinner Saturday night and lunch on Sunday at a neighborhood diner. He had photos of the people he had met Saturday night if I needed them. Sunday lunch was the interesting part. It was with Marty. And Jimmy had said he just ran the counter and knew nothing about anything else.

"Given that last tidbit, why don't you go next, Paul."

Paul never needed a notebook. It was all in his head. He ate while he talked.

"I have Marty. He only went out twice over the weekend, but who'd want to go out in this icebox? Saturday afternoon he drove to the Bear Arms gun range in Franklin Park. He took a black satchel out of the trunk and was inside for an hour and ten minutes. He went straight home and stayed in until the lunch on Sunday with Jimmy."

Chester took a plate of dessert out of the room and switched places with Helene. As soon as she filled her plate and sat down, she reported that the black Lincoln had just pulled up, and Joey got out. He was back in his lair.

Rebecca had nothing to report on Moose. Ralph had reported by phone that he had a journal of Danny's movements, but since the Eigen meeting there was nothing out of the ordinary. I set up the next meeting for Wednesday at noon.

Ben arrived when we were about done eating. He filled a plate and ate while the others left. I filled him in on the meeting.

"So, what did you learn?" he asked.

"I learned what I already knew. Everyone has something to hide."

"But there certainly are some interesting parts."

"Yup, I'd love to know what was said at the Jimmy–Marty lunch. And what was Moose doing out at night handing out envelopes? Paul thinks there's only one answer to why a man would hand a lady an envelope."

"Maybe he supports the neighborhood food drive," Ben said.

"Maybe, and maybe Paul's assumption is wrong. Maybe she was hired, but not for that."

"Like maybe she has ordnance in her closet?"

"Like maybe that. No saying women can't handle guns. But why would he go in and spend an hour if he was just paying for services rendered?"

"Lots of whys, Spencer."

"And then there's the gun range. Why does the books guy need a gun?"

"Well, he isn't exactly in the ice cream business."

"Nope."

"You know, I haven't shot in a while. I could use some range time," Ben said.

"I was thinking the same thing. You wanna join me tomorrow?"

"Love to."

As he finished his chicken and green beans, he handed me an envelope. I opened it. Inside was a blank piece of paper.

"I'll bite. What's this?"

"That's the detailed report on Loretta Hands."

"It's blank."

"Right. My source is the deepest you'll find. He'll tell you when someone sneezed. There's nothing besides what you already have. You want me to tail her?"

"Not yet. Let's see how she plays out. I might stop back at McGoon's. And if we do tail her, it can't be you—she's met you."

We arranged for him to pick me up at the office at ten in the morning, and I settled up with Mr. Chin. Helene had resumed her seat by the window. I stopped and made sure she was comfortable. She was, and not only comfortable, but by the look on her face she was enjoying it.

***

arol was always glad to see me. It had to be lonely by herself in the office. But Billy would be there at three. I told her just to go home when he got there. She handed me two messages, one from Mooneen and one from Joey, who was requesting my presence. I sat and filled her in on the highpoints of the meeting.

I pulled out my notebook and gave her the address on Belden and asked her to run down the owner.

"Did you talk to Ben?" she asked.

"Yeah." I told her about Loretta.

"Well, that's certainly odd."

"Certainly is. But as I learned at lunch, everyone has something to hide. Doesn't make them a criminal."

"Don't you want to know what she's hiding?"

"Curiosity killed the cat, and I don't have nine lives. I also don't have time unless it ties into Joey, and liking strawberry ice cream isn't a crime."

"That doesn't answer my question."

I gave her my best smile. "Yes, I'd like to know."

She tilted her head and looked at me sideways with a coy look. "And do you want to see her again?"

"Sure. But only to find out what's going on."

"Right. I'll remind you of that."

"I'm sure you will," I said as I walked to my office and called Mooneen.

"Hello, Spencer. I found something about our nasty woman. She had another working dog before this one."

"Any more information?"

"No. Same general stuff, but listen to this." She paused. I listened. "The dog died. Doesn't say how, but she was only four years old."

I didn't answer.

"You there, Spencer?"

"Yes, interesting."

"Also interesting is the lack of information. If a dog dies there's usually an investigation. These dogs are valuable."

"Gets more interesting all the time. Is there a signature on that application?"

"It's the same scrawl as on the other one. Can you do anything? There's something wrong here. I'd love to get this woman."

"Me too. I'll look into it. What was the address on the first form?"

"Same as now. If I can do anything let me know."

"You already have. Thanks, Mooneen."

"I mean *anything* else. I'd love to be a detective."

"It sounds better than it is. Sitting in a car all night in the cold doesn't make the papers."

"Well, you keep it in mind, and let me know what happens."

"I'll do that. Thanks again."

I told Carol about the dog lady.

She was disgusted. "Billy asks every day. I'm not going to tell him that."

"I agree. Just tell him I'm still working on it."

"Okay. You want me to get Mr. Mineo on the phone?"

I sighed. The last thing I needed at the moment was Mr. Mineo. "No, he can wait. Call and tell him I'll stop and see him sometime tomorrow."

"Sure."

I had found Carol by serendipity. I was glad I had.

***

S tosh wasn't in his office. I ran into Reynolds in the hall and asked if he had seen him.

"On his way down the hall with a newspaper under his arm. How urgent is it?"

"Not *that* urgent. I'll wait."

I chatted with Kate for a minute and closed my eyes in one of Stosh's chairs. I was still catching up from being up all night. I woke up to voices forty minutes later, stretched, and asked Stosh why he didn't wake me up.

"Best to let sleeping dogs lie."

"Nice, I—"

He held up his hand. "I've got a busy afternoon. The shot came from directly across the street. The occupant of the third-floor apartment works a second shift on the weekends and is always gone at that time."

"So, somebody did their homework."

"We found no signs of forced entry or any evidence that anyone besides the occupant had been there. The bullet was from a rifle. Two shots. The second shot was a waste of a good bullet."

"A pro."

"Looks like it."

"We're keeping the rifle to ourselves. I don't want it going any further than your ears." When I didn't respond, he said, "Got it?"

"Yup. You have any doubts that Joey was set up?"

"Why would I not consider that the mob ordered a hit on someone?"

I started to reply and he waved me off.

"I know… this is the new mob. They're all fancy suits and lawyers. But if talking nice isn't working, there's always the old way."

I sighed. "I know. If Joey set this up, what better way than to frame himself and make it look overwhelmingly like he did it." I stared past him at the picture of Dad in dress uniform on the wall behind Stosh's chair. He had taught me you had to think the way the criminal thought, and sometimes that wasn't all that easy.

"How about the phone calls?"

"The first was to a number that has been disconnected. The second was to the apartment across the street."

I took a deep breath and blew it out slowly. "Well that answers a few questions. Whoever pulled the trigger set up Glunner."

"It poses more questions than it answers," he said. He asked if I was getting anywhere, and I told him about what my team had seen.

"That's what makes this job so fun," he said. "Everybody's guilty of something. I hear Joey's out."

"Yup. He'll be sleeping in his own pajamas tonight."

"That warms my heart."

Kate leaned in the doorway and said, "Lieutenant, you have a meeting in ten minutes with the captain."

"Thanks, Kate."

"Just one more thing, Stosh."

"It's never just one more thing, kid."

"Well, for today."

He rolled his eyes.

"I'd like to see the warehouse. Mind if I poke around?"

He stood. "I don't think my saying yes or no would matter. So, to keep you legal, go with Rosie... during the day while she's working."

I frowned. "But that'll mean she'll have—"

"Suck it up." He slapped my shoulder as he walked past me.

"Oh—one more thing."

"Maybe you didn't notice me walking away." But he stopped.

"I'd like to read Glunner's statement of what he saw at the warehouse."

He asked Kate to pull it out and refile it when I was done. She handed me the file, and I sat in the wooden chair in the corner opposite her desk. Martin Glunner had been a very observant fellow.

***

I got back to the parlor at a quarter to five and parked in the restaurant lot where I could see the front of the parlor. Joey's Lincoln pulled up five minutes later and parked in Joey's spot next to his hydrant. Ralph pulled into the lot, parked next to me, and got into the Mustang. He tossed his brown cap on the dash, and I filled him in on my chat with Marty. His money was on the kid being fired. A minute after Danny parked, Moose came out and invited him inside. I was glad I didn't bet. Twenty minutes later they all came out and piled into the Lincoln. Danny was still driving.

"He doesn't look happy," Ralph said.

"But he's still walking," I said. "That's more than some."

"You're okay with getting him fired?"

"We don't know that, but I'm not the one meeting with Eigen. Things needed stirring."

Ralph wasn't asking because he disagreed. He really did want to know if I was okay.

"Let's both follow," I said. "If he was fired he'll also be clearing out of the mansion. Let's see where he goes."

Ralph didn't answer. He just got out and into his Chevy. He had left the engine running. He was a man of few words who didn't need something explained twice and had never made a mistake while working for me.

The Lincoln stopped in front of Joey's house and parked. Parking spaces were hard to come by, especially in the winter, but I figured the neighbors respected the spot. A half hour later a cab pulled up and double parked next to the Lincoln. Danny came out with two suitcases. Mike was carrying a box. The cabbie opened the trunk, and the bags and box were put in. Mike had nothing to say to Danny who looked pretty damned angry. He stared at the house before getting in.

***

We followed the cab to Lake Shore Drive where it headed south. It wasn't Highway 1 in California, but it was still a pretty drive. The contrast between the city on my right and the lake on my left was drastic. Every time I was on it, "Lake Shore Drive," by Aliotta, Haynes, and Jeremiah, ran through my head. At night in the winter the lake was just a lot of black, but during the summer it was dotted with boat lights.

Traffic slowed a bit at the s-curve as we crossed the Chicago River, and I thought of the engineering feat of the lock system that had reversed the flow of the river and sent the water and whatever else was in it south to the Illinois River, the Mississippi, and eventually the Gulf. Back in the late 1800s, water pumping stations were built out in the lake to supply the city with clean water. It had taken some time for them to figure out that people were dying because the waste they dumped into the river was getting into their water supply. So the natural flow of the river into the lake had been reversed.

The museum campus to the left of the drive was lit up in white lights. When I was a kid I got to pick from the museum of natural history, the aquarium, and the planetarium, and once a month we'd spend a Saturday exploring.

Ralph stayed right behind me as we kept heading south. There were a few brave souls jogging along the blacktop path along the shore through the longest park in the world, which had been laid out by Daniel Burnham in the early 1900s. Of Chicago's twenty-nine miles of shoreline, all but four are public park.

The cab turned off the drive at the Museum of Science and Industry, and ten minutes later stopped in front of a run-down apartment building on Kenwood. The cabbie helped Danny unload, and Danny hauled everything he had in the world up the steps. After he was in, Ralph joined me. I told him he could knock off after he got me a sandwich from the diner on the corner, and I'd watch Danny until midnight when Ralph could relieve me. I'd be back at six unless he called before that. After he left I checked the apartment tags. There were two Primos, Carla and Maxwell. I walked around the back through the alley and looked at the rear exits. But since Danny had no idea he'd been followed, he'd be using the front door.

I had parked one building down and across the street, twenty feet from a streetlight and next to a four-foot mound of dirty snow. The seven o'clock newsman said the temperature was eleven heading down to zero. Winds were negligible, and Tuesday was expected to be sunny with a warming trend into the twenties. But that wouldn't help me at the moment. I'd have to leave the car running most of the time.

I listened to WGN as I usually did when I was in the car. Chicago's top-rated radio host, Bob Collins, signed off at six thirty when Chuck Swersky took over with *Sports Central*. They talked Cubs for the first hour. Chuck was picking them to win the World Series, but the big story was about WGN raising a sixty second ad during the games from $110,000 to $145,000. *They* expected the

Cubs to do well also. The Cubs were also raising ticket prices. I was looking forward to the start of Eddie Schwartz's overnight show at eleven because I'd only have an hour left.

A few people came and went, but none of them were Danny. About ten I called Rosie. I figured that gave her enough time to lose Gabriel. She sounded glad to hear from me and laughed when I told her where I was.

"All that money and you're sitting in a cold car instead of your warm house."

"Well, the heater is on, and this cold car has one advantage over my warm house."

"And that would be?"

"I don't have to share it with memories." We had talked about selling the house, but I wasn't ready to think about that.

After a pause, she said, "I'm so sorry, Spencer. I wish I could help."

"I wish you could too. But there *is* something you can help with."

"If I can."

I told her about the warehouse. She said no problem. I asked if there was a day Gabriel would be otherwise busy, and she said it would be good experience for him. I said I guessed it would. Ben and I would be at the range Tuesday morning, so we set it up for Tuesday afternoon.

I was watching the lights in the neighborhood go off, and by eleven when Eddie Schwartz came on the air there were only a few left. A city of three million going to sleep.

Ralph relieved me at 11:50. I had nothing to report and was sure the night would be quiet. I told him I'd see him at six.

Chapter 14

It was still dark when my alarm went off. The only thing to do would be to throw off the covers and get up. One more minute of cozy warmth always turned into at least an hour.

When I turned onto Lake Shore Drive the sun was streaking through the clouds that hung over the lake, painting the clouds orange, red, and yellow. As long as the temperature kept rising there was the possibility that spring would again arrive. The days were getting longer, but there were still too many of them before Mom's tulips would make an appearance.

That early in the morning, traffic was light, and I pulled alongside Ralph's old Impala at ten to six. He nodded at me. I parked four spaces ahead of him and walked back to his car. There had been no traffic in or out of the building until twenty minutes ago, and none of them were Danny. I thanked Ralph for doing extra duty and told him the plan, which was that I was going to play it by ear. He could have said that wasn't much of a plan, but Ralph knew who the boss was. He also knew I already knew that. I asked him to be back by nine so I could get back to meet Ben. He just nodded and gave me a short salute.

A crowd came out of the building a little after seven. The fourth person was Danny. He turned to the south and walked down the block. I followed him to the diner on the corner and followed him in. I had told Marty I wanted to talk to all the employees, of which Danny was no longer one, but that wasn't going to stop me, so I sat next to him at the counter. We both ordered, and I waited for him to get a dose of coffee in him before I took in some coffee and started the conversation.

"Hits the spot on a day like this."

He didn't respond.

"Sorry, didn't mean to intrude. Just being friendly."

He stared straight ahead. "Well, be friendly somewhere else." He sipped his coffee.

I guessed that was a polite way of telling me to shut up.

I sipped mine and after a minute tried again. "You hear what the Cubs did to ticket prices?"

"I don't give a damn what the Cubs did with ticket prices. The Cubs never done nothing for me." He pushed his coffee ahead on the counter and turned to me with a disgusted look. "If it'll shut you up, I got fired yesterday, and I'm not in a mood for friendly."

"Gee, that's tough, kid."

He turned away.

I figured he'd be angry and want to share his anger with someone so I kept pushing. "What'd you do?"

He sighed and pushed the coffee to the side so the waitress could put his plate down.

"I was a chauffeur."

I poured syrup over my pancakes. "Nice job. What happened?"

"My boss didn't like a deal I was working on."

He was started. I could stop pushing. He just picked at his eggs, but I ate like I was hungry.

"It's a real sweet deal. Lotsa money involved, and I didn't have to invest much."

"Sounds perfect. What kind of deal? Maybe I'd be interested."

He took a bite of toast and washed it down with coffee. "A horse. This friend of mine knew where we could get a real runner for cheap. Some guy died."

"What does that have to do with being a chauffeur?" I knew darned well what that had to do with.

"Nothing." He tried some eggs. "It's complicated."

Yes, it was.

"This is a sure deal?" I asked, knowing there is no such thing as a sure deal.

"Locked up."

"Then I'd be interested."

He shook his head. "We don't need any interest. It's already split enough ways."

"Okay, just asking."

That was all he had to say, but it was enough. Marty had looked into whatever Eigen was cooking, and Joey had fired Danny because of the horse. I never figured Danny was smart enough to set up Joey, but knowing what was going on was better than guessing.

When I finished eating, I gave the waitress a ten and told her that covered both breakfasts. Danny thanked me and I wished him luck.

When I got back to the Mustang, I called Ralph and told him we were done with Danny. Anyone else would have asked why. Ralph just did his job. If the job was over, he didn't care why. He said he'd drop the cell phone at the office and would be at the pool hall if I needed him. I had been wondering why that was his point of contact, but he didn't mind my life, and I didn't mind his.

"Well," I said, "if you can keep your stick in mothballs for a few more days, there's something else I'd like you to look into."

"Sure. Business before pleasure."

I told him about the dog lady and that she appeared not to be handicapped. He joined the rest of us on the side of outrage. I gave him the address and asked him to check with neighbors and keep a watch on her and see what was what. Same pay. He agreed.

***

The sun was high in the eastern sky, and the temperature had warmed to the low twenties by the time Ben and I pulled into the

Bear Arms parking lot. I picked up my folder with the photos, and we got our bags from the trunk. We registered to shoot, asked for the manager, and looked at shotguns while we waited. A few minutes later a large man with a long ponytail and a pistol on his belt introduced himself as Walter, the manager, and asked how he could help.

I showed him my license and introduced Ben.

"We're looking into something that involves one of your clients and want to have a chat."

The "happy to be of help" look on his face disappeared pretty fast and was replaced by what I would call unfriendly.

"What my clients do is their own business. Now if you'll—"

"Hang on a second, Walter. We're going to do some shooting, so we're clients too. I do understand and agree with your views. But we're actually working for one of your clients."

After a long ten seconds of silence, he asked who the client was.

"Marty Sparin."

I expected to hear that he had no idea who that was and was surprised that he did.

"Is Marty in trouble?"

"You know all your clients by name?"

He laughed and shook his head, which sent his ponytail over one shoulder. "No. Just the ones who place in tournaments. We have quarterly shooting tournaments, and Marty has come in second place in the last three. He'd really like to win."

"Would you look at a photo?"

"Sure, but let's go to the office."

As we walked toward narrow stairs at the back of the room, I wondered how Walter was going to fit. He did, but not by much. His office was the only room at the top. It was over the range, and we could hear the constant, muffled sound of gunfire. It was a bit unnerving, but to Walter it was the sound of money. We all sat, and I laid the stack of photos on his desk. Marty's was on top.

"Yup, that's Marty. Nice guy. You didn't answer if he's in trouble."

I shook my head. "No, he's not. We're working on something for his boss."

The intercom buzzed. Walter leaned down to it.

"Yeah."

"Boss, I've got a questionable ID. You wanna take a look?"

"Yeah, I'll be down in a few." He sat back up and looked up at me. "His boss is in trouble?"

Ben and I looked at each other and Ben said, "You don't know what Marty does?"

"Don't know and don't care. Why? Any reason I should?"

I figured Marty had a right to privacy. "No, no reason at all."

I reached to pick up the photos, and the bottom two separated from the pile.

"Hey," said Walter, "that's Jamie."

Walter didn't see my surprise. He had picked up the picture and was studying it.

"Jamie?" I said. "Two of your clients are in my stack?"

He looked suspicious and defensive. "You trying to pin something on me?"

I quickly reassured him. "No, not at all. Just seems odd them being in the stack and you knowing both of their names. You told us how you know Marty. That makes sense. But how do you know Jamie?"

He laughed. "I told you he came in second place, right?"

I nodded.

"Well, she came in first."

This time he noticed my surprise and smiled. "Gotta love a woman who can shoot."

"That opens up more questions. Can you spare a few more minutes?"

"Sure. But I gotta take care of an ID. You gents wait here. I'll be back."

Ben had a smile on his face. "This keeps getting better."

"Sure does. I think I've used up my quota of coincidences for the month. Jimmy told me she had never been in the back room, and he was the only one she had ever talked to. Somebody's lying."

"Maybe everyone," Ben said.

We both looked around the room. Lots of pictures, many signed by some big names. As I looked, I let my thoughts wander.

"I just had a bizarre thought, Spencer."

"So did I. You first."

His eyes narrowed as he turned toward me. "If Joey was going to hire a bodyguard, it'd be someone who could shoot, right?"

"Right. And if you want someone who would be inconspicuous, why not get someone who would be inconspicuous in plain view?"

Ben just nodded.

I thought back to my meeting Joey at Riverview. I had looked for a bodyguard as he walked away… but I wasn't looking for a woman.

"You think it's possible?"

"Anything's possible. But likely?"

He shrugged. "Answers all the questions."

"The biggest one of which is why she hangs around the parlor so much."

Walter's slow footsteps were obvious coming up the stairs.

"Bad ID?" I asked as he sat down.

"Couldn't tell for sure. But I don't take any chances. The kid was pissed off that I wouldn't let him shoot, but better one pissed off customer than paying fines and being investigated."

"You think it's possible the state sends in ringers to test you?"

I think Walter shrugged, but it was hard to tell for sure. Nothing moved much.

"I've thought of that. Anything's possible."

"We were just discussing that," I said. "Would you give us a little more information about Jamie?"

"Maybe. Depends on what it is."

"Fair enough. I'm wondering if she and Marty knew each other outside of here."

"How would I know?" He moved his bulk around in the chair until he was comfortable.

"Did they come in together? Leave together? Were they here separately?"

"Well, I don't remember too far back, but they were pretty friendly at the last tournament, and they left together."

"Your records would show when they were here, wouldn't they?"

"They would, but that's not something I share with the public."

Ben was looking at the pictures on the walls.

"I can understand that. But the police would be a different matter."

The unfriendly look was back. I had no doubt that a person in Walter's business would not be happy to even hear the *word* police. He answered with something close to a sneer. "I thought you said you were just looking into something. Now we're talking police. I think we're done talking."

I tried to reason with him. "Walter, we're not accusing you of anything, and you've been very helpful. I'm just saying if something comes of this that'd be something the police will be interested in."

"Well, if they are, they are. I'm sure they'll have no trouble walking in the front door with a warrant and telling me that. You boys have a good day."

I put my card on the desk and asked him to call if he thought of anything else. He didn't answer.

Ben and I shot for a half hour, and that was about all I could handle. My Smith and Wesson .357 Magnum was a powerhouse, but it was heavy and wore my arm out. I only used .38 Special cartridges on the range. The .357 cartridges were eardrum shattering, even with ear protection, and the extra residue from the explosion made cleaning even more of a chore. I used a Smith and Wesson Model 60 for work that fit nicely in a shoulder holster. It only had five shots instead of six, but I figured if I needed that extra shot I was in more trouble than I could handle anyway. The magnum was more accurate, but the Model 60 was easy to carry, and if I was in the kind of trouble one might get into in this job, my target would be bigger than a nickel, and accuracy wasn't that important. But when I shot with Rosie, I used the Magnum, and all the shots were in the bull's-eye. We were both expert shots. The winner had the smallest tear. I didn't like carrying a gun and only took it when I thought the situation might be dangerous. But I did realize that couldn't be predicted.

We picked up sandwiches on the way back to the office and ate with Carol. Joey had called twice wanting to know when I was coming. I knew going in that I'd have to babysit Joey, but I was hoping it would be interesting, and it had been so far. The puzzle was waiting for me to put the pieces in the right spots.

Carol asked what happened at the range, and we all asked questions that had no answers while we filled her in. The big one was whether or not we had identified Joey's bodyguard, and if so, why was she such a secret? Carol suggested that Joey wouldn't want the world to know he had a woman bodyguard. That seemed logical. If she was, it also seemed logical that Jamie and Marty had met each other at the range and one thing had led to another. Marty would appreciate someone who could shoot better than he could, dress or not.

Rosie was picking me up at two. That didn't leave enough time to pay a visit to Joey. He'd have to settle for a phone call, so I called. But there wasn't much I could tell him. We had discovered things that might or might not be important and things that probably were none of his business, like that Mike was handing envelopes to a certain woman, or that Marty had more than an ice cream relationship with one of the customers. Or that maybe that customer was more than a customer. But then, if she was, he already knew that.

The phone rang a little after one. After answering, all I heard Carol say was okay, thanks, and goodbye. She came into my office a minute later.

"The address on Belden?"

"Yes."

"The ownership is in a trust. Denver says I should call him back if you want him to dig deeper for the usual fee."

I sighed. "Damn. It'd be nice if something was easy for a change. No, odds are he wouldn't find anything but red tape. Thanks, Carol."

She smiled. "I think you're in the wrong business for easy."

"You think right."

I called Joey and wasted the next twenty minutes trying to convince him that we were doing something without telling him what exactly that was. That we were watching select people didn't satisfy him. He wanted to know who and what we had seen. He wasn't happy that I wouldn't tell him. I appeased him a little by telling him I'd stop by in person tomorrow. He ended by telling me he expected more then and hung up. He wouldn't get any more, but that gave me time to think of something else.

At a little after two the back door opened, and Carol said hi to Rosie, who entered my office and asked if I was ready.

"Yup. Where's your shadow?"

"Detective Clements is keeping the car warm. And don't sell him short. Did you know there are only four angels identified in the Bible? Gabriel is one. He was a big deal."

"Pardon me if I don't see the connection," I said in my best surly tone.

"No connection… just saying."

"Who're the other ones?"

She smiled. "Hey, you're the detective."

"Like I don't have enough trouble. Let's go."

Carol told us to have fun. I wasn't putting my money on fun.

Chapter 15

The sky had turned gray, and a few snowflakes were in the air, but not enough to use the wipers. During the ride, Gabe—he asked me to call him Gabe—said he had heard a lot about me and tried to make conversation. I tried to be polite. With youthful good looks, he looked like he could still be in high school—very angelic. Rosie shot me a few looks, pleading for me to be nice.

There were plenty of parking spaces next to the warehouse, and Gabe parked next to a snow pile that we could hop over. The three-story brick building took up half a block of wasted real estate. More than half the windows were boarded up, and the front door was padlocked. There was no yellow tape and no crime scene notice. This was still a secret. Rosie had the key but had trouble getting the door open. I could have picked it faster and would have if Gabe hadn't been there. I didn't want to set a bad example. The rest of the neighborhood wasn't in much better shape. There were only a few buildings on the block with lights on. While Rosie was fumbling with the key a gust of wind blew off my Cubs ball cap.

The body of Max Schloff had been found on the second floor, face up on the concrete. We had to walk through the offices to get to the stairs. The rooms were bare except for a few metal desks and file cabinets with some of the drawers half open. An assortment of trash was everywhere.

"I wonder when this place was abandoned," I said.

Gabe answered, "About ten years ago is what the records show. It was a clearing house for office supplies. The owners—"

"Okay, I got my answer."

Although Rosie was leading the way, I was pretty sure about the look on her face.

Another doorway brought us onto a large, open floor space that extended in both directions to the ends of the building. Rosie dropped back and let Gabe lead us to the stairs.

"Jesus, Spencer, lighten up. He's just trying to help. I don't know what your problem is, but if you keep this up we're leaving."

"Okay. Got it."

She shook her head and followed Gabriel up the stairs.

With a concrete floor and a high ceiling with square, cement pillars every fifty feet or so, the second floor was just like the first except for less office space. Large, horizontal, crank-out windows filled the walls above six feet. The big difference was a section near the south end where the pillars were wrapped with yellow tape. Near the middle of that section was the chalk outline of a body. It wasn't the first time I had seen a chalk outline, but the effect was always the same. It was so impersonal. Max Schloff had lost his life there, and all that was left was the chalk outline.

I asked about Glunner, knowing that Gabe would answer. He did, and Rosie gave me a warning look.

"Glunner came into the station at eleven at night saying there was a body here on the second floor. Patrol officers found the victim lying face up in a pool of frozen blood. The temp was twelve that night."

I had been looking around. There were signs that someone had sheltered here—ragged blankets, empty bottles, cardboard on the floor, even a shopping cart. Boarded up or not, there was always a way into an empty building, and even a bed of cold concrete was better than outside in the wind. I bent to look closer at the floor.

"What was Glunner doing here?"

Gabe answered. "He said he used to live here when he was on the street. He came back to check on his friends."

I nodded. "Any sign of the shooter?"

"We—" Rosie started, but Gabe interrupted.

"They had a team in here—"

Rosie looked at him and held up her hand, stopping Gabe from continuing and me from giving him a piece of my mind. Gabe walked off toward the north end of the warehouse.

She turned back to me. "No. Not a thing."

"A phantom shooter. A lot of that going around." I stood up. "Entry?"

"No help. There are several broken windows that could have been used. Probably how the street people get in."

"Did they find anyone to interview?"

"Nope, the place was empty."

"Not surprising, given the temperature. Did they get anything from neighbors?"

"I don't know. I'm not the lead on this."

"Right, you're just babysitting Gabriel."

I got a stern look. "What the hell does that mean?"

"You've been spending a lot of time with him."

"Just breaking in a new partner."

I took a deep breath and didn't say what was on my mind. "Right. He's pretty pushy."

"He's just trying to learn, Spencer. Maybe he's a bit... energetic, but he's smart and will be a good detective."

"Okay, we'll call him energetic."

I stared at the outline some more. "Face up."

"Yup."

"Two shots?"

"What?"

"Schloff. How many times was he shot?"

"Right... two. From a distance. Nine millimeter."

"I bet the second shot was a waste of a good bullet."

"If by that you mean the first was enough, then yes."

"Lots of that going around too."

She looked to the north. "I wonder where Clements has got to."

"Even when we're alone he's on your mind."

She glared at me with her hands on her hips and her lips pressed tightly together. When she relaxed a little, she asked, "Are we done?"

"I don't know… are we? I bet the women are jealous of you, spending so much time with him."

"What are you talking about?"

I shrugged. "He's good looking and available."

As she turned and started to walk away, she muttered "Jesus" under her breath.

I followed ten feet behind her, and we met Gabe just before the stairs.

Since I hadn't answered her the first time, Rosie asked again if we were done. I was pretty sure she had meant with the warehouse.

"I'd like to see the third floor."

Gabe looked excited and started to say something, but Rosie cut him off.

"I've seen it. Third floor is just like the second floor and the first floor. Nothing there."

"I haven't seen it," I said. "You two do whatever it is you two do. I'll be down in a few minutes. Don't leave without me," I added with a laugh.

"Don't bet on it," said Rosie, without a laugh.

I didn't blame her—if the roles had been reversed, I would have left.

The third floor was just like the second… same signs of being lived in. I wandered aimlessly, not looking for anything in particular. The shooting had happened on the second floor, so I didn't expect to find anything, which is the best time to find things.

There was still a bit of late-afternoon light, and as I was walking back to the stairs, I thought I saw a shadow move to the side of one of the pillars. I gave it a wide berth and came up on it slowly from the side. There was a person hiding behind the pillar. I saw him before he saw me.

"Excuse me," I said softly, not wanting to scare him. Despite that, he jumped and turned out not to be a him, although it was hard to tell. Her clothes were dirty, and she was wearing a shabby coat that didn't look real warm. A scarf was wrapped around her head.

I held my hands up in front of me. "I'm sorry to bother you. I don't mean you any harm."

She backed off a few feet, looking scared.

"My name's Spencer. I'm a private detective. I'm looking into the shooting."

She still just stared, wide-eyed.

I lowered my hands and asked, "Would you mind if I asked you a few questions?"

She shook her head slowly.

I walked a little closer. "What's your name?"

"Angie," she said hesitantly.

"Hi, Angie. Do you live here?"

She nodded.

I kept walking slowly. "Are you the only one here?"

"There's me and Slim. There used to be more, but when it got cold they all went to a shelter. If it wasn't for Slim I'd leave too. I don't want to be by myself."

I stopped when I was five feet from her. "I can understand that. Were you here when the shooting happened?"

She shook her head violently. She was lying.

"It's okay if you were, Angie. I'm not going to hurt you."

She shook her head more slowly. "It's not okay. Whoever killed him would kill me too."

"I won't tell anybody. And whoever it was is long gone. Did you see it happen?"

"No. I saw him, after he was... lying on the floor, looking right at me."

"Had you ever seen him before?"

"No."

"Did Slim see him too?"

"Yes." She looked around nervously.

"Did Slim know him?"

"No. He wasn't a… like us."

I felt sorry for her. I of course knew there were homeless people, but standing next to her and talking was different from just knowing.

"Why didn't you go to a shelter?"

"Shelters won't let men and women stay together. We go and eat and then come back here. Are you going to tell the police?"

"No. If you didn't see the person who did it, it wouldn't do any good." I knew that wasn't true. They'd definitely want to talk to someone who was at the scene. She knew that wasn't true also, and why should she trust me? She just wanted to be left alone. I couldn't think of anything else to ask, and I knew if I came back tomorrow, she and Slim would be gone, and I would be the one responsible for them leaving a place where they felt safe.

I took my money clip out of my pocket, pulled off the clip, and held the money out to Angie. I didn't count it but knew it was around eighty bucks.

"I don't take charity."

"It's not charity, Angie. It's for helping." I stepped closer.

She reached out and took it. I thanked her and wished her luck.

She just looked at me with empty eyes. As I walked back to the stairs, I felt just as empty and a little guilty.

***

Rosie and Wonder Boy were chatting in the office by the front door.

"That was more than a few minutes," Rosie said.

"Yeah, my apologies. Angie and I were chatting about old times."

Gabe jumped on that. "Somebody's up there? Let's go get her! She needs to come to the station and—"

"Slow down, kid. She wouldn't go. She was scared enough just talking to *me*. And she told me all she has to tell."

"But she might be a witness. We need to—"

"We need to go, Clements," Rosie interrupted. "If Spencer says she has no more to say, she has no more to say."

It was nice to know she still had faith in my detective judgment. But I was sure she questioned my relationship judgment.

"I have one more question before we leave," I said. "Gabe, what's on the pillar to the left of the body?"

He looked confused and flustered. "What?"

"The pillar twenty feet from the body. What's on it?"

"Well, I don't know. It's just a pillar. Just cement."

I nodded. "Rosie?"

There were questions in her look, but she wasn't flustered. "A raised red fist. The Prophets' gang sign."

I nodded some more. "Now why did Rosie notice that and not you, Gabe?"

Now he looked embarrassed. "I don't know. I guess she's been doing this longer."

"Yes, she's more experienced. It takes a trained detective to notice the little things. Now, do you think Glunner, seeing someone with a gun and probably hiding behind one of the pillars and then seeing someone killed would notice that?"

"I…"

I shook my head. "No. He wouldn't. But he said he did. Does that make you wonder? It does me."

The sidewalk was covered with less than an inch of snow, and Gabe brushed the windows. He did come in handy for something. The ride back to the office was quiet. Not one word was spoken until Gabe pulled into the alley.

"Thanks for the tour," I said.

"Sure," said Rosie. "We'll talk later."

I wasn't looking forward to that. She'd have things to say she wouldn't say in front of company.

"See you, Spencer," said Gabe.

"Probably," I said, knowing he wasn't going anywhere soon.

I didn't waste any time out in the cold and was inside before they backed out. There was one message on my desk, a reminder from Joey to see him tomorrow. I had pleasantly forgotten about him.

I was hungry and considered three options... something frozen at home, dinner with Stosh, or dinner at McGoon's. I needed some company which was guaranteed with Stosh. There was always Jack at McGoon's, but he wasn't really company, just somebody to talk to. Now, Jamie would be company with her red lipstick and lips to go with it, but there was no guarantee she'd be there. I ruled out a frozen dinner and flipped a coin. McGoon's. But I didn't always listen to the coin. I called Stosh and asked if we could switch our Wednesday gin and dinner night to tonight. No problem. I told him I'd pick him up in a half hour.

Chapter 16

S aving me getting out in the cold, Stosh came out when I honked. Saturdays were sandwiches at his place. Weekdays we ate out. We had been doing that since Mom and Dad died. We decided to drive down to the near north side to Gino's East for deep-dish pizza. It had been Dad's favorite pizza place. We had been going there since its opening in the mid-sixties. We had to wait fifteen minutes for a table, but I remembered nights with Mom and Dad when we had waited an hour.

As we drove, the conversation turned to the leaded gas situation in Chicago.

"What are you going to do if the city's ban on leaded gas holds up, kid?"

I finished a turn and answered. "I guess I'll have to buy gas in the burbs. But I gotta think over two thousand angry station owners will have something to say about this."

"Yeah, lawsuits have been filed. And remember the courts ruled against the same ban in New York ten years ago."

"Yup. But I have mixed feelings. It would be inconvenient, but the reports say lead is really bad for the environment. And the guy who added lead to gasoline developed lead poisoning." I pulled into the parking lot.

"Who knows what we're doing to the environment in the long run?" Stosh said. "All I know at the moment is there's no lead in Gino's pizza."

After we ordered the supreme with sausage, onion, mushrooms, and peppers, and our beer was delivered, he asked how the trip with Rosie went.

"Which part would you like?"

"What the hell does that mean?"

"Well, there's the Spencer Manning detective part, and then there's the Spencer Manning romantic lover part."

"Since I've already counseled you about the romance, and you don't listen to me, get to the detective part."

I took a long drink of beer and said, "I don't understand women."

"So much for what I like." He took a drink. "You're not going to understand them. I'm having enough trouble understanding *you*."

I slowly swirled my beer. "That Clements is a pain in the ass."

"He's learning, Spencer, and Rosie is a good teacher."

"He needs to learn to shut up once in a while."

"He will. Is that all that's bothering you?"

"She's broken three dates. And this afternoon she stuck up for him."

"Well, he *is* her partner. That's what partners do. I'm sure she'll have a talk with him. She wouldn't want to embarrass him with you there."

I nodded and sipped the beer.

"So, what did you learn?"

"Not much. But everything supports Joey being framed."

"I understand he's your client, but isn't that your preconceived notion? You're supposed to be impartial, not look for evidence to fit your theory."

"Of course. Remember, there's a part of me that would love to see Joey behind bars. Here's what I saw. You tell me what it supports or doesn't."

"I'm all ears."

"Max was shot in the chest and fell on his back. He was facing the shooter, someone he probably knew who somehow lured him to that warehouse." I took another drink. "What was Martin wearing when he came into the station to tell you what he saw?"

"Regular clothes. Winter coat. Why?"

"Did he look like a street person?"

"No."

"So, he didn't live there. And if that's so, and he *did* see it, what was he doing there? It's not a place the average person goes to spend time. Gabe said Glunner came to check on friends, but that doesn't make a lot of sense. If he had lived on the street, he'd know his friends would have moved to a shelter because of the cold. And if he wasn't there, somebody had told him what to say, right down to the graffiti on the pillar."

"Nothing new to me, Spencer. But which is it?"

"I'm betting on the latter. Someone told him what to say." I told him about my experiment with Gabe and Rosie.

The waiter arrived and placed the pizza in the middle of the table. I was hungry.

"And then there's Miss X." I told him about Angie but didn't mention her name. "Rosie said you interviewed people in the neighborhood."

"We've interviewed thirty-two homeless people within a ten-block distance of that warehouse. No one knows anything."

"Not surprising since they weren't there," I said. "And even if they did know something, they may be having tough times, but they're afraid—they may not want those times ended. You showed them Max's picture?"

"Yeah. Nobody knew him, or nobody is willing to say they did. We've pulled in known associates of Max. While most aren't doing too much grieving, there's nothing that would point to killing him."

"What about Joey's crew?" I asked.

"We've talked to them. So far, nobody knows anything, or if they do they're clammed. If we, or you, find something that points to one of them, we'll look harder. We've also looked into murders using those two weapons. Lots using nine millimeter weapons, of course. Less using that rifle. But only one person who had used both... a man named Rockton. His latest address was the state prison."

That got my attention. "Was? He's out?"

"Yeah, he's out."

"Do you have an address?"

"Yeah. A cemetery somewhere in Kansas. He died in prison two years ago."

"Damn." I put another slice of pizza on my plate. There were only two left. "There *could* be two shooters."

"Could be, but not likely. How many people shoot like that? And the fewer people involved the better for whoever's behind this."

I nodded. "Those homeless people you interviewed."

"Yeah?"

"Did you show them Glunner's picture?"

He took a big bite of pizza, washed it down, and looked at me with squinted eyes. "No. What are you thinking?"

"I'm thinking that if Glunner wasn't there he was picked by somebody to be the witness. How was he picked? Maybe he has some connection to that building. Would you say his clothes were typical for someone living off of social security?"

"I'd say he was clothed beyond his means."

"So, someone clothed him. Wouldn't hurt to show his picture around."

"No, it wouldn't."

We finished off the pizza and declined dessert, but got refills on the beer.

"There's one big hole in your frame scenario, Spencer."

"Only one?"

"Only one big one. Why go to the trouble? If someone has it in for Joey, and I could find a hundred who do, it would be much easier just to shoot him. Why go to all this trouble?"

I took a deep breath and let it out slowly. "Exactly. I have no idea. But if someone did, they killed two innocent people to do it."

"That'd be one cold bastard," Stosh replied. "And again, if someone was that angry at Joey, just take out Joey. Why the frame? If it *is* a frame, what's the motive?"

"No idea. Maybe it's not anger. Maybe it's revenge. Just flat out, cold-hearted revenge."

"Revenge for what?"

I shook my head. "Who knows. Revenge is taking the law into your own hands. I think someone might want revenge if they think they didn't get justice."

"If that's the case, someone has killed two innocent people. Again, why not just shoot Joey?"

"Maybe dying is too easy. Joey was a basket case in jail. That's worse than killing him."

"If that's true, someone is risking the death penalty for two murders," Stosh said.

"If that's true, that someone may not care."

"So we're back to someone wronged by Joey."

"Yeah. And since you're taking care of the rest of the world, I'll keep working on the crew."

"How's that going? Anything new?"

I ordered coffee for me and another beer for Stosh. I was driving.

"A few things, but I have no idea if they're related."

"Most of the job is sifting through the chaff. What do you have?"

"Mike DaVita is having some sort of dalliance with a woman a few blocks away from the mansion. He walked there Sunday night and handed an envelope to a woman, much younger than he, who answered the door. He stayed a little over an hour."

Stosh shrugged. "Gotta get old living in a house with men. Can't blame him for getting some attention. You're thinking he's paying for it?"

"Looks like he's paying for something. But I've had a man on the house, and no one else has shown up. If it's a brothel, it's not doing a very good business with just one customer."

"You want me to look into it?"

The coffee came and I took a sip—too hot.

"Not at the moment. If there's something that falls in your direction I'll let you know. I ran the ownership and hit a dead end. It's in a trust. Marty has raised two red flags. He met with Jimmy for lunch on Sunday."

He picked up his glass and asked, "What's red about lunch?"

"Jimmy told me he had nothing to do with any of the people at the parlor aside from manning the counter."

"That's what makes this job so much fun... everybody lies, and we have to figure out which lies matter. What's the second thing?"

I told him about the firing range and the tournaments with Loretta.

"So, more to your stalker than you thought. Maybe she's a split personality... Loretta the marksman and Jamie the soda lover."

"And Loretta the phantom."

"Pardon?"

I told him about the lack of history.

"There's just nothing straightforward about this case, is there? Where did you get your information? I'll run her."

I laughed. "I'm not saying. Thanks for the offer, but don't bother."

He shook his head. "I won't ask who in my department is spending taxpayer money on you."

"Good, but we're all after the same thing. And Danny is no longer Joey's driver."

"It's like a soap opera over there. He quit?"

"I may have gotten him fired." I told him about my chat with Marty.

"So he fired Danny for fraternizing with a known criminal? I imagine the irony of that was lost on him."

The waiter refilled my coffee and asked again if we wanted dessert. He may have forgotten he had asked, but more likely it was a hint that we had been there long enough—there were people waiting for tables.

As I sipped the cooling coffee I asked, "How much do you know about Joey?"

"He's been doing this a long time. What do you want to know?"

"He has the reputation of not carrying a gun. He has no permit. There must have been a time he carried a gun. What's the history?"

The waiter stopped again and said, "If you gentlemen are finished, I'll bring the check."

I can take a hint. "That'd be fine, thanks." He had it in his hand and laid it on the table. Stosh had paid at Carsons, so it was my turn to buy. The other paid the tip, which always worked out nicely for the wait staff. If you thought about it, it made no sense in the long run, but we figured if we were getting a free meal, we could leave a large tip. Stosh left even more than he would have to cover the use of the table.

As I was peeling off bills he asked if I had time for some cards.

"Sure. I'll play through a beer. And we have more to talk about."

***

I set up the card table and got out the cards and scorecard while Stosh got a couple of bottles of Schlitz. We played a penny a point. He owed me $3.84. As he dealt, he asked what else was on my mind.

"Back to Joey. What do you know about his job history?"

"He's been around as long as I've been on the job. That'd be twenty-six years. He was a two-bit hood, the Max Schloff of his day but with higher hopes. He took over the gambling, mainly the horses, about ten years ago. Since he became a big shot we've gone after him more times than I can remember, but no convictions."

I filled a straight and discarded an ace. "How about a gun? Would you run the permit history?"

"Sure. What are you looking for?"

His discard gave me my third king, and I laid down my cards.

"Crap. Needed one more card."

As I shuffled, I said, "No idea. But information is good, and somewhere here pieces have to start going together."

"One can hope."

I didn't have to arrange my cards—there was nothing that fit. "You know, there's always the chance that Joey is playing us. No reason he couldn't be the shooter."

"No reason at all," Stosh said with a big smile. When he picked his first card his smile got bigger. "Gin!"

I pretended to be upset, but I liked him to win once in a while. "I'm meeting with him tomorrow. I'll lean on him a little."

I thought while he dealt. "I haven't seen anything new in the papers. They're still sitting on the location?"

"Yeah, hard to believe that hasn't gotten out, but the public still thinks it happened in an alley."

"Good. Maybe I can use that."

"Maybe you can." He fanned his cards.

"Do you have any books on mob murders?" I asked. Two shelves of Stosh's bookcase were filled with books on Chicago crime and one picture of Francine. I always wondered why there were no other pictures of his family, but I never asked, and he never talked about anyone else. Evidently, he didn't have any kids.

He picked a book off the shelf and held it out to me. *Murder in the Big City – Unsolved Mob Hits*. "I just finished this. Some new information and some new angles on some old ones."

"Thanks. Mob murders tend to have a lot of things in common. Maybe I can find a thread that makes some sense. Why did they order hits?"

Stosh laughed. "Just about any reason you can think of, or no reason at all. Somebody saw someone someplace that made somebody wonder. Easier to kill him rather than spend time looking into the someone and the someplace. You looking for anything in particular?"

"Well, back to the revenge angle. If that's the case, no one is going to go to this extreme over something trivial like a gambling debt. It has to be something big, like murder, and it has to to be personal."

Stosh handed me the book and looked at me with squinted eyes. "Is this about your folks?"

"You got that guy."

"But you were after him before we got him. Is there a difference between our getting him and your getting him?"

"What do you mean?"

"He died, but not by your hand. Did that settle it, or were you still angry?"

I hadn't thought about it and didn't answer.

"If that theory is correct," Stosh continued, "maybe it's not an unsolved case. Maybe it was solved, but whoever did it is back on the street."

"Thanks for making it even muddier. But that would let Joey out. He's never been convicted."

We finished the hand and the beer.

On my way home I got a call from Chester. Mike had taken another walk to Belden. He didn't hand off an envelope, and he was still inside. Chester wanted to know if I wanted to join the party. I declined. Then he asked if I wanted him to have a chat with Mike. I thought not. I'd have to at some point, but I wanted to get an angle on what was going on before having a chat with Mike. Chester had been watching the house since our lunch meeting, and no one else had visited.

***

I got home by ten and glanced at the telescope as I walked onto the porch. It was a perfect night for viewing, clear and cold… little heat in the atmosphere made for better viewing. But little heat in the atmosphere meant little heat on the ground, and I'd had enough cold for one day. And I still wasn't ready for the memories. The last time had been with Dad looking at the Andromeda Galaxy.

I left Stosh's book on the kitchen table and went to sleep hoping to dream the solution to the case, because so far dreams were my best bet.

Chapter 17

arol was already in the office when I got there. She was telling
me about Billy's science project at school when the phone rang.
It was Ralph.

"Morning, Spencer."

"Morning, Ralph. Got anything?"

"Not much. I've talked to three of the five neighbors in her building. None of them like her. Two of them called her names I'd rather
not repeat. And they all feel sorry for the dog. She puts it on a leash
in the yard and leaves. One of the neighbors brought it into his own
apartment during the cold just before Christmas and caught hell for
doing it. He tried to reason with her but got nowhere. He called the
SPCA and was told they'd follow up. As far as he knows they never
did. Could be that's how the dog got loose last week... outside and
slipped his collar."

"Lovely. What a piece of garbage." While he was talking, my
brain was working. "Do you have a name for the man who took the
dog in?" I knew he did.

"Cyrus Jennings."

"Phone?"

He read it off and I jotted it down. "Okay, good job, Ralph.
You're done. Get your time to Carol. Still at the pool hall?"

"Yup."

"Okay. But keep the phone. There's something else I may need you for, and if I do it'll be short notice."

"Sure thing." He didn't ask what I had in mind, and I didn't say. It's best no one knows about some of the things I do… for my sake *and* theirs.

***

R osie was working the middle shift so was probably still at home. I called to see if she wanted to have a late dinner. She agreed and said we needed to talk. She suggested McGoon's. I suggested anywhere else.

When we hung up I called in Carol and asked her to get me an appointment with Maggio, for the afternoon if possible. I had a question.

A little before ten I was getting up to get my coat and head for the parlor when the phone rang again.

"It's Kate, Spencer. Says she has information for you."

"Thanks, Carol." I sat back down and punched the lit button. "Hi, Kate. Staying warm?"

"Just fine, Spencer. The lieutenant asked me to call concerning Mr. Mineo."

"Great. Watcha got?"

"He had a gun permit that he let lapse in 1978 when it was up for renewal. Hasn't had one since."

"Interesting. Thanks, Kate."

"I hope that helps."

"Not at the moment, but it's another piece to put on the table."

"Okay. You be careful, Spencer."

"Always, Kate. Thanks."

I added that bit of information to my notebook, and since I hadn't dreamt the solution, went back to work. I wanted to meet with Joey before the noon lunch meeting. Fifteen minutes later the phone rang again. Carol told me Stosh was holding.

"Morning, Lieutenant. Thanks for the permit info. Are you calling to arrange time payments for the gin money you owe me?"

"I wish I was. A matter has come up."

I tried to think what his serious tone would lead to and had a few guesses. I wasn't even close.

"Internal Affairs is conducting a hearing. I'm pretty sure you're on the list."

"IA? What do they want with me?"

"Your input."

"On what?"

"They're investigating Rosie."

"Rosie! What the hell for?"

"For the death of Steele. Why wasn't she there when her partner killed himself?"

"Are you kidding me!" They probably heard me across the street. Carol came in looking concerned. I gave her a wave meant to say okay, but she stayed in the doorway. "Stosh, she saved my life."

"Yes, but they're not concerned about your life. They're concerned about the guy with the badge who ended up dead."

"But she didn't kill him. He would have killed himself no matter *what* she did."

"You don't have to convince *me*, kid. I'm on your side."

I was still fuming. "This makes no sense."

"Nope, it never does. Let me know if you get the letter." He hung up.

Rosie had said we needed to talk. I had assumed it was about my behavior. Maybe it was, but maybe it was also about this.

Carol was still standing in the doorway. "What was that about?"

"Remember last year at Riverview when Steele killed himself?"

"Sure. How could I forget?"

"Seems Internal Affairs is investigating Rosie. They say if she had been with her partner he wouldn't have died."

"What? She saved your life."

"Lieutenant Powolski seems to think IA considers my life irrelevant."

Her mouth opened, but no words came out.

"He also agrees it makes no sense," I said.

"Can't you explain it to them?"

"Oh, I'll get the chance. He thinks I'll be called. But they're not known for listening to reason, especially from someone whose life is irrelevant."

Her hands were balled into fists. "I'd like to give them a piece of my mind."

"Tell you what… I'll give them a piece of mine and let you know how that turns out."

"Can they do anything to you?"

"Other than make me feel irrelevant… no. But it's not me I'm concerned about."

"Well, Rosie couldn't have a better person on her side."

"Thanks for the confidence, but my personage won't interest them. They have an agenda and will hear what they want and disregard the rest."

"How do you know they won't listen? Have you done this before?"

"No. But, having a dad who was chief of police, I've been around cops all my life. I've seen the results of a lot of these so-called hearings. It's not usually pretty."

"What can happen to her? Can she go to jail?"

"No. Worst, she could lose her job. More than likely she'd get a suspension or be demoted."

"None of which would be fair, Spencer."

"Carol, my dear, Mom told me more than once that life's not fair. Sometimes you just have to make the best after getting punched."

We were chatting about the dog lady when the phone rang. She got it at her desk and came back in after a minute to tell me I had a three o'clock appointment with Mr. Maggio. It had turned into a busy day.

***

Mike just nodded toward the door as I walked to the back of the parlor. And this time he let me do my own knocking. Jimmy didn't turn around from whatever he was doing. No one else was in the place. The slide opened and Marty let me in.

"You're hard to get ahold of, Manning," said Joey.

"You look good too, Joey." I had a few smart-ass comments about jail, but I kept them to myself. "I've been busy with this case I'm working on."

"Okay. So, give me a report."

I sat without being asked to. "I gave you all I have, Joey."

He stared at me and said, "Marty... go get a soda."

Marty didn't point out that it wasn't a good soda time. He just went.

When the door closed, Joey said, "You gave me what you wanted to give me. I'm asking for what I want to get. You've been looking at my boys. I don't mind that... you never know who needs looking at. But I want to know what you got."

"Nothing that pertains to the matter at hand, Joey." I didn't need to ask how he knew I was looking at his boys—Danny Premo.

Just like it wasn't soda time, it also wasn't scotch time, but Joey got up and poured a glass from the bar behind his desk. He raised the bottle toward me. I declined.

"There are two problems with your stance on this issue, Manning. One, I'm paying the bills. And two, you already spilled information on Premo. So why not the rest?"

"Maybe because of what happened to Danny. I wouldn't have said anything if I knew he'd lose his job."

"He deserved to lose his job. He's lucky that's all he lost. He knew the rules. He's the one who got mixed up with Eigen and a horse."

"Maybe, but unless it's something relating to the frame, I'm keeping it to myself."

"So, you do have something?"

"Sure. Notebooks full. People do things—boring, meaningless things that no one else cares about."

He sipped the scotch. "So you got nothing on the frame?"

"I have lots of questions and lots of pieces to a puzzle. I just don't know if they're all to the same puzzle. And since you're giving me nothing, I'll just keep collecting pieces and see if any of them fit."

I watched him sip.

"I do have a question about one of the pieces," I said.

He nodded.

"You let your gun permit lapse in '78. I'm wondering why."

He took more than a sip. "Why is that any of your business?"

I shrugged. "Maybe it's not… it's just one of the pieces. Two people dead so far… both shot. Guns interest me."

"And what does people getting shot have to do with my permit?"

"Probably nothing."

"You're damn right, nothing. You might remember, when that rat piece of garbage was shot I was in jail. So maybe a visit to County was a good thing. No way they can pin that on me."

"No, not directly. But your hired help wasn't in jail with you."

He slammed his glass down, and some scotch spilled out. "Who the hell are you working for, Manning! Doesn't look like me!"

"I just ask questions, Joey… of everybody, including you. The question about the permit is still on the table."

"Well, it should be under the table. How the hell am I supposed to remember back that far?"

"I have an easy, logical answer."

"Yeah? What?"

"I'd rather not answer my own questions."

"Well go ahead. You have my permission."

I was thinking I should have taken the scotch. "If it was me, and I was the boss and had hired help who had guns, why would I need one? And if I didn't need a gun, why would I need a permit?"

He took another sip. "Yeah, yeah that's right, why would you?"

"There's another part of the puzzle that keeps eating at me. You're a smart guy, smart enough to set all this up. No one would expect you to do any of the things the cops say you did. Even one of the cops agreed that it's ridiculous to think you'd be out late at night in an empty warehouse looking to kill Schloff."

He cracked a smile for the first time. "Yeah, why would I be—? Hey, what did you say? Warehouse? I thought that scum Schloff got it in an alley."

"Warehouse? Did I say warehouse? I don't know where that came from. Right, alley. Nobody I've talked to sees you stooping that low."

"Damned right. What's next?"

"There is no next. We keep looking. It would help if you'd tell me who your bodyguard is."

He just laughed.

"One more question. If you were to say... have an unfortunate accident, or end up in jail, who do you think would take over?"

He wasn't laughing anymore. "You say the damndest things, Manning. Pardon me if I don't get up. Have a soda on your way out."

I didn't say goodbye. I just let myself out. Mike was at his post with the paper, and Marty was at the counter not having a soda. I didn't say goodbye to any of *them* either. For an ice cream parlor, there was a lot of tension in that room.

***

I again entered the restaurant by the side door. I was twenty minutes early, so I sat with Helene at a front table. She was having a grand time, what with a warm spot for surveillance and good food. She gave me what she had to report, which wasn't much. Loretta had shown up Tuesday afternoon and stayed for twenty minutes. Other than that, there was nothing out of the ordinary. I was going to reassign people, but Helene would stay at Chin's.

While we were waiting, we saw Mike walk to the front door. It looked like he was locking it. He then disappeared toward the rear of the parlor, and Jimmy left his post behind the counter. After a minute, I asked Helene to use the side door and walk past the parlor and see what was going on. She passed it once going west and then again coming back east, that time reaching out to try the door. She was back three minutes later.

"There's nobody there, Spencer. And the door is locked. Do you know what's going on?"

"I stirred Joey's pot a bit. He may be wondering if one of them wants his job. He's having a heart to heart with the hired help. You won't need to be in the meeting. Order some lunch."

She shifted in her chair and scrunched up her face.

"Problem, Helene?"

"I'd actually like to be in the meeting, if you don't mind. I've been looking forward to it."

That seemed odd. "You have? There's no need… I'll share your report."

"Well… I…"

"Out with it. What's the problem?"

She took in a deep breath. "I'd like to eat where I won't be seen by Mr. Chin."

I had no idea what she was talking about. "It's okay with me, but you'll have to explain that," I said with a smile.

"I have in my purse a peanut butter and jelly sandwich. I don't want to see another egg roll for months."

I laughed. "No problem. Someone will switch with you."

"Thanks, Spencer."

"Sure, but I can't help you tomorrow."

"No, I'll have to be creative."

The front door opened, letting in a cold draft. Rebecca was the first to arrive. The rest followed within five minutes, and we adjourned to the meeting room.

***

When everyone had filled their plates, I started.

"First, we have ruled out Danny, so Ralph is done for the moment. Priorities have changed a bit, so I'll be reassigning some of you."

I told them about what Ben and I had learned at the range and that Mike had paid another visit to the mystery lady, but this time there was no envelope. I told them Helene had seen Loretta once at the parlor and asked them to let me know if they saw her with any of the crew outside the parlor. Rebecca had nothing further on Mike, and Paul had nothing further on Marty. That left Jimmy, and Morrie had a report.

He pulled out his notebook. "Last night he left his house at twelve past seven, made three stops, and was home at twenty past ten. The first stop was Carlucci's on Halsted. He stayed twenty-two minutes. The second was Emo's steak house where he stayed only ten minutes, and the third was Vinnie's Pool Hall on Western. He was in there a half hour. From there he went home."

"Thanks, Morrie. I had planned on paying more attention to Jimmy after that meeting with Marty. This adds fuel to the fire. I don't know of the pool hall, but the restaurants are favorite eating places of certain crime figures."

"So is the pool hall," said Paul. "High stakes poker in the back room run by a punk named Harvey who'd like to make a name for himself."

"Joey know about this?" I asked.

"Sure. Harvey cuts him in, and Joey figures it's easy money. The guy is too small to be much competition."

"But maybe several small guys together make a big fish. Maybe Marty is trying to make a bigger fish," I said.

"Do we care?"

"If Marty wants to make a business decision based on circumstances, that's not our concern. But if Marty set up the circumstances, that's a different ball game. We'll tighten up surveillance on both of them. Chester, you'll stay on the mansion from five to midnight. Helene will stay here during business hours. Paul, you stay on Marty, but I'm guessing he's got Jimmy running his errands and won't do anything out of the ordinary. Rebecca, I'm trying to get information on our mystery lady, and since that seems to be Mike's only extracurricular activity I'm not concerned about him as much. That may change. But for now, you help Morrie out with Jimmy. Run a double tail. With two, one of you can follow inside and see who he's meeting with. You two figure it out. Any questions?"

There weren't any.

"Chester, please take Helene's window seat for a bit so she can eat."

"Right."

"Thanks, all. Call the office during hours if anything comes up. Otherwise my car phone or at home. Let's meet again on Friday, same time."

Helene came in and unwrapped her sandwich. With the first bite she looked like she had just taken a bite of prime rib.

***

I arrived at Larry Maggio's office a half hour early. I got a quick glance from the muscle sitting outside Maggio's office, and he went back to his paper. His secretary told me I was early, but Mr. Maggio would be available in a few minutes. I sat and looked out the glass wall at the scenery. But not all the scenery was outside. Ten minutes later she told me I could go in.

Larry looked like he was having a tough day. The knot on his tie was loosened, and his suit coat was on the back of his chair. Usually, everything was perfect. And it was the first time he didn't offer me a drink. He looked like he could use one.

"Bad day at the office?" I asked as I sat in one of the plush green chairs in front of his desk.

"You have no idea. You're lucky you don't have employees. Never a dull moment."

Not having employees who had constant need of lawyers may have helped, but I didn't give him that advice.

"My secretary said you have a question."

"I do. Why did Joey let his gun permit lapse?"

Larry's eyes opened just a hair wider for a split second. It wasn't much but it was enough. He quickly looked confused.

"That's a strange question. Why do you think I'd have any idea about Joey's gun permit?"

I shrugged. "No particular reason. Just thought you might, being the head of the corporation."

He shook his head. "Not a clue. I didn't even know he had let it lapse. Why are you asking?"

"It came up while I was looking into something else, and the question has been hanging there waiting for an answer. Things like that keep me awake at night."

"You need to do something about that. Let go of things that don't matter. There's too many things that do."

"Ah, but there's the problem. In my business, I have no idea what matters and what doesn't until the pieces of the puzzle start coming together, and so far all I have is a bunch of pieces."

He picked up a gold-plated pen and rolled it between his fingers. "I wish I could help, Spencer, but I have no clue. You're not making any progress?"

"Given that it's been less than a week, we've discovered quite a lot. There are several pieces on the table. It's putting them together where I earn my money."

He opened a silver box on his desk and offered me a cigar. I took it and put it in my jacket pocket.

"I understand one of your discoveries left us one man short."

"Really? Who would that be?"

He just smiled and asked if I had any more questions. I said I had lots but none for him.

"Okay, drop by again if you do. And look into that sleep thing. I have all the problems that come with running a big company, and I sleep like a baby."

I wanted to point out that he of all people had reason not to sleep like a baby, but I kept that to myself too. "I'll do that. Thanks for your time."

I have a habit of making people uncomfortable, and when they are, interesting things happen. I had no idea if Larry Maggio knew anything about Joey's gun permit, or even cared if Joey ended up in jail because of a frame. All Larry cared about was whether it was good or bad for business. And in the long run, Joey was a small cog in the machine.

Chapter 18

I stopped at home to change into something dressier for dinner. There was an official looking envelope from the Chicago Police Department in the mail. It was a summons to appear before the Internal Affairs board on Friday at ten in an incident concerning Detective Rosie Lonnigan. It gave no further information. I was glad Stosh had filled me in. I dropped it on the table on top of the rest of the mail.

Rosie buzzed me into her building a little after six. I climbed to the third floor and knocked. A tired looking Rosie answered the door.

"Come on in, Spencer." She sounded dejected. "I'm beat and upset. Would you mind if we eat here?"

"No, of course not. Can I help?"

"Sure, once we figure out what to have. There isn't much, but I just don't feel like going out."

She searched the refrigerator and pantry, and we decided on tomato soup and roast beef sandwiches. The thought crossed my mind to ask if I should make a sandwich for Gabe, but I kept that to myself. It was witty as long as it stayed in my head. I handled the sandwiches, she took care of the soup, and we ate at the kitchen table. After a few minutes of silence, I thought I'd better break the ice.

"I got a letter from IA today."

She nodded. "When?"

"Friday at ten."

She slowly stirred her soup as steam rose from the bowl. "I have to be there Monday."

"I wonder who else they're calling. This is just insane." I dug into the sandwich.

She looked dejected and far away.

"I suppose I should have been with him," she said.

"Rosie, don't even think that. The plan was between him and me. You had no way of knowing about it."

"I guess." She took a spoonful of soup and continued stirring. "But if I had been there…"

"Rosie, he didn't plan on coming out of there alive. You couldn't have done anything. I think he planned it when you wouldn't be there so you wouldn't have to be involved."

"But now I am."

"Only because of this witch hunt. They should be investigating Steele."

"But he's dead."

"Exactly. And they can't investigate me, so you're the next best thing."

She took a bite of her sandwich. I had finished my first half.

"Even so," I said, "this seems nuts. Stosh agrees. You'll get off."

"Maybe. But in the meantime what a pain in the ass."

I finished my soup and concentrated on the sandwich. "I wonder if there's more going on than meets the eye."

She had put her spoon down and was just staring at the table. "Meaning what?"

"Is there anybody who might have a grudge against you for anything?"

"There's always the people we've arrested, but nobody on the force."

"Maybe someone you put in jail has connections."

She let out a long sigh. "Who the hell knows. You know, we're all supposed to be on the same team, but Internal Affairs isn't part of the team. I get that there are bad cops, and there needs to be a way of dealing with that. But I've heard so many stories and seen good cops thrown under the bus by these morons. They just seem to be trying to justify their existence."

"I'm so sorry, Rosie. I'll get the names of the people on the board and run them by you."

She just stared.

"You need to eat, Rosie." She had only taken one bite of her sandwich and not much soup. She absentmindedly took another bite.

I tried to lighten up the conversation. "Have you heard about the cold front coming in tomorrow night?"

She nodded. "Yes, a record low is predicted, along with wind chills in the minus fifties."

"Yeah, sounds like a good time to stay in. They're already talking about closing schools."

"A bad night to be living in a warehouse."

I had thought about Angie and assumed it would be a night they would agree to staying in a shelter.

Rosie ate some more soup. "Spencer, about Detective Clements."

I was wondering if she would get around to that. I just listened.

"I'm sorry I've had to break some dates. I guess I'm spending more time with him than I have to, but he's so energetic and excited. He'll make a very good detective. I wish you wouldn't take it so personally."

"I know you're just trying to help, but it's hard not to take personally. He's a good-looking guy who gets to spend a lot of time with you. I'd rather it were me."

She reached out and took my hand. "That's sweet. And when we figure out these two killings, things will calm down. You're busy now, too, you know."

"I am. But I'm not the one who broke the dates." As soon as I said it I wished I hadn't. Sometimes my mouth opens before my brain has a chance to process. My brain always wonders how that happens.

She took her hand back. "I'm too tired to argue about it. And with this IA hearing this isn't a good time to have a talk like this. I'm already at the end of my rope."

"I'm sorry, Rosie." I pushed away from the table. "I'll clean up and get going so you can get some rest."

She didn't respond.

I rinsed the dishes and put them in the dishwasher. She was still sitting at the table.

"Well, I guess I'll get going. If the hearing happens on Friday I'll get back to you with the names."

"Why wouldn't it happen?"

"The cold."

She nodded. "Oh… I forgot. Sure, thanks."

I gave her a kiss on the forehead and then had a thought. "How about dinner Friday, and I'll fill you in then. I'll pick you up at—"

She wearily held up her hand. As she slowly lowered her head she said, "I can't, Spencer. I'm so sorry, but there's a district dinner for new officers and detectives."

I tried to smile, but it wasn't a good one. "Last I checked, you're not that new."

She gave a feeble laugh. "No. I'm… well…"

"You're going with good old Gabe."

"Spencer, I… he had no one else to go with. I didn't want him—"

"That's enough. I get it." I wanted to take back my kiss on her forehead. I turned and let myself out. I stood outside the building and stared at the dark sky. It had never looked darker.

The radio had been on in the kitchen, and the announcer had said the temperature was nineteen. There was no wind. When the front arrived, the wind would pick up and bring the deep freeze with it. I found it hard to think that in another day I'd be wishing it was nineteen again.

***

The light on my answering machine at home was blinking. I pressed the play button and listened while I looked through the unopened mail. Jimmy had gone out again after dinner. Morrie and Rebecca had followed him back to the pool hall. Morrie followed him in and saw him talking to the bartender who picked up a phone. Jimmy sat at the bar for two minutes but didn't order. After the two minutes a door at the rear of the hall opened, and the bartender nodded toward it. Jimmy slid off the stool and disappeared into the back room. That was at seven thirty. He had come out a little before eight and headed home.

It was now close to nine, and it was time to have another chat with Jimmy. I called Morrie and asked for a suggestion of how to make that happen. He told me Jimmy had breakfast every day at a quarter to eight at a little joint called the Blueberry Diner, halfway between home and work. He gave me the address, and we chatted for a minute about the cold. I told him I might be shutting things down for a few days. He said if I wanted him on the job he'd be on the job. Evidently double pay trumped cold.

While I had the phone in my hand I called Stosh, told him I got the letter, and asked for advice.

"Two things. Just answer questions. Don't volunteer any extra information. And for God's sake leave your smart-ass comments at home."

"Me? Smart-ass comments? You must have me confused with someone else."

"Right. They *are* going to piss you off. Remember Detective Lonnigan is in their hands."

"I got it, Stosh. I'll behave. This is all so idiotic. It makes no sense."

"No argument there. The real issue is what was Steele doing there? They should be investigating him, but that's obviously not possible."

"He was rescuing a kid from a kidnapper and breaking up that ring."

"Obviously. And it's also obvious that he threw procedure under the bus when he teamed up with you."

"But he—"

"I know. The job got done, but you don't do things by the book, and a detective who is supposed to do things by the book joined you in that."

"That was his choice," I said.

"Yes, and also obviously he decided to do it knowing he would never be investigated."

"Then there's the history with his son."

"Yup. Sad and complicated."

"And it has nothing to do with Rosie."

"It does now. Keep that in mind, Spencer." He hung up.

While I had the phone in my hand, I opened my notebook and dialed Cyrus Jennings. My brain had finished working, and I figured if he had been willing to take that dog in out of the cold he'd be willing to help. He wasn't only willing… he was thrilled. That dog lady sure was good at making enemies.

I went to bed with Stosh's book and read the first chapter about unsolved murders in Chicago. The preface stated that the book would concentrate on the more interesting of the thousands of un-solved murders on the Chicago police books. Chapter one dealt gen-erally with murder history in Chicago and stated that there had been around one thousand mob murders since 1900. There were seven-ty-nine mob murders during the reign of Sam Giancana, mob boss from 1957 to 1966. Giancana was reported to have said that seven out of ten hits were the wrong guy, but the other three made up for it. It didn't take a lot of evidence, or even any, to order a hit. If a boss thought the mob had been wronged, a hit was ordered without any investigation. The mob was the judge, the jury, and the execu-tioner of the death warrant. FBI agent William Roemer had said that Giancana would kill someone at the "flick of an eye." I read for another fifteen minutes but had to reread the last two pages as I realized I was thinking about Rosie and didn't remember what I had read.

Chapter 19

At seven in the morning Thursday, the temperature had climbed a bit to twenty-two… the calm before the storm. I parked across from the diner and listened to WGN. All Wally Phillips talked about was the coming cold. Schools were closing on Friday, and the weather experts were telling people to stay in if at all possible.

Jimmy was a minute late. I followed him in. He slid into a booth with his back toward me. As I walked by his booth I did a double take and acted surprised to see him.

"You eat here?" I asked.

He didn't look surprised to see me. More like wary. "Evidently."

I gestured at the seat. "Mind if I join you?"

"Do I have a choice?"

"Sure. We all have choices. You just have to live with the consequences."

"Yeah. Thanks for the wisdom."

A waitress arrived just as I slid in.

"The same for you, Jimmy?" she asked.

"Sure, Wanda. Thanks."

"How about your friend?"

He just stared at me.

"I'll have coffee and two eggs over easy with bacon and wheat toast."

"Got it," she said with a warm smile.

Jimmy was still staring. I figured I might as well get to it.

"So, Jimmy, I hear you've been out making the rounds."

His eyebrows raised. "What are you talking about?"

"Your evening activities. I hear you've been making new friends."

He bit his lower lip and lowered his hands under the table. I was pretty sure they were clenched again. He looked away, and I could see him trying to decide.

When he looked back he asked, "So, what do you want?"

Wanda brought my coffee, and I wrapped my hands around the cup. Nice and hot.

"I'm a curious fellow. Just looking for some answers to satisfy that curiosity. I figured a talk with you was the best way to do that... since you were the one doing the visiting."

"And what if I don't feel like talking?"

I took a sip. "Hey, no problem. If my curiosity isn't satisfied when I walk out of here I'll ask Joey if *he* knows."

I knew his hands were working because his shoulders were moving, and I wondered how he was going to eat with his hands under the table.

"Okay, okay, don't get all excited. I'll talk."

But he didn't talk. He looked around the room, and his shoulders kept moving. I figured he was trying to decide how little he could say to shut me up. He didn't have to worry about anyone else hearing. The place was full... and noisy.

I sipped my coffee. "How about this, Jimmy. Joey is paying me well. I've got a hundred in cash to help satisfy my curiosity."

He laughed—not long and not loud, and it wasn't because he thought it was funny. "Dead men can't spend money, Manning."

I couldn't argue with that. "Are you worried about Marty?"

"Wouldn't you be worried about Marty?"

I shrugged. "Not particularly."

He looked around some more. Every five seconds or so his eyes darted back to me. Our food arrived, and he had to show his hands when the waitress handed him the plate. He made a show of putting butter and syrup on his pancakes and took a bite.

I started on my eggs. "Listen, Jimmy, I'm going to find out about what's going on. The only question is how I find out and whether or not Joey finds out. You're involved in something. If it has nothing to do with the murders—"

"Murders! I got nothing to do with any murders. It's just business, that's all."

"You sure about that?" I swallowed toast and washed it down with coffee. "I'm working on the murders and the frame. I don't care about business. What you do is not my concern if it has nothing to do with my case."

He put his fork down, looked around some more, and leaned toward me. "Okay. He's just covering his bases. If Joey goes to jail, Marty wants to be ready to take over. He wants to expand the business. He thinks Joey is being too soft on some of these guys, just taking a percentage. He thinks there's more money in a syndicate."

"With him sitting in Joey's chair."

"Yeah."

"And you sitting on the couch instead of behind the counter serving ice cream."

He took a deep breath. "Yeah."

I nodded. "I can see why you're talking to Marty. But I can also see a couple of problems."

He didn't ask. Probably didn't want to know, but I was going to tell him. I ate some egg first.

"One, you may not be involved in the frame and the murders, but somebody is. And that somebody might be Marty. If he is, then you're an accessory."

He stopped his fork halfway to his mouth and all of a sudden looked older. "Hey, I got nothing—"

I held my hand up. "I know, you got nothing to do with it. But what you don't know might hurt you. Second, I wonder what Mr. Maggio might think about all of this."

He set his fork down. "I wondered that too. I asked Marty. He said it wouldn't be a problem. All Mr. Maggio is concerned about is money. If Marty brought in more money, Mr. Maggio would be happy."

"Perhaps. Perhaps not."

"What do you mean, not? Why wouldn't he be happy about more money?"

I ate the last of my eggs. "No reason, but he might not like the way it was done. I think he likes Joey. And if it gets out that Marty was making moves to take over while Joey was still sitting in the chair… well…" I spread my arms out, palms up.

"Jesus, Manning. I didn't think of that."

"I guess not."

He looked worried… real worried.

"You're not going to say anything to Joey, are you? I mean now that I helped?"

"Don't see any need to, but better be careful who you're seen with. If I were you, I'd be happy serving ice cream for a while."

"But what am I going to tell Marty?"

Wanda asked if we wanted anything else. We didn't. She left the check.

"No clue. But if it helps any, I'll buy breakfast." I picked up the check and handed him my card. "Call me if you see or hear anything you think I should know concerning the Joey issue."

He looked at my card. "Thanks for the grub. You still think it's a frame?"

"Most of me does, but I'm not totally convinced." I slid out and gave him a two-finger salute. When I walked along the front windows he was still sitting in the booth. I had ruined his day, but I got what I was looking for. The only question left was whether Marty was just playing the possibility or had he had a hand in setting it up.

***

I got to the office just before nine thirty and asked Carol to call everyone and tell them to stay home Friday and Saturday, with pay, and we'd meet again Monday at noon. I told her to have them back to work on Sunday if the temperature warmed above ten. If not, take

Sunday off also. And I wanted to talk to Morrie, Paul, and Rebecca. I told Morrie and Rebecca about the chat I had with Jimmy. I asked Morrie to stay with Jimmy, but I was reassigning Rebecca. I asked her to start surveillance on the Belden house from seven a.m. to noon but to be at the meeting. I reassigned Paul to the house from noon to seven and asked Chester to start at seven instead of five. I was no longer concerned about Marty. He was still a possibility, but we wouldn't learn anything more by following him. If I wanted more I'd have to think of something else.

The temperature had risen to twenty-two, but the forecast hadn't changed. The temperature would start to drop by early afternoon. I called the number on my Internal Affairs letter and asked if the hearing would be postponed. No such luck. When I had first learned about the investigation I was ready to charge in on my white horse and rescue Rosie. The facts were still the facts, and I would report those, but I couldn't stop thinking about her Friday night dinner date, and I no longer felt like saddling my horse. What I felt like was having dinner at McGoon's. But I didn't make a reservation. Nobody in their right mind would be out in the deep freeze, including Miss Hand.

I told Carol to leave at noon, but she said she could brave a walk across the street and would stay until Billy got home from school. I took the rest of the day off and went home to read.

***

I made a ham sandwich on rye and watched the noon news, which was mostly Tom Skilling talking about the weather. A big dip in the jet stream was going to funnel arctic air into the Midwest. At twelve thirty the temperature had already dropped to ten. Skilling wasn't sure about breaking the record, but he was guaranteeing we'd get close. The record low of twenty-six below had been set in 1982. I decided to reserve the right not to go out for dinner.

I cleaned up lunch and settled in the recliner with *Murder in the Big City*. I was on the second chapter, which was about the bungled hit on Ken Eto, known as "Tokyo Joe," two years ago in 1983. Eto had set up a gambling racket in 1949 that had netted up to two hundred thousand dollars a week, less three thousand in payoffs to corrupt cops. The FBI arrested him in 1982. Afraid that he would talk, John Gattuso and Jasper Campise, a Cook County deputy sheriff and mob associate, were given the task to make sure he didn't. In February of 1983, Eto was invited to a dinner party. He never made it.

Campise and Gattuso attacked him while he was sitting in a parked car and fired three shots into his head. They left him for dead, but all three bullets only grazed his skull. They had handloaded their ammunition to keep it from being traced, and it was thought they hadn't used enough gunpowder. Eto agreed to turn informant and entered the witness protection program. He identified Campise and Gattuso, with Gattuso being the triggerman. They were arrested and charged with attempted murder.

The FBI offered witness protection to Campise and Gattuso in exchange for who had ordered the hit, but they said they weren't in danger and refused. Five months later their tortured bodies were found in a car in Naperville. Eto helped to put away fifteen mobsters and corrupt policemen and was still in witness protection. The murders of Campise and Gattuso had not been solved.

I got up and uncapped a bottle of Pabst Blue Ribbon, also brewed in Milwaukee. By 1980 Pabst had passed Schlitz in sales. At a little after two, I had just started on chapter three about the murder of Sam Giancana, killed in the basement of his Oak Park home in 1975, when the phone rang. Mike had left the parlor, taking the Lincoln, and Rebecca had followed him to the house on Belden. He was parked in front and had entered the house.

"What happened to knocking off at noon?" I asked.

"I figured I was already out and might as well finish off the day," she said. "I'll stay with him."

"Okay, thanks, Rebecca. Keep me updated." I hung up and thought about a couple of odd things. One, I had to find out what was going on at that house. And two, Mike didn't have a driver's license. One of the main rules of being a criminal was you don't let the cops pick you up for something stupid, like driving without a license.

Rebecca called fifty minutes later to tell me Mike was back at the parlor. She had nothing to report concerning the trip other than it had happened. Since we had been watching the parlor that was the first time someone had left during business hours. I wanted to get surveillance on the house during the day, but it was just too cold. It would have to wait until Monday.

I went back to the book. Sam Giancana, also known as Momo, was the Chicago mafia boss from 1957 to 1966. He loved the spotlight and dated movie stars and associated with politicians, including John F. Kennedy. But he had made enemies in the organization. He had made a fortune in offshore casinos in Central America and had refused to cut in his underlings. And then after President Kennedy was assassinated, Giancana was called to testify. He was getting much more attention than the organization liked, and they were afraid of what he would say to the Senate committee. Tension didn't lessen over the years, and in 1975 he was shot in the back of the head while cooking Italian sausage in the basement of his Oak Park home. He was then shot six more times in the face to send a message about too much publicity. No one was ever arrested.

I finished the chapter and walked to the front picture window. I watched the trees swaying and could hear the wind blowing. I turned on the TV for the news at five. Winds were gusting to twenty, the temperature was two below, and the wind chill was minus thirty-five. I decided that if I went to McGoon's one of the people not in their right minds would be me. I settled for canned chili and wondered what Loretta was doing.

Chapter 20

The Internal Affairs office was located downtown in the same building as the permitting section, so I parked in the same garage as when I had lunch with Mooneen. This Friday would go down in history as the coldest day in Chicago on record. A little before five a.m. the thermometer had hit minus twenty-seven, and the wind chill was minus fifty-four. It had been very hard getting out of a warm bed. That would have been easier if I was meeting Rosie for dinner.

It had warmed to minus twenty-five by the time I left at nine. It was a one-block walk from the parking garage, but the wind was at my back. The walk back would be brutal.

I took the elevator to the fourth floor and looked for room 416. The woman at the desk in the outer room told me they were running a bit behind and to have a seat. I picked up a *Field and Stream* magazine and waited patiently. I was called in fifteen minutes later, ten minutes after my ten o'clock appointment.

I hadn't thought about what to expect, but I wasn't surprised by three people, two men and a woman, sitting behind a long glass table. There was one wooden chair in front of the table. Theirs were upholstered. There were no windows, and there was a picture of the current chief of police on the wall behind them. He seemed to be staring at me, and I wondered if my dad's picture had been on that wall staring at others on the hot seat. The only items on the table were a tray with a pitcher of water and glasses, a tape recorder, and notepads in front of everyone but me.

They introduced themselves as August Lee, Eloise Maher, and Alexander Welch. All three were middle-aged, but Maher was less so. Lee wore a tan suit coat over a white shirt with a sort of matching solid tan tie. He was kind of pudgy with wavy brown hair and a solid square jaw that invited an uppercut. Many in this room had probably been tempted. Welch was too skinny, wore a three-piece blue suit, and with a pointy nose and eyes too close together reminded me of a certain bookie who was a good source of information. His slicked back black hair added to the likeness. Miss Maher looked to be the friendliest of the group, but no one entered that room expecting a friend. She wore a tweed jacket over a white blouse, and her brown hair was pulled back tightly into a bun. I thought it stretched the skin on her forehead too tight. None of them smiled.

Welch was sitting in the center and appeared to be in charge. He started by asking me to state my name and profession. I did. He then tried to put me at ease.

"We thank you for coming in, Mr. Manning, especially on a day like this." There was certainly a perfect chance to talk about the weather, but that was as far as he went. "We will be tape recording this. Do you have any objection to that?"

"I have plenty of objections to that, but do my objections matter?" I also objected to his voice. It had a staccato effect, like a typewriter.

He took a deep breath. I have no idea what he expected me to say. Does everyone just say *sure, no problem*? Stosh hadn't warned me about the tape recorder.

"Certainly your objections matter, Mr. Manning. But there are alternatives should you object."

"And what are those alternatives?"

"The woman in the outer room is a stenographer. We could do it that way."

"And if I didn't agree to that?"

"Then there are further measures that you would like even less." No one was smiling, and it was obvious no one felt at ease. Lee was pinching the skin on his chin and staring down at the table.

I didn't know what difference it would make if I opted for the stenographer. I decided the goal was to stand up for Rosie, and pissing them off wasn't going to help that.

I sat back in the chair and said, "Go ahead with your recorder."

He pushed a button and, looking down at his notes, said, "We want to start with verifying facts. State your name and profession again please."

I did.

"You were in the room when Detective Steele shot himself, correct?"

"No, that is not correct."

He looked up suddenly. "Not correct? You weren't there?"

"Depends on how you define *there*. Yes, I was there at the scene. But you asked if I was in the room. I was not. Detective Steele left the room so no, I was not in the room he was in."

He made a note on his pad and continued. "And if Detective Lonnigan had been with her partner he would not have died. Correct?"

I took a breath and did my best to stay calm. I looked at the other two behind the table. Lee was doodling on his notepad and every few seconds pushed out his lips in a fish imitation. Maher was looking back at me. She looked concerned, and I felt she didn't agree with the line of questioning.

"With no disrespect meant, I don't think that is correct or not correct. I think it is simply not valid. If someone wants to kill themselves they're going to find a way to do it."

"And you have a degree in psychiatry?"

I had to take a deeper breath. "No."

"Then I suggest you stick to the facts. I'll repeat my question. Do you think if Detective Lonnigan had been there Detective Steele would have killed himself?"

"That's not a fact… what I think would be an opinion."

That brought a slight smile from Miss Maher. I thought he would have shot himself, but I ran that by my brain before I opened my mouth, and it didn't look good. "Psychiatrist or not, I think your premise is illogical. Ros—Detective Lonnigan wasn't there, so it's a moot point. Do you think he would have killed himself if *you* had been there?"

That brought an even bigger smile from Miss Maher. I just got a stare from Welch.

Making an effort to control himself, Welch asked, "What was Detective Steele doing there in the first place? And what were you doing there?"

"Rescuing a kid and breaking up a kidnapping ring."

Lee was still doodling. It was obvious who was leading the charge.

"All on your own."

"Was that a question?"

"No. All on your own? Do you think your father would have condoned that level of irresponsibility?"

"You mean rescuing that kid and saving many other kids' lives?"

A longer stare with his jaw clenched. "We are not debating the outcome, Mr. Manning. We're questioning how it was handled. If Detective Steele had handled it by the book he might not have died."

I crossed my left leg over the right. "He wasn't killed by the bad guy. He was killed by his own hand, and he had thought about it enough to set it up that way, which, by the way, saves you a lot of trouble."

"So you are saying that Detective Lonnigan had nothing to do with what went on in that room?"

"Correct, she knew nothing about it."

"Don't you think if she did know about it things might have turned out differently?"

"Again, asking for an opinion. It only happened because Steele didn't care about the consequences to himself and knew he wouldn't be worried about his job when he was done. But he would have found another way someday."

"Which brings up another question. Why didn't he care about his job? Why did he make that decision? No one gives up their own life purposely to catch a criminal."

I knew why. Steele had never gotten over losing his son to a kidnapper, and putting a bullet in his head was his way out. But that was none of Welch's business. "Don't know, I'm not a psychiatrist." I stared back at him.

"You say Detective Lonnigan knew nothing about the plan, but she *was* there. That seems odd. How do you explain that?"

I had asked Rosie that exact question. She had explained that she had been assigned to shadow me because I always seemed to find trouble, and the police had been having trouble finding any.

"I don't know. You'll have to ask someone else."

"But she wasn't there when Detective Steele killed… I'm sorry… murdered Walters?"

He was trying to bait me, but I knew he was right. It was murder, and I had warned Steele of that at the time. I hadn't known that part of the plan. "She was not."

"Or when Detective Steele took his own life?"

"She was not."

"But then she magically appeared."

That wasn't a question, but I answered anyway. "Nothing magic about it. She was…"

He looked up with wide eyes and raised eyebrows. "She was what, Mr. Manning?"

"I forget."

"You forget what you were just about to say?"

I shifted in the chair and uncrossed my legs. My left foot was falling asleep. I think Lee was also. "Yup. I have trouble with that. I've been thinking of seeing a psychiatrist."

Miss Maher was looking down, but I again thought I saw a smile.

"But if she had been with her partner, Steele would probably be alive."

I had to remember I left my smart-ass at home. "That's conjecture. No one will ever know. But I've already said Steele was planning on killing himself. He would have done it no matter what."

"Why do you think he went into the other room?"

I had thought about that and decided I respected Steele for it. It would have been a shock for everyone in that room. I don't know if he considered me, but there was a kid in there who had already seen one man die. Welch was throwing jabs at Rosie and trying to distract me with feints at Steele. Not a bad strategy. I had to think about every response. A person not used to thinking so much might slip up. He was tapping his pencil on the table waiting for my response.

"No idea."

"Was Detective Steele a friend of yours?"

"We worked well together."

"But he was a policeman. You're not. So what was it you worked together on?"

There had to be a trick there somewhere, but I couldn't find it. And no matter what I said, Steele was dead. They weren't investigating him.

"I'm a private detective. Just because I don't have a shiny badge doesn't mean we're not after the same thing. Our paths crossed." I wasn't about to tell anyone how much. I get results by bending the rules once in a while, and Steele had helped when I needed it. The last time had led to the rescue of a kidnapped detective.

"Just like they cross with Detective Lonnigan?" he asked.

"Or anyone else on the force who happens to be working on the same case."

"But more so with Detective Lonnigan, I hear."

That was personal, and it was harder not to tell him to go to hell, but I didn't respond.

"My apologies. That wasn't a question. Do you have a personal relationship with Detective Lonnigan?"

"Yes."

When he smiled his eyes seemed to get closer together. "And just how personal is it?"

"And just why is that your business?"

"Just how much information about cases do you get from Detective Lonnigan outside of business hours?"

The answer was just as much as I get from anyone else at the station who wanted to solve a crime, including Lieutenant Powolski. And I had been very successful with their help.

"I am offended by the question."

"Is that your answer?"

"Yes."

He smiled again. "Sometimes the lack of an answer makes the answer clear."

I had a comment but kept it to myself.

"So Detective Lonnigan is at the park, but isn't with her partner. She, a trained detective, is somewhere outside while a murder and a suicide happen inside that room. That seems negligent to me. Doesn't it seem so to you?"

"I've already explained she knew nothing of the plan. She—"

He held up his hand and was no longer smiling. "The point is, Mr. Manning, she was not where she should have been, and two people died violently... two deaths she may have been able to stop. She had obviously been watching her partner yet let him walk into that shack alone."

That wasn't a question, but my string was pretty taut. "He wasn't alone. And when she heard the shots she ran to the shack and was in time to keep Marcel from killing me and the other two in the room. She didn't—"

"She didn't. Exactly." He stood and talked down at me. "She didn't follow procedure, or she would have been with Detective Steele, and we could have taken two criminals out in cuffs instead of bags."

I stood and pushed the chair back. "So instead the state was saved the expense of two trials." I guess I hadn't left all of my smartass at home.

He leaned toward me, hands on the table. "Listen here, Mr. Manning, I—"

"No, you listen here. You have the report of exactly what happened and why it happened that way. If you're looking for help in crucifying Detective Lonnigan, you're talking to the wrong guy. And you're done wasting my time."

I glanced at Miss Maher who seemed to have a sparkle in her eye, turned, and walked out.

Welch said, "You're not done here, Manning."

I kept walking and let myself out, not taking any care to close the door quietly. Just before it slammed I heard him warn me not to talk about what had taken place there. I was plenty steamed, and the walk against the wind back to the car felt good for the first half block. After that it felt like thirty below or whatever ungodly temperature it was.

The Mustang cranked a bit slowly, but she started. I let the fluids circulate for a minute and then headed for the station. I decided to see if I could kill two birds with one stone. If Rosie wasn't out galavanting with Gabe, I could fill her and Stosh in at the same time.

***

Rosie's car was in the lot, and Gabe was talking to the desk sergeant who nodded to me as I walked by without Gabe noticing. I had no desire to chat with him. Stosh was putting on his coat as I walked into his office.

"Hi, kid. You wanna get some lunch?"

"No. I just stopped by to tell you and Rosie what happened at the hearing."

"Oh yeah. How'd that go?" He took off his coat and sat on the chair next to the door.

"Well, if we can find Rosie I'll just have to tell the story once."

He asked Kate to page Lonnigan, and she walked in a minute later. She looked at Stosh, not noticing me on the other side of the room.

"What do you need, Lieutenant? I was just going to find Clements and get some lunch."

"Great," I said. "Maybe we can all make a party of it."

She turned suddenly with a look of surprise. "Spencer. What are you doing here? Was there no hearing?"

I spun a chair and sat on it backward. "There was."

"Well that was pretty quick. That must be good news."

"You can decide about the news, but it sort of ended suddenly."

Stosh rolled his eyes to the ceiling. "Oh, Jesus. What did you do?"

"I told them if they were looking for someone to crucify Rosie they'd have to find someone else and left."

"Why am I not surprised? What led you to that opinion?"

"It's not an opinion. Those people are morons. Well, at least one of them is."

"Only one?" Stosh asked.

"Only one said anything, and his voice rubbed me the wrong way… staccato, like someone banging on a typewriter. I don't know about the other two voices… they never used them. The man on the right never even looked up at me. The woman did look me in the eye and didn't seem hostile, but she never spoke."

When I looked over at Rosie I saw her jaw had dropped and her eyes were open wide. "What's the matter, Rosie?"

"The guy with the voice… skinny, pointy nose, black hair combed back?"

I nodded. "How do you know?"

"Damn," she said quietly. After a pause, she said, "Well, that answers why this is happening."

"It does? Why?" Stosh asked.

She took a deep breath and blew it out slowly, puffing out her cheeks. "Welch, right?"

"Right."

"About a month ago we met at a city dinner function. He was very attentive and at the end of the event suggested dinner the next night. I turned him down, making some excuse. He kept trying. The last time he asked I was pretty blunt, and he got huffy… said something about being better than him. The guy makes my skin crawl."

Shifting in his chair, Stosh asked, "Why didn't you tell me about this?"

"It wasn't a big deal. I'm a big girl and thought I had it handled."

Stosh shook his head. "I hate this crap. I'll take care of it. What a waste of time." He started to get up.

"Hang on, Lieutenant," said Rosie. "Are you sure you want them to know what my assignment was?"

He sat back down. "The truth will set you free, Rosie."

"Okay, I appreciate that, but either way we lose. My assignment was to follow Spencer because he does things outside of the rules, and he'd lead us to trouble. That admits we condoned Spencer breaking the rules by doing something we couldn't."

"Not couldn't, Rosie. Shouldn't. We follow the law."

"And Spencer doesn't, and we let him."

I chimed in. "Two bad guys were taken care of, and we rescued numerous kids, and—"

Stosh held up his hand. "Nobody is denying that." He turned to Rosie. "I don't think you'll have to go, but if you do just tell the truth. If there's fallout I'll deal with it. I'm hungry. Anybody interested?"

We both declined. I was anxious to get home.

"Okay. Good luck Monday, Rosie. We still on for cards tomorrow, Spencer?"

"Sure. See you at noon."

"I got fresh pastrami from the butcher."

"I'll skip breakfast."

"You do that."

I also wished Rosie luck on Monday if she had to go.

"I won't see you before then?" she asked.

"I don't know. I'm not the one whose dance card is full."

She just looked at me as I turned and walked out. I stopped in the hall and went back. "I would like to see you, Rosie. Call if you find time."

She nodded. "I'm working the weekend. I have Monday off."

That meant she didn't have much time, at least for me, but it was a good weekend to stay in. The predicted high through Sunday was minus fifteen. The jetstream was supposed to shift back north by Sunday night.

I fell asleep reading about the 1929 St. Valentine's Day Massacre. Most people send candy on Valentine's Day, but not Al Capone. The

Irish gangster, George "Bugs" Moran, Capone's main rival on the north side, had called a meeting at his garage headquarters, and Capone had found out about it. It was time to settle an old score.

A little after ten thirty in the morning, two uniformed policemen entered the garage, told Moran's gang it was a raid, and lined them up against a wall. They then opened up with Tommy Guns, leaving seven bullet-riddled bodies lying on the concrete. Capone wanted to send a message, and bullets were cheap. Ironically, Bugs was late to the meeting and arrived to find his gang dead on the floor. With most of his gang wiped out, the gang wars were over, and Capone became the boss of the Chicago underworld.

The cops knew who did it, but knowing and proving are two different things, and I have to wonder how much effort they put into it. Seven gangsters were dead. No one was ever arrested, and Capone got away with it. But the massacre had an effect Capone hadn't seen coming. The public was outraged about the Chicago mob wars and demanded action. Elliott Ness was sent to Chicago. He attacked Capone from every angle, and two years later Capone was convicted of tax evasion and sent to Alcatraz.

Chapter 21

I took care of a few chores Saturday morning and headed for Chez Stosh at half past eleven. The bright midday sun had no effect on the temperature. The thermometer on the porch read minus sixteen.

Stosh had the cards out on the table. We made sandwiches and ate on trays in the living room watching Northwestern and Michigan play basketball. Everybody looked forward to playing Northwestern. We watched with the sound down and talked about the case.

"Good pastrami, Stosh."

He took a swig of beer and said, "Nothing beats a good butcher. You have your people out working in the cold?"

"Nope. I gave them the weekend off. I think we've learned all we're going to learn from the tails anyway."

"And what would that be?"

"Well, everyone has something suspicious going on, and almost everybody has a motive."

"Who doesn't?"

"The driver... Danny Primo. He's been hanging around with Jack Eigen." We both took a minute to eat and wash it down with Schlitz. "I had a chat with him. While he could choose better company, it seems to have nothing to do with Joey. They have some scheme to buy a horse. I hope it works because he lost his job when Joey found out about the horse."

"And you think Primo's going to tell the truth to an investigator, especially one working for Mineo?"

"He didn't know who I was. We were just two guys having breakfast at a diner."

He finished his sandwich. "You wanna split another sandwich?"

"Split? You on a diet?"

"I'm watching my figure."

"That's not hard. There's a lot to watch." I got a look that wasn't too friendly. "Sure. Hate to see good pastrami go to waste."

Stosh headed for the kitchen, and I turned up the sound on the TV. Northwestern was actually winning by four halfway through the first half. I wasn't going to get excited. He was back in a few minutes, and I continued.

"DaVita has been out taking late night walks to a house a couple blocks away." I told him about the lady and the envelope.

"You think she's running a house?"

"Seems unlikely. My people haven't seen anyone else there, but maybe Mike has some special deal. And maybe it's something else." I took a few bites. "The most interesting is Marty, who is the most obvious to benefit should Joey be inconvenienced by a jail term. He pretty much runs things now… I'd think he'd want the prestige that goes along with that."

"You'd think. But Marty isn't stupid. I can see him taking advantage of misfortune, not causing it."

"Agreed." We ate and watched the game. By the time we were done with our sandwiches Michigan was ahead. I muted the TV.

"Then there's Jimmy Smith, the soda jerk who told me he knew nothing about what goes on in the back room. But he's been out at night talking to the competition."

"Lining up a stable?"

"Looks like it," I said.

"Joey never has been interested in expanding. He's content with letting everybody do business as long as they don't get greedy."

"Right. But Marty isn't so understanding. I think he's been after Joey to expand. He sees dollars. And if Joey is out of the way…"

Stosh stretched out the recliner that also served as his bed ever since Francine had died.

"Which leads me to believe he knows something we don't," I said. "And if that's so, maybe he's the one who set it up."

"Maybe. But I don't see him getting involved with murder to do it."

"I don't either, but who knows?"

"So you've got nothing."

"Pretty much. You making any progress?" I asked.

"We're doing better on the second shooting than the first. Not that we even have a hint of someone to look at, but there is more evidence, and we're working on it."

"I'm halfway through your book. If these were mob hits, you can add them to the list of unsolved murders."

"Yeah, they tend not to make mistakes. Or their mistakes get buried."

"Well, the book quotes Giancana as saying that seven out of ten of their hits were on the wrong guy."

Stosh grunted. "Yeah, I misspoke. They make a lot of mistakes… we just have trouble catching them at it."

"And even more trouble with a dead witness."

He sighed. "Yeah, that sure doesn't help, but we have a signed statement. The DA isn't giving up." He looked at me with squinted eyes. "Tell me."

I looked back. "Tell you what?"

"You've been scratching at this for more than a week. There must be something keeping you awake at night."

I watched the clock on the wall behind Stosh. It was exactly thirty seconds before I replied. "Permits."

"I figured you'd be working on that."

"You know I'm not fond of coincidences. Loretta gets a permit in 1977 as soon as she is twenty-one. Joey lets his lapse in '78. Why?"

"Why don't you ask him?"

"I did. He wasn't too happy about it."

"What a surprise."

I stared at the wall.

"What?" he asked.

"There had to be some reason, which leads me to wonder what happened back then. And there's one elephant in the room."

"Sure there is. Sam Giancana. Gunned down in '75. But I don't see the connection."

"Joey was Sam's driver, right?"

"Right."

"So they spent a lot of time together. You could assume they were buddies to some extent."

He shrugged. "Or not. But if you make that assumption, the last thing you'd expect Joey to do would be to give up his gun. If my buddy is killed I'm looking for the guy who did it."

"I assume they talked to Joey," I said.

"Sure. Oak Park asked a lot of questions."

"And he had no ideas about who did it?"

"Of course not. The mob solves its own problems."

"Yeah. And maybe they just did. Maybe it took ten years for Joey to figure out that it was Schloff who killed his pal. Revenge has no expiration date."

"And maybe the Cubs'll win the pennant this year."

"It would make sense," I said. "The guy puts on a big show of not having a gun just waiting for the one day when he takes the shot. Speaking of revenge, Sam have any kids?"

"Three. All girls. And girls don't hold onto grudges, or set up hits."

"Really? I could name—"

He held up his hands. "Okay, okay. Most girls."

"How about brothers?"

"One."

"Was he in the business?"

"No. Car salesman."

I thought for a minute. "Do you know what happened to them all, and his wife?"

"His wife moved back east. I don't know about the rest."

"Would you find out? I'd like to know where they are."

"Sure, I'll add it to the list. You want me to see who he played with on the playground in first grade?"

"No thanks. Just relatives."

Stosh took in a bushel of air and let it out slowly. "You keep scratching, kid. Let's play some cards."

While he was shuffling, I said, "But I *am* making progress with the dog lady."

He looked up. "What the hell are you talking about?"

"The husky that showed up at Carol's door. You remember—the lady with the bogus working dog permit?"

"Oh yeah." He dealt. "What kind of progress?"

"You don't want to know."

"I don't want to know most of the things you do. Next time don't bring it up."

As he spread his cards, he asked, "You seen your stalker lately?"

"Nope. But I haven't been looking. McGoon's seems to be her pub of choice, and I've either been too busy or it's been too cold to go out for dinner."

He dealt. I had two pair.

"But you'll go back to McGoon's one of these days?"

"Of course. One of my favorite places." I discarded a queen.

He picked it up. "And that would have nothing to do with the lady?"

I didn't answer. He discarded one of my pair. I picked it up and he swore.

"And what about Rosie?" he asked.

"What about Rosie?"

"You still playing the jealous lover?"

I discarded a king that he picked up with a big grin. "Gin! Add up those points."

I had the three fives and filled a straight. He got six points and swore again.

"So?" he asked.

I shuffled. "I'm not jealous. I'm just upset and disappointed. I've lost count of the dates she's broken because of this Gabriel guy."

"There is that work thing, Spencer. It's not like you work regular hours either."

"But I'm not hanging around with Gabriel."

He sighed. "I hope not. How many times you gonna shuffle those cards?"

I straightened the deck and dealt. "I told her to call me if she has time this weekend."

"Well if that doesn't have her falling all over you, nothing will."

"Did I ask you?"

"You never do. Gin." His smile widened. "If you only have six points again I quit." He didn't have to quit.

At the end of the afternoon I had lost and so had Northwestern. And there were no messages on my answering machine. I heated some mushroom soup and spent the evening with the book.

***

My phone rang at ten minutes after nine. It was Cyrus Jennings. The dog had been tied up out in the cold for fifteen minutes. I gave him instructions and called Carol.

"Evening, my right-hand woman whom I can't work without."

She responded by saying she wanted a raise. I told her I had to talk with the board of directors. I also told her I wanted to make sure she would be in the office at nine Monday morning. She would. Then I told her there might be a red bandanna next to the door and not to pick it up. One of the reasons she was my right-hand woman was that she didn't ask questions. I wouldn't have answered even if she did—it was much better that she didn't know, for several reasons.

My next call was to the pool hall. It took six minutes for Ralph to come to the phone. He had been in the middle of a run.

***

I thought about going to McGoon's Sunday but decided to stay home. I was hoping to hear from Rosie. I didn't. I finished the book while I was eating dinner, a bowl of tomato soup and a ham sandwich. About eight I decided to swallow my pride and call her. She apologized for not calling. Something about helping her sister, and the weekend had just gotten away from her. She thanked me for calling and said she'd make it up to me. She also told me she had received a call from Stosh—the hearing was over.

When I suggested dinner Monday to celebrate, she hemmed and hawed and finally admitted she was going to dinner with Gabe. It was his birthday, and he had no friends or family, and she felt sorry for him. She was sorry. So was I.

I hung up and decided I hadn't been to McGoon's in a while. I was thinking about a good meal. If Loretta happened to be there it was just fate, and I had no control over fate.

Chapter 22

I got to the office Monday morning by eight. I didn't have anything to do, but I was anxious and full of adrenaline. Everything depended on my instinct about people, in this case the dog lady. I could usually count on people to behave consistently. I went to the front picture window and waved at Ralph, parked across the street. As soon as traffic cleared he pulled away. I sat at Carol's desk so I could watch the front door.

Carol arrived at ten to nine, glanced down at the cement, and unlocked the front door.

"Good morning, Spencer. How do you like sitting in the boss's chair?"

"Too stressful. I'm going back to my office."

"You have a nice nap. I'll let you know if anything important happens."

I smiled as I stood. "Oh, I think I'll know."

"Any instructions?"

"Only one." She hung up her coat, and I held the chair out for her. "Make sure nobody except the right person picks up that bandanna."

"Is the right person who I think it is?"

"Entirely possible."

"I don't need to know anything about this?"

"Nope. Better if you don't. Just react normally to whatever happens. You need to know nothing, and since you *do* know nothing, that'll be easy. Just a normal day at the office."

"Got it." She sat and started in at the typewriter.

I heard the steady rhythm of the keys until eight after nine when the door opened, and I heard the bell. If I was right, the next voice would be angry. I was right.

"What the hell did you do with my dog?"

"Excuse me?" Carol answered.

I got up with a smile and wiped it off before I left my office.

"Don't give me *excuse me*! You know damned well what I'm talking about."

I joined the party. "Excuse *me* too. You are?"

Carol held out a hand toward the lady with the angry eyes. "Mr. Manning, this is Miss Knox. It was her dog Billy found last week out in the cold."

"Ah, yes. Poor dog. I hear he doesn't like being dragged across the floor."

"You people have a lot of nerve. You have no idea who you're dealing with." She was gesturing at me with her left fist. The other hand was in the pocket of her coat. I kept an eye on the pocket.

The energy coming from her was intense, and I was enjoying every second of it. And I *did* know who I was dealing with—that was exactly the point. My whole plan depended on knowing not only who I was dealing with but how she'd behave. And so far she was right on target.

"I'll give you one more chance. What have you done with my dog?"

I sat on the edge of Carol's desk, between the dog lady and Carol just in case she decided to use the fist.

"Miss Knox, if you can find a dog in here you are more than welcome to him."

"Really? Maybe he's not here, but you know where he is."

"And what makes you think that?"

She pulled her hand out of the pocket and held out the red bandanna with just a violent stare.

"I'm sorry, is that meaningful?"

"You know damned well it is. This is my dog's bandanna, and I found it by your front door. How do you explain that?"

I gave her a puzzled look. "I can't. Perhaps he remembered where he was treated well last time and sat by the door, and the bandanna came loose."

Her hand was shaking. "Or perhaps you hid him somewhere. This is your last chance. Where is my dog?"

"Does your dog have a name?"

"What the hell does that mean?"

"Simple question, but perhaps a bit sarcastic. My apologies. How about this? Do you know your dog's name?"

Now her whole arm was shaking. "Are you insane? Of course I know my dog's name. What does that have to do with anything?"

I shrugged. "You never use it. People who care about their pets actually call them by their names."

"Well he's not a pet. He's a working dog."

"Working at what?"

"What is the matter with you?" she yelled.

"Ah," I replied. "Exactly what I was wondering about you. Working dogs have a reason for being with someone. What's the reason with you? You seem to be pretty functional."

She opened her mouth, but no words came out. She shook her fist at me and said, "You'll be sorry. I'll be back. You'll be real sorry!"

She stuffed the bandanna into her pocket and stomped out.

I turned to Carol with a smile. "That's the most fun I've had in a long time."

Carol shook her head. "Whew. That's one angry woman."

"That's what I was counting on."

"What do you think she means by we'll be sorry?"

"Oh, I think she thinks she has a wild card to play that I'm unaware of."

"But you are aware?"

"I am if my plan works."

"Are you going to fill me in?"

I stood up and turned to face her. "Again, it's better—"

She held up her hand. "I know, I know. Better if I don't know. But if I may ask, do you know where the dog is?"

"I do not."

"Then I'm worried. He's out in the cold somewhere, maybe even…"

I put a hand on her shoulder. "I don't know where he is, Carol, but I do know he's okay."

"How do you…?"

"I just do. Trust me?"

She nodded.

"Okay. If all goes according to plan, it'll all work out. She'll be back with her wild card."

"When?"

"That I'm not sure of. Maybe today. Tomorrow for sure."

"I don't know that I want to handle her and her wild card by myself. She scares me."

"I don't want you to either. I have a lunch meeting. I'll be back after that and stay until you leave. And I'll be here tomorrow if need be."

"What if she comes during your meeting?"

"Good point. When I leave, lock up and go home for lunch. I'll call you when I get back."

"Okay. I hope your plan works."

"Me too."

I called Stosh and gave him a heads-up about what was going on and told him I might need some support from Chicago's finest. He gave me a number to call, made some remark about taxpayers' money, and hung up.

I gave the number to Carol and told her to keep it handy.

***

I met Mr. Chin as I came in the back door and handed him five twenties. He bowed several times. Joey was a generous client. My team was all there, and everyone had full plates. Rebecca was just sitting down as I walked in.

We chatted for a few minutes, and I gave everyone the update. When I asked if anyone had anything new to report, Rebecca was the only one who responded. She raised her hand and finished chewing.

"I got to the house on Belden at seven this morning. At a quarter to eight the woman came out with a little girl who appeared to be eight or nine. They walked to the corner, and the lady waited with her until a school bus came five minutes later."

I asked if they were affectionate.

"If you mean hugs and kisses, no. But they did wave as the bus took off."

"Interesting. So we have Mike visiting a house with an envelope that he hands to a lady and that same lady seeing a little girl off to school." I finished an egg roll.

"Would you like me to stay on the house, Spencer?"

"Yes. Let's see if that continues."

As the temperature had climbed to the teens, I told everyone to continue their assignments, and we would meet again on Thursday. Morrie remarked that he'd probably be hungry before then. I told him Mr. Chin would be happy to take his money any time. He was certainly happy to take mine.

***

Moose was in the middle of a roast beef sandwich when I made my obligatory stop at the parlor. I wanted to ask him about the lady and the girl but decided a few more days might give me more information. Marty was eating at the counter. When Mike saw me, he just nodded to the door and I knocked. I had nothing new to report and realized the purpose of my visit was just to let Joey blow off some steam. But with Sam Giancana in the back of my head, I had decided that maybe his steam would hold some droplets I could use. Joey looked up at me, wiped his mouth with a linen napkin, and washed his last bite down with bourbon. Nothing as fancy as Maggio's.

"I hope you got more than last time, Manning."

"Things are still coming together, Joey."

His look wasn't anywhere near happy.

"What do you mean, coming together? That doesn't sound like a five grand statement."

I looked around the room. "It's like arranging furniture. You got this place the way you like it, right?"

"Sure. Comfortable."

I sat on Marty's couch. "Exactly. It's comfortable because everything fits, and everything's in the right spot. But it maybe took a little rearranging to get it like that, right?"

He squinted and slowly shook his head. "What the hell are you talking about? I'm paying you to find out who framed me, not decorate my damn office."

"Same principle. I collect pieces and move them around until they make sense, until they're comfortable."

He took a big gulp of bourbon. "You're giving me a headache. You got something or not?"

"I do."

"Good. Who?"

"I can't say yet... not until all the pieces fit."

He took a deep breath. "I'm paying for you to say."

"I'm reading a book about Chicago crimes. It says Giancana once said when they took care of a problem, seven out of ten times it turned out to be the wrong guy. I can't work like that. I need to be sure before I give you a name."

"Yeah, well, you're being sure with my life here. You're not the one spent time in jail."

"I know. I'll have something soon." I hoped I would. "Speaking of Giancana, you were his driver, right?"

"So?"

"So, was it just a job or was he a friend?"

He shifted in his chair. "It was a job, but the guy was okay. I had no beef."

I nodded. "That's good. But it must have been a shock."

"Yeah, a shock. What do you care about Momo?" He took another big drink.

"I don't. Just interesting… you working for him. And then you go from driver to gambling boss. Seems you made out pretty good by Sam's sudden demise."

"His sudden what?"

"Death."

"Why the hell don't you just talk plain in the first place? And why are we talking about me?"

"Just passing time, Joey. Like I said, it's interesting. Then there's the gun permit."

He banged his fist on the table. A picture fell over. "I'm done talking about the damned permit! You better stop passing time and start doing what I'm paying you to do, or else."

I could have asked what he meant by that, but I wasn't concerned. "Okay, Joey, I'll have something soon."

"You'd better. Send Marty in here!"

I asked Marty to join us, sat back down, and waited for everyone to get comfortable.

"What are you still doing here, Manning?" Joey asked.

"I have one more question."

Joey let out a big sigh. "I hope it's better than your last one."

"Oh, I think it is." I looked at Marty and then back at Joey.

"I don't have all day, Manning."

I nodded. "How long you been using a woman for a bodyguard?"

"How did you—?" Marty said.

"Shut up, Marty!" Joey was fuming. I'd never seen Marty flustered, but he was now.

"But, Boss, he knows—"

"I said shut up. I used to think you were the smartest person I knew. Manning just pushed you over. He didn't know nothing… he was guessing. But he knows now." He turned back to me with fire in his eyes and took a drink. He put the glass down but didn't let go of it. He was squeezing it hard… hard enough to break.

"I have one more question," I said.

Joey said, "You're out of questions, Manning."

"I'll ask anyway. You can pretend not to listen. I know what the connection is. She keeps beating a certain someone at target shooting. What I'm wondering is—who approached who?"

"What does that mean?"

I guess he had decided to listen.

"That means did she ask for a job, or was she offered one?"

"Who cares? What do you got against a woman bodyguard?"

"Not a thing. Anyone who wins contests is a candidate. But back to my question."

Joey shifted in the chair and raised his arm toward Marty. "You hired her. You answer."

"That's a stupid question, Manning. She didn't even know about the job. She didn't even know what I did. I ran it by the boss and then I asked her."

"What was her response?"

"What do you mean what was her response? She's working here isn't she?"

"Did she accept right away? Was she surprised?"

"What does it matter who asked what?" Marty asked.

"Oh, it matters—you figure it out."

Marty was about to say something else when Joey butted in.

"Enough about a bodyguard, Manning. What do you think you're doing?"

"Just moving the furniture around, Joey."

He rolled his eyes. "Great. For five Gs I get a decorator. You wanna know if she was surprised, you ask *her*."

"I might."

"Now you done? We got business."

"Sure."

As I started to get up, Joey said, "I got something bothering me, Manning. Sit down a minute. Marty, go get some ice cream."

Marty left without any interest in what was bothering Joey.

"Manning, you've been following my people."

That didn't need an answer, so I didn't give it one.

"How about Mike?"

"What about him?"

"I saw him one night leaving the mansion and walking down the block. You know where he went?"

"I'd have to check with my operative. Was he smoking?"

"Yeah."

"Well, then probably just went out for a smoke."

"Maybe. But maybe not. You check and let me know."

"Okay." Given the mob's record of going after the wrong man, I didn't want to tell him what Chester had seen. But he *was* paying me. I'd have to find out what it was about. Asking Mike might be the best way to do that.

I stood and left without a friendly goodbye.

Chapter 23

I called Carol and made it to the office in fifteen minutes. All was quiet. She had nothing new. I sat at my desk and added notes about the Joey meeting to my file. Ten minutes later the quiet was interrupted by the doorbell and then shattered by the same angry voice.

"I'll give you one more chance—what have you done with my dog?"

I picked up the file on my desk and hurried to Carol's aid as she said, "I've already told you I have no idea what you're talking about."

"Do you deny that you had my dog last week?"

"Of course not. We took him in on a cold night after you mistreated him."

The dog lady turned to the lady standing next to her. "See! They had my dog!"

I joined the fun as I put my hand on Carol's shoulder. "*Had* being the key word. And you should be thanking us for saving him from freezing to death. Carol would you please make that phone call? Use my phone."

The dog lady pulled the bandanna out of her pocket and waved it at me. "And how do you suppose this got next to your door?"

"I already explained that. I'm guessing your dog escaped again and came to where he was treated well, and the bandanna somehow came off."

"So where is he? What have you done with him?"

With both palms turned up, I said, "I have no idea. I wish I did. I sure hope he's okay."

"The hell with you! You know darned well he's okay." She held out her hand to the lady standing next to her. The woman, trying her best to look threatening, but looking more scared, hadn't as much as twitched since I had joined the party.

Looking like she was playing her trump card, Knox said, "This is Mrs. Schenk. She's from the city... the permit section. You'll be in big trouble if you don't produce my dog, right now."

"Mrs. Schenk? May I see some identification?" I didn't care at all about her identification, but I did need to buy some time.

She fumbled in her purse and held out an ID card. I stepped closer and looked it over—City of Chicago, Permitting Section. Her picture made it official.

"And your purpose here is?"

Mrs. Schenk opened her mouth, but the dog lady didn't let her get any words out.

"Her purpose is to arrest you if you don't produce my dog."

Now the words came out. "Now, Miss Knox, I told you I cannot—"

The dog lady started in again, but I cut her off. I opened the manila file folder, removed the permit, and held it out to Mrs. Schenk. "Mrs. Schenk, is this your signature?"

She came up close to it and with a scrunched up face said, "Well, it's kind of hard to read in this light."

I dropped the permit on the desk. "It's not the light. It's hard to read because it's illegible." Over her shoulder I saw a patrol car pull up and double park. "Is this how you sign all permits?"

"Well, no, I mean..."

Two officers came in and stood just inside the door. They had already been briefed.

The dog lady saw them and said, "Good. Now we'll get some results."

I silently agreed and wondered if she thought they had just magically appeared. I went back to Mrs. Schenk.

"Mrs. Schenk, did you know Miss Knox before she came in wanting a permit for a working dog?"

The dog lady interrupted. "What does that have to do with anything?"

I calmly replied, looking at Mrs. Schenk who every minute seemed more and more like she wanted to be somewhere else. "It would have to do with special favors."

While Mrs. Schenk shrank into her coat, the dog lady became more belligerent. "For your information, the city runs on special favors. I—"

"Yes, that's politics. But when favors become fraud the scenery changes a bit."

"Fraud? Are you insane? It's just a dog!"

Mrs. Schenk had all but disappeared.

"It's a dog that is being abused. And there's a list of people waiting for working dogs, people who actually need them."

"Are you saying I don't?"

I held out the permit again to Mrs. Schenk. "Mrs. Schenk, please read the reason for wanting a working dog."

She just looked at me with eyes begging for mercy. She looked down and said, "It's blank."

"It's blank. Exactly." I turned to the dog lady. "What is the reason you need a working dog?"

Looking like she was about to boil over, she said, "Come on, Louise. We're leaving." She grabbed Mrs. Schenk's arm and pulled her toward the door.

One of the officers stepped forward and held up his hand. "I need to see identification for both of you, please."

"What! I'm not showing you anything! These people stole my dog. You should be arresting them!"

"There's two ways we can do this," the officer responded. "We're bringing you in for questioning on the matter of fraudulently obtaining a permit, and I need to see ID. If you want to do it the hard way,

I'm arresting you for resisting a police officer. I don't care one way or the other. Which will it be?"

Knox just stood with her mouth half open. Mrs. Schenk looked like she was going to cry. The dog lady opened her purse and took out her driver's license as did Mrs. Schenk.

Five minutes later, the office was back to normal. Quiet had returned.

Carol stood and gave me a hug. "That was fun, Spencer!" But her grin quickly turned to worry. "I know you said..."

I smiled. "He's okay, Carol. Ralph has him. We'll have him back soon."

She sat. "But what will happen to him? That... that... woman won't get him back, will she?"

"I can guarantee that. When she's done with this day she won't want to even *see* a dog."

She paused for a few seconds and shook her head. "So this was just a scam?"

"It was. And she would have gotten away with it if she had taken care of her dog."

"So what will happen to him?"

I sat on the edge of her desk. "I don't know. He's a working dog, and somebody who needs him should have him. They'll get him to the right person."

She nodded. "I wish Billy could have him. He won't quite understand the 'right person' thing." She sighed. "But even if we could get him, we can't have pets in the apartment. Such simple things can be so hard."

I put my hand on her shoulder and agreed. As I stood I picked a dart out of the tray and threw it at the board. It stuck just outside the bull's-eye. Better.

***

I had been wondering what to do about Mike. I needed some answers... for me as well as Joey. But getting him alone was difficult. I decided there was another way to skin that cat, and I'd try that first. As I was leaving to do that, the phone rang. Carol answered.

"Spencer, it's Lieutenant Powolski."

I picked up the phone. "Hey, Stosh. The dog lady is on her way to the station. It worked. A Mrs. Schenk is her contact inside city hall."

"Good. One thing to cross off the list. I've got information on your relatives. The—"

"Hold that thought. I'm on my way out. I'll swing by the station. You be there in twenty minutes?"

"Yup. But don't make it much more than that."

Traffic was light, and the sun was still out. The temperature was up in the twenties. The sun had gone back to work.

***

S tosh was sitting at Kate's desk looking at a file.

"It'd take three of you to do her job," I said.

"That's the truth. Maybe four." He closed the folder, walked into his office, and closed the door. "You talk to Rosie?"

"Sure. She told me all about her birthday party tonight for my buddy Gabe. Noisemakers, pointy hats. You probably weren't invited because she knows you don't look good in pointy hats."

He got comfortable in his chair, sighed, and said, "I met Francine when I was twenty. She was nineteen. We were married three months later." He was staring at her picture at the front of his desk. "We were married for thirty-seven wonderful years. It wasn't all perfect, but you have more drama in one day than we had in thirty-seven years."

I was sitting on one of the wooden chairs and was not comfortable. "What are you saying?"

He raised his eyes to the ceiling. "I'm saying God bless Francine."

He broke the silence by opening the folder on his desk. "Giancana's wife is still in New York as are all of his daughters. His brother is still in Chicago and still a car salesman. None of them have any ties that we know of."

"So nothing."

"Not there. But Glunner doesn't have a sister."

"Figured he didn't. So somebody set him up in that apartment. Somebody who used him… and then killed him."

"You're jumping to some conclusions."

"It's not a big jump."

"And one more thing. We have an informant who has been talking about Marty. Seems he is quietly setting himself up to take over."

I started to interrupt and he raised his hand.

"Even more than you had learned. At least two alliances are in place and ready to go as soon as Joey is out of the way."

"I'll have another talk with him."

He shook his head. "No, you won't. There are some things we're working on that depend on him not knowing that we know."

"Nice business they're in. You can't—"

We were interrupted by a knock on the door.

"Come in."

"Hi, Spencer," said Kate. "Meeting in five minutes, Lieutenant."

He nodded. "Thanks, Kate. Where to from here, Spencer?"

"Gonna stop and see a mystery lady and then dinner at McGoon's."

His eyebrows went up. "Stalker?"

"Not up to me."

"Sure it is." He walked out, leaving me sitting there looking at the back of Francine's picture. I could use less drama, but I needed a good meal.

Chapter 24

I had to park at the other end of the block from the mystery lady's house. But since the sun was back on the job it was a nice walk. Comparatively, twenties seemed like a spring thaw.

I rang the doorbell but didn't hear a bell, so I knocked, twice. It took a minute before I heard footsteps, and a woman's voice asked who it was.

"Spencer Manning. I'm a private detective, and I have a few questions."

Silence. No one wanted a visit from the cops, even the private kind. Everybody had something to hide.

"Ma'am?"

"Yes, I'm here. What about?"

"This would be better if we were both on the same side of the door."

She opened the door to the limit of a chain. "Can I see ID?"

I handed it to her.

She handed it back and asked again what it was about.

"Mike."

"Is he okay?" she asked with worry in her voice.

"He's fine." I was still looking at the chain.

"Then what...?"

"He takes walks. Those walks bring him here. I'd like to know why."

"You need to ask him," she said as she started to close the door.

I got my foot in and said, "I can do that, but not without his boss around, and I'm guessing he wouldn't want that to happen."

More silence. "If you remove your shoe, I'll let you in."

I did, and she did, but not happily.

She didn't look much older than me, not much more than thirty. Casual clothes that weren't fancy and brown hair pulled back into a ponytail gave her the look of any woman in any other house on the block. If she was running a house of ill repute this was her day off. She led me into a living room with the standard furniture and a fireplace. Several pictures of a little girl were on the mantel. I sat on the slightly worn green couch, and she pulled an armchair close to my end. She didn't offer coffee.

She sat on the edge of the chair, folded her arms across her chest, and asked what I wanted.

"Simple. Mike leaves his house and comes here. You let him in. Why?"

She unfolded her arms and sat back looking a bit relieved. She evidently had an easy answer.

"He's just visiting. We met at the grocer and discovered we lived near each other and stayed in touch. That's all."

"Ah, well that's pretty simple."

"Yes, it is." She smiled.

"What was in the envelope he handed you?"

Her smile disappeared, and she looked around the room. But there was no one there to help her.

When she had thought about it enough, she said, "I don't think that's any of your business."

"Maybe not. But I'm looking into two murders, and if there's a connection you could be an accessory."

She sat up straight. "Murder! I have nothing to do with murder! Who was murdered?"

"I'm sure you read about the murder of Max Schloff and poor Mr. Glunner."

She clasped her hands in her lap. "And what does that have to do with me?"

"Maybe nothing. But it might have something to do with Mike. I'm sure you also know his boss was arrested for the first murder."

She looked like she was trying hard to come up with a good story.

"Mike had nothing to do with that."

"Maybe not. But we'd like to know if Joey had anything to do with it."

"Well, obviously, he did… he was arrested wasn't he?"

"Plenty of innocent people get arrested."

She thought some more. "But Mike wasn't arrested… his boss was. And you're asking about Mike."

"We're asking about everyone associated with Mr. Mineo. Mike led us to your door."

"So you were following him?"

The question didn't need an answer, so I just let her sit with the thought.

"Would you tell me your name?" I said.

She looked down at her hands and after a pause said, "Karen… Karen Bedore."

"Okay, Karen." I moved to the edge of the cushion and leaned toward her. "What was in the envelope?"

She looked up and met my eyes. "That's not really my place to say. You need to talk to Mike."

I shook my head. "We're going around in circles, and we're back to asking him with his boss there." I paused. "And I'm not sure it's any of his boss's business."

She didn't respond.

I gave her some relief. "And if it has nothing to do with the murders I forget about it as soon as I walk out the door."

Looking back down at her hands, she sighed and said, "Money."

Of course. Everything's about money.

"But it has nothing to do with any murders."

I felt sorry for her and wanted to take her hand. I leaned a little closer. "Then what does it have to do with?"

She got up and walked to the fireplace and stood looking at it for half a minute. She reached out, took down one of the pictures of the little girl, and brought it back to the chair where she looked at it for a bit and then handed it to me. The smiling little girl looked to be around ten and was holding a doll.

Karen looked at me without saying anything.

I handed it back to her and asked, "She has something to do with Mike and the envelope?"

Obviously she did, but instead of answering she set the picture on the table and offered coffee. I accepted. While she was gone I looked around the room and wondered what kind of story Karen would come up with. I hoped the kid wasn't mixed up in this somehow. And despite what Joey did for a living, I knew he would hope so also.

Karen came back with a plastic tray, two cups, and sugar and cream. I declined the sugar and cream, took a cup, and waited.

She stirred in cream, set the spoon on the tray, and took a sip. Taking a deep breath, she touched the picture and talked.

"The little girl is Rachel. Her mother was Mike's sister's daughter."

"Was?"

Moving her eyes from the picture to me, she said, "A year ago Rachel's parents, Mike's sister and her husband, were killed in a car accident in Michigan. Rachel was the only survivor."

"I'm sorry, Karen. How awful."

With tears in her eyes, she said, "When I think of that little girl losing her whole family, I…"

"I know." I decided to be quiet and see if she would continue.

She wiped her eyes with a napkin. "Would you like more coffee?"

"No, thanks. So, Rachel is Mike's niece?"

She nodded. "Once removed."

I had pretty much guessed at what was going on when I heard about the little girl, and now I could fill in the gaps, but I needed to have her tell it. "So, Mike took her in?"

She nodded. "He bought this house and hired me to be with her. He pays me every week."

"But why so secretive?" I thought I knew the answer to that also.

With a shrug, she said, "He doesn't want Rachel to know what he does."

"But he comes to see her."

"Yes, not only to bring money. She loves him… really looks forward to his visits. And once in a while he'll take her out for something special."

I thought Joey would support what Mike was doing. Joey was what he was, but one of those things was a person who had a soft spot for kids. But I could understand Mike not wanting Rachel to know. Maybe it was better that way.

Karen looked up at me. "Do you have to tell about this?"

"No. It has nothing to do with what I was hired for."

She finished her coffee. "What *were* you hired for?"

"To find whoever killed Max Schloff."

"And that's not Joey?"

"Well, Joey doesn't think so."

We both laughed.

"Do you think so?" she asked.

"I don't."

"Well, good luck, Mr. Manning." She gave me a puzzled look. "Manning. Riverview?"

I smiled. "That would be me."

"That was an amazing story. I wish I had realized that earlier. I would've trusted you sooner."

"Well, that's okay. We got there."

I gave her my card and told her to call if there was ever anything I could do for her or Rachel.

Chapter 25

I got to McGoon's around five. Mondays were never very crowded. Only three people were at the bar, and none of them were Jamie.

Jack was pulling a Guinness before I got my coat off.

"Hey, Spencer. How do you like the summer weather?"

"Much better." I took a stool and a long drink through the foam. "Hey, Jack. Do you remember that woman I was sitting with last week?"

"You mean Jamie?"

The woman five stools away cackled at something she thought was funny.

"That's the one."

"Hard to forget. I wasn't here yesterday, but she's been here every other night since."

"She has?"

"Yup. Seemed to be waiting for someone, but that someone never showed."

"Barkeep. Another round, if you please," the man with the cackler said with a slur.

"Coming right up. I'll be back, Spencer."

I nursed my beer until he returned. "What did you learn about her? Did she say who she was waiting for?"

"No, she didn't. The only thing I know is she likes white wine."

"A man of your conversational skill and that's all you know?"

"Yup. Odd. She said a lot, but nothing of any value. A lot of fluff with no substance."

Or very careful, I thought.

Jack grabbed a towel and wiped down the bar. "But that might change if the right guy shows up," he said with a smile.

In the next half hour the bar filled except for two seats to my left. The cackling lady was drowned out in the din of conversation. I was about to ask for a refill when, with a wink, Jack caught my eye and nodded toward the entrance to the bar. I didn't have to look to know what he meant, so I just nursed the last inch of beer wondering if indeed I was the right guy. I was.

She sat next to me and asked if the seat was taken.

"It looks like it is," I said with a hint of a smile.

She hung her coat on the back of the stool. "Fancy meeting you here. Spencer, right?"

"Right."

"I came in for dinner. If you haven't eaten, would you join me?"

I looked at my watch. "I guess I have time. Do you want to eat here or get a table?"

"Let's get a table. It'll be more private."

I put a five on the bar and stood. I requested a table with Jane, and we were seated right away. Jane asked about drinks and was back in two minutes with white wine and a Guinness. I told her to give us a few minutes.

Jamie opened the menu and looked up at me.

"I feel a bit nervous, Spencer."

I let that sit.

She continued. "I have a confession."

I expected her to tell me she had been coming in every night, but she surprised me.

"I know some things about you."

I took a drink and let that lie too.

Looking right at me, she said, "For instance, I know you're a private detective."

Of course I already knew she knew. When I didn't react she looked confused.

"Don't you want to know how I know that?"

"I might if I didn't already know."

"You do?"

"You just told me I'm a private detective. I detect things."

"Oh… right." She sipped her wine. "I also know you're working for Mr. Mineo."

"You'd be pretty slow if you didn't, Jamie… or is it Loretta?"

That flustered her. "Pardon?"

I smiled. "I know some things too. Like that the tag on your mailbox says Loretta, yet you introduced yourself as Jamie."

She put down the glass and laughed. "Well, I can explain that, and then I want to know how you know that. I've never liked Loretta. Jamie is my middle name. Nobody ever calls me Loretta. Now how do you know about my mailbox?"

"I'm a detective. I—"

"Yes, I know. You detect things. I'm flattered that you wanted to know more about me. I'd ask how you know where I live, but I'm not as slow as you think. I know you saw me in the ice cream parlor. Even someone who wasn't a detective would see where I went if he waited and watched."

Jane stopped at our table, and we both ordered steaks.

Jamie gave me her pretty smile and asked, "Were you hoping I would be here tonight?"

I gave her my best shocked look and said, "I hadn't thought about it. I come here a lot."

Her smile turned coy, and she asked, "Not even a little?"

I smiled back. "Well, maybe a little."

The smile was back. "Good."

We talked about many things for an hour and a half. Jack was right… she was good at fluff. But I wasn't trying to pry. When Jane brought the bill I asked a personal question.

"If you don't mind my asking, what do you do for a living? I mean, besides eat ice cream."

She gave me a fluffy answer about one thing and another and having trouble holding down a steady job. She explained she wasn't cut out for eight to five. No, she was cut out for whatever Joey told her.

I paid the bill and asked if she had driven.

"No. I took a cab."

"Well, can I give you a ride home?"

"I would appreciate that, Spencer. I guess I don't have to give you the address."

We both laughed.

I pulled into Joey's private spot next to the hydrant and thanked her for a nice evening.

"Thank you for dinner. Would you like to come up for a nightcap?"

I looked at my watch again.

"Come on now, Spencer. It can't be past your bedtime yet."

"Well, I suppose so. Just for one. Do you have any pointy hats?"

"Pardon?"

I shook my head. "Never mind. Just being silly. You get the lights on, and I'll find a legal spot." When she had gone in I pulled into Mr. Chin's lot, stopped in the restaurant, and gave him ten bucks for the parking fee. He wouldn't take the money, so I left it on one of the tables.

***

The door was open, and I let myself in. It was a one-room apartment with an adjoining bedroom and a kitchen built into the back wall. She had poured wine and offered me a beer choice of Miller or Budweiser. I silently cringed, mentally flipped a coin, and went with the Miller.

While she opened the fridge I sat on the couch and looked around the room. Other than a few wall hangings and photographs on shelves, it was pretty stark. It didn't much look lived in. I felt a little sorry for her. One of the wall hangings drew my attention. It was a crocheted likeness of Uncle Sam. Lots of red, white, and blue.

Not that I had anything against patriotism, but I didn't know anyone else who had Uncle Sam on their wall.

She set the glasses down on the wooden coffee table and sat next to me. The couch was big enough for both of us to have breathing room, but her leg was touching mine. She had done that in the bar also, but then I figured it was because the stools were close. I decided I didn't mind.

"So, Spencer, do you have family here in Chicago?"

That was an innocent question but not something I wanted to get into, so I kept it short. "No, I don't. My only aunt is up in Wisconsin."

"Where's the rest of your family? Are you not from here?"

"Yes, I am. My parents were killed in a car accident a few years ago, and my sister died when she was young."

She put her hand on my leg. "That's sad. I'm so sorry."

I reached for the beer and reluctantly took a drink. "Thanks. How about you?"

"Me too, and most of my family is gone too. So I guess we have something in common."

"I guess."

She swirled her wine. "You know, what you do is so exciting. How did you get to be a detective?"

One of the disadvantages of being a detective is what it does to relationships. You wonder about ordinary questions, and that wonder gets in the way of conversation. Her question was perfectly normal and one that anyone would ask, but given the situation I was wary. You can't get close to someone if you're wary. But my goal wasn't to get close to Jamie. I wasn't quite sure what my goal was, and I decided some history wouldn't hurt.

"I was in the army... military police. I liked the investigation part of it so I decided to try my hand at working privately."

"And you like it?"

"I do. It's been interesting." And there was another relationship issue—I had left out more than I had told her.

I swirled my beer. I figured if I was swirling it I wouldn't have to drink it.

"That's great. Not many people like their job." She pulled her legs up under her, but her leg was still touching mine. "There's something else I'm wondering. You're a detective, but you don't carry a gun. Don't detectives carry guns?"

I laughed. "They do, and I do when I need to. They make me nervous."

She returned the laugh. "Perhaps not a good trait in a detective."

"Perhaps not, but things have worked out okay so far."

She took a drink and changed the subject. "There hasn't been much about Mr. Mineo on the news. Have you found out anything?"

That was innocent enough also, but...

"Not much. At least nothing that seems to help. Do you think he did it?"

"Oh, I have no reason to think he did or didn't. But I've learned that most of the time things are actually the way they appear."

I agreed.

"I know you can't tell me what you've found out, but you must know more than what's on the news."

I laughed. "That's not always the case. Sometimes they know more than me."

She finished her wine. I had barely started the beer.

Turning toward me, she put her hand on my shoulder and said, "For instance, the man was killed in an alley. You must have looked at the alley and found something you can't talk about."

Her touch was electric, and her eyes were like a puppy that just wanted you to pet him. In a normal situation I would have returned the touch. And then there was Rosie, but whenever I thought about Rosie I saw Gabriel. Her hand was still on my shoulder.

"I'd love to look at the alley with you and have you tell me what you found."

When I looked away from her I was being stared at by Uncle Sam and wondered what he would think about relationships.

I put my glass back on the table and turned toward her. She moved her hand from my shoulder back to my leg.

I took a deep breath and said, "I'm feeling a bit nervous."

She looked confused. "I make you nervous?"

"No, Uncle Sam does." I pointed at the hanging. "I feel like he's staring at me."

She laughed.

"It's the first time I've seen Uncle Sam up on someone's wall. Are you that patriotic?"

She shook her head and smiled her pretty smile. It was very endearing. "No, not really. But I do love Uncle Sam. Kind of a strange looking fellow, but he's done a lot for me. I thank him every day for what I have."

"Well, I can't argue with that."

"I'll take it down if it'll make you feel better."

I put my hand on top of hers and said, "No, that's okay."

"Good." She cocked her head with a little smile and said, "I'm just wondering... and it's okay either way... it *would* be fun to look at the alley with you. I've always been interested in things like this. Maybe if someday you need a partner..."

I laughed. "I have enough trouble taking care of myself."

Her face lit up. "Which is why you need a partner! You could teach me."

Either this was the start of a beautiful relationship or she was fishing for something. If it was the first, I didn't know what to do. I kept thinking about Rosie and Gabe and wondering if he was doing the same thing to her that Jamie was doing to me. If it was the second, I was the bait, and I needed to know what she was fishing for. I remembered her statement about most things being the way they appear, but there was that word "most." I looked over at Uncle Sam, but he had no advice. I decided to take the hook and see where it led.

"I don't know what I could teach you, Jamie. And it's not very much fun. It's mostly drudgery, just asking a lot of questions and seeing what makes sense."

"Sounds like putting a puzzle together, and I love puzzles."

I nodded. "They can be fun. But sometimes they can be frustrating."

Her face lit up again. "I know... I can help with some questions!"

I cocked my head and shifted on the couch. "I don't know, I—"

"Come on. It would be fun."

It didn't sound like fun to me, but I didn't see the harm. And maybe she'd ask something I hadn't thought of. "Okay, go ahead."

"Hmmm, well, let me think for a minute." She got more wine while she was thinking. "You're not drinking your beer."

"Oh, no, I guess I was distracted by the company." I was hoping not to have to finish it, but I picked up the glass and took a drink.

She sipped her wine. "The papers haven't said much about all of this. I know someone needs a motive. Does Mr. Mineo have one?"

"Not really. But there may be an old grudge nobody knows about, or maybe Schloff was getting in Joey's way."

She squinted her eyes. "Anybody else with a motive?"

"None that makes it worth killing a guy."

"Maybe not to you."

"What do you mean?" I asked.

"A person's motive might not seem like a big deal to someone else, but it might be a real big deal to that person."

"That's true." I hadn't excluded any possibilities, but there were no smoking guns.

"How about the witness?"

I was a little wary about the questions, but conceded that if I were sitting next to someone who was investigating a big murder case I'd be doing just what she was. "What *about* the witness?"

She shook her head and frowned. "Some guy does the right thing and comes forward, and he dies. That's just awful."

I agreed.

"Why didn't the police keep him somewhere safe?"

"They thought they did."

"Then how did he die?"

"He was shot, but I assume you are wondering how someone got to him."

"Yes."

"Good question."

She drank and thought some more. "If Mr. Mineo killed Schloff, then he would have killed the witness too, right?"

"Not necessarily, I think—"

"Does Mr. Mineo have an alibi?"

"The best. He was in jail."

She laughed. "Hard to beat that. But what about his gang?"

"His boys were at his mansion. They hadn't left all day."

"Mansion? Mr. Mineo lives in a mansion?"

"He thinks he does."

"And you believe them?"

"I didn't ask them."

She looked puzzled. "Then how do you know?"

"I had someone watching the house."

"That's awesome. You're their alibi!"

"Well, my man is."

She thought some more and finished the wine. "Schloff was shot with a handgun, right?"

"Right."

Tapping the empty glass with her fingernail, she asked, "So if the witness was shot with a rifle, wouldn't it be two different shooters?"

"Not necessarily. The witness was shot from farther away, across the street. A rifle is more accurate."

"I see. And couldn't the witness getting shot have nothing to do with Schloff?"

"You mean someone completely unrelated to the Mineo case had a reason to kill the witness and happened to find where the police were keeping him?"

She scrunched up her face. "If you put it that way, I guess that would be a little far-fetched."

"It would be a lot far-fetched." I forced down the rest of the beer. She asked if I wanted another. I declined.

She looked disappointed. "I guess we haven't solved the crime, huh."

I laughed. "No, I guess not. And some crimes never get solved."

"Must be some smart criminals out there."

"Some. But luckily most aren't. Most make mistakes."

She took her hand off of my leg, folded her arms across her chest, and, with a smile, said, "You must know some things nobody else knows."

I smiled back. "I know some things even the police don't know."

"Aren't you supposed to tell the police?"

"Only when I'm sure they're pertinent."

"Like what?"

After a few seconds of thought, I decided to share one thing.

"Okay, I'll tell you something that the public doesn't know."

She grasped my arm and looked excited. "What is it?"

"Max Schloff wasn't killed in the alley." The week was up, so it would be in the morning papers anyway. I wasn't really giving up anything critical, but she was excited.

"See! That's what I mean about your job. You get to know things like that. Where *was* he killed?"

"In a warehouse over on Cambridge, a block east of Broadway."

"Well why did they say he was killed in an alley?"

I shrugged. "Beats me."

She looked coy again and took my hand. "Could you show me the warehouse? It could be my first lesson!"

"I suppose I could."

Her excitement faded, and her look turned from coy to seductive. She reached out and gently touched my cheek as she leaned in and kissed me. And after a few seconds I kissed her back. Maybe that was the reward for the inside information, and maybe what she was fishing for was me. But I wasn't sure if I was landing a tuna or a barracuda.

We made plans for the next day. I'd pick her up after lunch.

***

started the Mustang, and while it was warming up I picked up the phone and called Rosie. She answered on the third ring.

"Hi, Rosie, how was the party?"

"It wasn't a party, Spencer. Just dinner."

"How many?"

"How many what?"

"People at dinner."

Silence for five seconds and then a sigh. "Just two."

"So, no funny hats or noisemakers?"

More silence. "Is that what you called for? To harass me?"

"No. We need to talk. Can I come by?"

More silence. "Sure."

The drive was only twenty minutes, but it seemed like an hour.

Chapter 26

I was in the office before Carol, taking care of paperwork and throwing darts—mostly throwing darts. I had just hit two bull's-eyes in a row when she walked in.

"Good morning, Spencer. Tough job you've got."

"Glad you noticed. It's very stressful." Actually, throwing darts gave me a chance to think. I thought about adding the time to my Joey time sheet.

As she hung up her coat, she asked, "Any news on the dog?"

"There will be soon. The wheels have to turn." I put the darts away. "I know Billy is excited about the dog, but he'll probably go to someone who needs a working dog."

"I know." She sat and opened her drawer. "At least he won't be mistreated anymore."

"We can hope."

She opened her schedule book. "Nothing on the schedule for you today. More darts?"

I laughed. "No, I actually have a full day. Phone calls to make this morning and an errand this afternoon that will take a few hours." I didn't want to tell her what it was. Me bending the rules was one thing... her knowing about it was another.

"Well, I'd practice up on darts if I were you. Billy wants a rematch, and he's been practicing."

"Tell him we'll do it soon."

The mailman came in with the mail as I was heading back to my office. We hardly ever got anything Carol needed to ask me about.

My first call was to Mooneen at city hall.

"Oh, hello, Mr. Manning. I was wondering if I'd hear from you."

"Hi, Mooneen. Anything new in the office?"

"Nothing you don't probably already know. Mrs. Schenk is on administrative leave pending an investigation into the business with Knox. I assume you had something to do with that."

"Not a bad assumption."

"Then thanks. I hate to see animals being abused. I also hate to see people abusing their public trust."

I smiled, but she of course couldn't see it. I was pretty cynical about public trust. A lot of people serving the public were giving themselves a pretty big helping at the same time.

"I do what I can, Mooneen."

"On another note, we'll need the dog back. I assume he's safe. Do you know where he is?"

"I do. And I assume I'll get a call today about that. I'll turn him over, but there's a little boy who would love to have him."

She paused. "Mr. Manning, I've been thinking about the little boy. I'm not promising anything, but I have an idea."

"Anything you'd like to share?"

"No, I don't want to get anybody's hopes up. It's a longshot."

"Okay. Good luck with that. Thanks for all your help, Mooneen."

"You are welcome. And thanks for yours."

When I had hung up Carol came in with two messages. One was to call Stosh. The other had a number of a Mr. Gillery from animal welfare. My conversation with him was brief. He was nice enough, but he was all business. I explained about Billy. When I asked if there was any chance we could keep the dog his response was to tell me he'd be coming for the dog just after lunch. I told him that wasn't possible, and he told me about defying a city official. I wanted to tell him what I thought of that, but kept it to myself. I told him the soonest I'd be able to have Spot back in my office would be Wednesday at four. He admitted that since I was holding the cards, or in this case the dog, there wasn't much he could do about it. I agreed.

I decided to get some exercise and walked out to the plush lobby.

"Carol, what time does Billy get home from school?"

"About three."

"Okay. Please call Ralph and tell him to bring the dog Wednesday at two."

Her face lit up with a smile. "Sure. Billy will be so happy."

"Well, I'm not sure Billy should see him. A Mr. Gillery is coming at four to get him."

The smile disappeared. "Oh. Well, I guess that has to happen."

"Yes. Do you think Billy should see him? It might be harder to see him and then have to say goodbye."

"Yes, it probably would. But I think that's up to Billy. I'll talk to him about it and see what he wants to do."

"I'm sorry this is so hard, Carol."

She tried to smile. "I know. Thanks for all you've done, Spencer. Do you want me to get the lieutenant for you?"

I took a deep breath. "Nope. The lieutenant is the last person I want to talk to."

I got a very quizzical look, but she didn't ask why. She also didn't ask why I closed my door when I went back to my office. It had never been closed.

I spent the next hour talking to Ben, telling him about the evening with Jamie. Rosie and I had always had a strange relationship, and it looked like that hadn't changed. I felt a bit guilty, and it helped to have someone to talk to. I wanted someone to know what was going on, and Ben was the best person to tell. He always had been.

Chapter 27

On the way to the warehouse I gave Jamie some rules about what not to do. *Don't touch anything* was first on the list. I parked on Cambridge about a hundred feet from the door and remembered the snow that was falling the last time I was there. Today the sun was shining, and the wind had calmed to a slight breeze, so the cold wasn't as bitter.

Jamie put her arm around me, and her boots clicked on the concrete as we walked up the block. "This is very exciting," she said, giving me a squeeze, her shoulder purse digging into my side.

I had the lock open in less than thirty seconds, opened the door, snapped the lock back in place, and pulled the door closed. The last time it had taken a minute for my eyes to adjust to the dim light. Today there was plenty of sunlight streaming in the windows. I could almost hear the sound of forklifts. As we exited the offices I motioned to the left. "Stairs up to the second floor." She followed me.

"This is kinda spooky, Spencer... you know... knowing someone died here... all alone."

"Not quite alone."

"Well, you know what I mean."

"Yup."

"Where did it happen?" she asked as we reached the top of the stairs.

I pointed to the right and started walking. The yellow tape was still strung around the pillars. As we got closer I could see the graffiti and the body outline on the floor. I wondered if Angie and her friend were upstairs. If they were they wouldn't be making their presence known.

She took my arm and said, "So that's all that's left of a man... a drawing on the floor."

I didn't respond. Death was something I didn't want to think about.

She stopped short of the tape and looked around. "You know, there's something wrong with this picture."

"And what would that be?"

She touched the tape and shook her head. "I just can't see Mr. Mineo and his fancy suits in a place like this."

"I agree, but like you said, some things are more important to some people. Maybe this was important enough to Joey to be here."

"Can I go inside the tape?"

"Sure." The police were done with this place. The tape would stay up until someone found a use for it.

She ducked under the tape and walked to the drawing. She was about ten feet from me. Looking back at me, she asked, "And where was the witness?"

"I'm not sure. Behind one of the pillars, I guess." Each one was a hiding place.

She turned away from me and reached down to her purse. When she turned back to me she was holding a gun, and it was aimed at *me*. I didn't react.

"What? No surprise?" she said.

I just looked at her.

She smiled at me. "You know, that habit you have of not carrying a gun doesn't serve you well. Not that it would do you any good at the moment."

I shrugged and took a step to my left. "Better to be smart than armed most of the time."

"Don't move. This time you were neither. You know, I didn't learn anything from you about detecting."

"No, I guess not. We talked about motives. What's yours?"

"You'll die wondering that, Spencer."

Most people liked to talk about their plans so I kept talking.

"Not quite. I can guess at most of it. I just don't know why."

"And what are your guesses?"

"Uncle Sam. I just can't see any taxpayer having a picture of Uncle Sam on their wall. Who crocheted that for you? Your aunt?"

"Well, you're not as dumb as I thought."

"Thanks. Sam Giancana was a thug. I'm wondering why you've made him into an idol."

"Because he wasn't a thug to me. He was my favorite uncle who loved me more than my own father." Her stare was lost in memories, but the gun didn't move an inch.

"You killed Schloff and framed Joey with that phony witness. Why?"

"Because Joey killed my uncle."

"How do you know that?"

"I saw it. Uncle Sam and I were cooking sausages for lunch. He was at the stove, and I was playing behind the bar. We were the only ones home. We heard footsteps coming down the stairs, and he told me to get down. He ran for his gun, but the door burst open before he got to it. I could see past the end of the bar. Joey Mineo shot him once and he fell. Then Schloff came up and shot him six more times in the face. They didn't check to see if anyone else was in the room."

"How old were you?"

"Twelve."

I couldn't bring myself to say I was sorry. "I gotta tell you, you've caused a lot of conversation with the bodyguard thing. Lots of theories and wondering if Joey even had one or not." I shifted my weight from my left foot to the right.

She laughed. "Yes, that was a plan that didn't work out. I was sure I'd get a chance to get him, but I was never alone with him in the right spot. That guy is either holed up in that room or in a crowd. I wonder what he's afraid of."

"You."

"But he had no idea who I was." She brought the gun down to her side, but it was still pointed at me.

"It's the business he's in. He had Sam hanging over his head, and I'm guessing he didn't like it. If it helps you any, I'm guessing killing Sam wasn't his idea and not something he was happy about."

"I couldn't care less how happy he is. Then I figured if he was convicted of murder, being in prison would be worse than death."

"That's true. So you get Joey and Schloff. What about Glunner?"

"He was a bum. He had nothing to live for. And one of the things about a successful criminal is that they leave no one behind to talk. Which is why *you* have to go."

"But you didn't know if I knew anything, and I didn't know anything. At least I don't have any proof."

"I had a feeling. And I knew you'd keep digging until you found what you were looking for."

"That's what I do. I must say, the way you got the job was brilliant. You got Marty to ask you, didn't you?"

"Yeah. He's good with numbers, but not too smart when it comes to life. I played him for months. It was set up so well I just had to wait for him to ask."

"Which makes nobody suspect you of anything. You're just a woman who can shoot a gun."

She nodded again and raised the gun. "That's all the questions you get, Spencer."

"Then how about a last statement."

"Sure. I'm not in a hurry."

"There are three things that a successful criminal needs to pull something off."

She moved to her left and took the gun in both hands. "Okay, I'll bite."

"No witnesses, no emotions, and no little mistakes." I let that sit for a few seconds. "You took care of the first, but the last two are your downfall."

She kept moving slowly. I turned to face her.

"I agree with you, but I don't see the downfall."

"You let your feelings for Sam get in the way. Granted, the wall hanging isn't a picture of your uncle, but it's odd, and it caught my attention… and I'm not stupid."

She shrugged. "So what. Your attention isn't my downfall."

Through this whole thing her eyes hadn't changed. They were cold and showed no emotion. The only thing she cared about was revenge for her uncle.

"No, but it added a piece to the puzzle, and I like pieces to fit. The downfall comes in the third."

She just looked at me.

"The fact that the second shooter used a rifle was not made public," I said.

She kept looking and twenty seconds later said, "And given that, you walked in here without a gun. I hope you didn't think I put my arm around you to be romantic. And bottom line is, none of that matters, does it?"

"It matters to me," said a voice from off to the side.

Jamie turned toward the voice and fired. The roar in the empty space was deafening. But the voice had the protection of a pillar. Jamie was out in the middle of the floor. The return shot hit her shoulder. As she dropped the gun and knelt on the floor, Rosie stepped out from behind one of the pillars and walked toward us. She keyed the mic attached to her shoulder, reported what had happened, and asked for an ambulance. Out of the corner of my eye I saw another person step out from behind a pillar on the other side of us, and Gabriel joined us. His gun was pointed down at the floor. We nodded to each other. Everyone was silent for a good half minute. It was such a sad, strange situation.

Jamie just sat on the floor on her knees holding her left shoulder with her right hand. There must have been blood, but I couldn't see it through her heavy coat.

With her gun still pointed at Jamie, Rosie asked Gabriel to cuff her. He holstered his gun and started toward Jamie. In one quick motion, she reached back into her boot and pulled out a knife. A split second after it was visible, Rosie shot her in the chest, and she slumped to the floor. Gabriel froze wide-eyed with his right hand on his cuffs.

I knelt down and touched her arm. She was trying to say something. I leaned in close and faintly heard her last words.

"I... win... both... ways. I either... get... you... or you get... him."

"How do we get him, Jamie?"

"If you... knew what you were... walking into... you'd be re... cording what I... said. I hope he rots... in..."

Her head rolled to the side. I reached out and felt for a pulse. It was faint, but it didn't last long. She was dead in ten seconds. I took a deep breath and said, to no one in particular, "What a bizarre ending to a bizarre story."

"And the next story is just beginning," Rosie said.

"What story is that?" asked Gabriel.

She pulled the tape recorder out of her pocket. "We now know who killed Sam Giancana."

"Would her confession be enough?"

"Probably not," I said. "But it will make Joey's life hell for a while, and he'll need a new bodyguard."

"Pardon?" said Rosie.

"I'll explain later."

Rosie called back in and told dispatch not to hurry on the ambulance.

Help had been staged just up the block, and a few minutes later the place was full of cops and medics.

"You okay, Spencer?" Rosie asked.

"Sure. Just hot." Part of that was adrenaline, and part was the bulletproof vest that Jamie hadn't felt under my bulky coat.

"After we get this wrapped up, we'll probably have to spend an hour with the lieutenant. Then I'm buying dinner, just you and me," said Rosie.

"Sounds good. But why don't you invite Gabriel?"

"What?"

I smiled and put my arm around her. "I'm thinking the three of us should spend some time together so I can see that I'm not as big a jerk as I think I am."

"I'll pretend I understand that."

"Good luck. And I'd like to invite Ben. He'll want the story."

"Sure. We'll make it a party."

"I'll bring the hats." Before we ventured back out into the world I took off the vest and handed it to Rosie. "Glad we didn't need this."

"Me too."

As the Mustang warmed a bit I called Carol. I liked listening to the way she answered the phone. It still sounded good—"Spencer Manning, private detective."

"Hi, beautiful. Anything you need me for?"

"Not a thing. Anything you need *me* for?"

"Everything. But for the moment, call the gang off. We're done. Tell them to figure their time through the rest of the week and stop in for their checks." I gave her the short version, ending with me still being here to talk to her, and told her I'd give her the long version tomorrow.

Chapter 28

We spent two hours with the lieutenant. The state attorney's office was already talking about the confession.

Ben was waiting for us at McGoon's. I found him in the bar. I told Rosie and Gabe to get a table, and we'd be there in a minute. Ben was talking with Jack as the televisions over the bar ran the story of the shooting in the warehouse.

"Hey, Spencer," said Jack.

"Jack." I slapped Ben on the back.

"Looks like you have one less admirer," said Jack. "Strange."

"More strange than you'll ever know. Those kinds of admirers I can do without."

He laughed. "I always thought you could use all you could get."

"Nice. Ben, let's take our business somewhere else."

"Don't piss off the king, Jack," Ben said. He put a ten on the bar, and we headed for the dining room where Jane was chatting with Rosie.

Rosie introduced Ben to Gabriel as a retired state's attorney. I was anxious to get his input on Joey's new predicament. Ben listened through my telling of the story, accompanied by great food. Ben and I had bangers and mash, and Rosie had shepherd's pie. When Gabe ordered the vegetarian Irish stew Ben gave him a sideways look. I laughed and shook my head. Irish brown bread topped things off nicely. Gabe was nursing a Harp while the rest of us were on our second Guinness.

As I soaked up the juice on my plate with the bread, I asked Ben for his opinion on Jamie's confession and what would happen to Joey.

He shrugged. "The confession is pretty worthless. He said she said. Unless Joey breaks down in tears and confesses, he just has to live with the fact that everybody knows."

"Not that he's going to care about that as long as he stays out of jail. The only thing he'll care about is that he doesn't have a body-guard. And he'll blame all this on Marty."

Gabe, who hadn't said anything up until now, set his glass down and said, "The good thing is, we have a bunch of dead criminals."

"Except for Mr. Glunner who happened to be in the wrong place at the wrong time," I said.

Jane convinced us to order dessert. It didn't take much.

"There are some answers we'll never get," said Ben. When no one responded, he continued. "Like how did Jamie know where Glunner was, and how did she get him in front of that window when she happened to be set up in the room?"

"Maybe she kept a journal," said Gabe.

"I doubt it," I said. "If she was willing to kill the people who knew anything about this, she sure wouldn't write anything down. But I've thought about that. She was taking a chance on all of it. And if it didn't work out, she'd find another way."

"Probably a leak somewhere on the force," Gabe said.

"Probably not," said Rosie.

"Then how else?"

"That's what I mean by chance," I said. "Remember, Glunner made some calls. I'm thinking Jamie told him to find a way to call her once he was placed. If he couldn't call she'd plan something else. Glunner took advantage of a Reynolds pee break." I took a long drink. "And the other was even more chancy. She had to have a vantage point to set up with a phone. She would have told Glunner to keep in touch when he could, and when she had the apartment she gave him that phone number. We know the second call was to the apartment across the street. She got lucky on so many counts. But if that didn't work she would have done something else."

"Revenge," said Rosie, as she finished the last bite of pie. "It consumed her, and look where it got her. She spent all of her happy teen years plotting revenge. She's dead, and Joey will be just fine."

"And she took two other people with her," I said.

"Yup, it's a dead end path with no other solution."

"Well, there is one other," I said.

"And what's that?" she asked.

"Forgiveness." I raised my glass. They all followed.

Chapter 29

The sun rose Wednesday in a cloudless sky, but the bright sun didn't help my mood. I wasn't looking forward to the day, which would start with a meeting with Joey. I didn't want to see the smug look on his face. I was tired of him. But I mostly wasn't looking forward to the afternoon appointment with Mr. Gillery. Ralph was bringing Spot at two, so Billy would have some time before Gillery arrived.

***

I parked in the restaurant lot at ten and walked across the street. As I opened the door I glanced up at Jamie's window. The curtain didn't move.

Mike pointed at the door without taking his eyes off the *Tribune*, and Marty let me in. Joey was on his throne with a drink in his hand. I was right about the smug look.

"Well, Manning, looks like you earned your money after all."

"I always do, Joey. But I'm not always happy about it."

"You're not happy I'm not behind bars?"

A part of me wasn't. "I'm not happy so many had to die along the way. There's four people, starting with your buddy Giancana."

"Momo? What do you care about him? We could spend hours telling you about the people he had killed. And that crazy broad…"

He glared at Marty. "Imagine making up that story and going to all this trouble to frame me."

"If it is a story," I said.

"What are you talking about? Who are you working for?"

"I'm not working for anybody at the moment. And we'll never know if her story is true or not, luckily for you." I paused and stared right at him. "But I figure it *is* true. I figure you were just carrying out orders. And I figure you weren't happy about it, and it's been eating at you ever since."

"That's a lot of figuring, Manning. If I did do it, what makes you think I'd care?"

"You gave up your gun."

He just stared at me.

"And there's Mr. Glunner. He had nothing to do with this except he was in the wrong place at the wrong time."

"Yeah, well the cops talked to me and my lawyer for hours. They got nothing and they know it. Read the papers, Manning. People getting shot every day in this city who had nothing to do with nothing. It's a disgrace. Somebody oughta do something."

I agreed and said goodbye. I was glad to get out of there. Mike didn't look up from the paper, and Jimmy didn't look up from drying glasses.

***

When I got to the office I chatted with Carol for a few minutes, threw a few darts, settled into my chair, and called Stosh. The evidence team had only found one thing of any interest in Jamie's apartment. Inside the back of the Uncle Sam hanging was a photo of Sam Giancana with his arm around Joey.

After finishing my notes on the case, I gave them to Carol who started at the typewriter while I went to the deli for sandwiches.

Always punctual, Ralph arrived at two with Spot, who ran to Carol with his tail wagging and then sniffed at the bed that was in front of her desk. After enough sniffing, he circled a couple of times and lay down. I invited Ralph to stay, but he had a date with a pool cue. He gave Carol his time sheet and his phone, and she wrote him a check.

Billy arrived a little after three with a big smile on his face when he saw Spot. Carol had explained the situation and given Billy the choice. He wanted to see him, even knowing he'd probably have to say goodbye.

When Gillery arrived a few minutes before four, Billy and Spot were playing catch with a rawhide bone. Both boy and dog were happy. Gillery introduced himself and bent to pet the dog. Billy didn't take his arm from around Spot's neck.

I led Gillery to my office and closed the door.

"Looks like you've made a home for Spot, Mr. Manning."

"Well, just trying to make him comfortable while he's here."

"Yes, and perhaps trying to influence me?"

I spread my hands, palms up, and smiled. "Hey, I do what I can. But it's all for a good cause."

"Yes. But I do have my job to do. Usually that job is rewarding, placing dogs with people who need them. This case obviously isn't typical."

"No, it isn't. But we did get him away from someone who was abusing him. That has to be worth something."

"That's worth a lot, Mr. Manning. And if he wasn't a trained working dog, this wouldn't be an issue. There are lots of dogs out there that need good homes."

"I understand. But I'm not sure Billy will."

"Yes, that makes this harder, and easier."

"Pardon?"

He leaned back in his chair. "I had a chat with your friend Mooneen about our guidelines for working dogs. One of them is age. We train dogs when they're a year old. After that they just don't learn as well. So, Spot is obviously too old to get into the program now. But since he's already been trained that isn't an issue."

"So, what *is* the issue?"

"There's another age stipulation. We don't want to change owners after the age of four. We've found an older dog isn't able to adjust to a new owner as well."

My hopes rose. "And how old is Spot?"

"Three and a half."

I was sure my face showed my disappointment. "Well, could we
wait six months?"

He laughed. "No. But I talked to people in my office, and we
decided that the extenuating circumstances were worth six months."

"So, what are you saying?"

"I'm saying the criteria here today was to decide if you all would
give Spot a good home."

"And?"

"And you made it easy. Looks like he already has a good home.
Hard to beat a boy who loves a dog. Where do the boy and his mother live?"

"They have an apartment right across the street."

"And there are no issues with the apartment? I know a lot of
landlords don't allow pets."

"Nope. No issues with that."

"Well then, I see no problem with the little boy getting his dog.
We'll just have to do the paperwork."

"I do have one issue."

"Yes, sir?"

"Do you have any rules about us renaming Spot?"

He laughed. "I wish you would."

I got up. "Okay, we're good. Let's go tell Billy."

Billy still had his arm around Spot. I was glad I didn't have to
watch him say goodbye.

"Billy, Mr. Gillery has something to tell you," I said. He looked
very sad, and I could tell he was trying hard to hold back the tears.

Mr. Gillery knelt and patted Spot on the head. "I can tell you
love this dog, Billy."

Billy nodded slowly.

"Would you take good care of him?"

Billy's eyes opened wide. "I sure would!"

"There's a lot to do, Billy. There's walking and picking up and feeding. There's a lot more than just playing with him."

I looked at Carol. She had a huge smile.

"I know that, sir. I'd take good care of him."

"Well then, Billy, I know you'll enjoy your new dog."

Now the tears fell, but they weren't from the sad face Billy had a few minutes ago. Mr. Gillery talked to Carol and me about paperwork, the first of which she filled out right then. He told us Spot could stay, but it would take a month or so to get all the paperwork done. After he left, Carol gave me a long hug.

"I can't tell you how much this means, Spencer. Thanks so much. But there's a problem you haven't thought about."

"And what would that be?" I asked with a smile.

"Our building doesn't allow pets."

"I *have* thought about that. I think you should move to a building that does."

"Oh sure, I'll just run out now and find a place. This one was hard enough to get even without pets. It's close to Billy's school and—"

"Whoa. Would you consider moving across the street?"

She looked confused. "Across the street? This building is across the street."

"It is."

"First, we looked here, and not only do they not allow pets, but it was more expensive. And second, there aren't any vacancies."

"You're forgetting about the apartment I have."

"Okay, assuming you were willing to sublease that, there's still the pet problem."

I smiled. "Is that all you do? Think of problems?"

"Just facing reality, Spencer."

"Well, that may not be a problem."

"How could that not be a problem? I can't hide a dog."

"No, but the new owner allows pets."

"New owner? Who...?" She figured out my smile. "You didn't."

"I did, and I'm giving you a raise and reducing the rent. You'll have a bigger apartment, and you won't have to walk across the street to get to work. It's going to take a bit of time to get all this done, so in the meantime Spot can stay with me."

She wouldn't stop thanking me. "How did you...?

"Well, when Mooneen told me she had an idea, so did I. I called the owner of this building and made him an offer he couldn't refuse. But there is one thing," I said. "Billy needs to find a new name for Spot."

We both watched Billy hugging Spot.

"Well, Spencer, we already talked about that. We decided if Billy got him his name should be something that would be fitting for you since you made all this happen."

I was sure my surprise showed. "I'm honored, Carol, but it should also be something Billy likes."

She smiled. "Oh, it is."

"So you decided?"

"He did." She held out her arm toward Billy. "Spencer, meet... Watson."

Please go to *Cold Justice* page on Amazon.com
and post a review.

Also, sign up for Spencer news at RickPolad.com.

Acknowledgements

This book would not exist without the help and support of several special people. To my first readers and friends, Mike Polad, Carol Deleskiewicz, Gary Lindberg, Ellen Tullar Purviance, and John Zelman. Thanks for your edits and input. Any remaining errors are the property of the author. And, as before, to all my friends and readers who have asked for more Spencer, my undying thanks.

About the Author

Rick Polad worked as a geologist, taught Earth Science and Astronomy at a junior college for twenty-nine years, and volunteered with the Coast Guard Auxiliary on Lake Michigan. Rick edited the English version of Living With Nuclei, the memoirs of Japanese physicist, Motoharu Kimura, and currently works as chief editor for his publisher, Calumet Editions. Rick also worked at Fermilab, the country's highest energy particle accelerator, and currently volunteers at Microtrace, one of the world's premier forensic chemistry labs. You can find more information on the Spencer Manning mysteries at rickpolad.com.

www.ingramcontent.com/pod-product-compliance
Lightning Source LLC
Chambersburg PA
CBHW022013010726
47494CB00003B/1014